For those who have magic living in their souls.

~

Before it was forbidden,
A goddess loved a mortal.
A king of his kind.
While their love was still new,
He was slain.

Pierced by grief,
The goddess transformed his body
Into an incarnation of the World Tree,
Weaving their love into the cosmos.

As the goddess mourned, she faded out of time.
Her tears filled an underground cavern
That welled into a spring that flowed
In several worlds at once.

At the roots of her beloved,
Submerged in sweet water laced with sorrow,
The goddess birthed their daughter,
And bound her to wander the World Tree
Until she found her way home.

~

PART I

~

CHAPTER 1
STORM AND SWORD

THERE WAS NO END to the beauty of the fjords. Sun-kissed clouds stretched pink and gold across a sky of deepening blue. Gentle winds filled the sails, pushing the dragon ship through a colossal cradle of steep mountains and flowing water, with a god-blooded Viking at the helm.

Breathtaking though it was, I couldn't stop thinking about what had happened last night.

The oath. The goddess. The watchers in the stars.

The dragon.

I'd flown with Eirian, and he'd promised to help me return to Killian and Troy. I'd been too drunk on magic to ask how, but I'd find a way.

The vow Nikolas had made went beyond the bonds of any one world. Already proven.

We'd woven our souls together.

Nikolas glanced down from his spot at the ship's wheel, his beard half-concealing his smile. I sat in a nest of furs on the deck with young Brendan, who was busy gnawing on a wooden spoon. The weightlessness of the night before had left me sore from the strain of being pregnant and the long journey to the stone circle at the convergence of valleys.

Love shone in Nikolas's eyes as he looked at us. He recognized Brendan as his own, like Troy had. The confounding part was how true it was, even if the child's dark hair and eyes were Killian's. Worlds away.

My mind tripped over the bending of time.

Nikolas relinquished the helm to his first mate, Alexandra, and came over. He kneeled next to me, his big hand dwarfing mine. "Are you alright, Shelta?"

"Tired." I shrugged it off. "Where are we going?"

Instead of answering, he touched my temple, and a map formed in my mind. An aerial view of the fjords showed the ship headed along an illuminated path toward a narrow channel.

"You see?" Nikolas dipped his face down, close to mine.

"I do. And what will we find there?"

"Dragons." He cracked a roguish smile.

"Eirian?" I whispered his name. My dragon. The one I'd sought my whole life.

"Likely." Nikolas rubbed his thumb over my knuckles, the bass of his voice rumbling in my ribcage. "Dragons possess an essence not so different from our own. We each have souls made of stars."

"Souls made of stars?"

His beard gently scratched my cheek as he snuck a kiss. "Didn't you see it last night?"

My breath caught at the glacier blue of his eyes and the gravity of memories spinning through me. "I saw the glow, but that was the magic of the stones, right? The moon, the offering, the goddess?"

My mother was a goddess. How long until that felt normal?

Nikolas ran a hand along his belt. He didn't wear his hammer, but the gems on either side sang, fully charged, as did the crystals in the pouch nestled in my right pocket.

When I took my sword from the altar this morning, it had vibrated in my hand.

"Nature's energy amplified what you already are," said Nikolas. "Your essence. Your star-self."

"Like, a real star?" I lifted a finger toward the sky.

"What do you think the stars are made of?"

How absurd would the science I knew sound to him? "Big balls of chemical elements burning in space, mostly?"

He shook his head. "They are conscious beings of light, Shelta. Each and every star."

I held my tongue. Maybe he was right. The gods had looked down on us last night, no question in my mind. The goddess and her kin. Our kin. I looked at Brendan and tried to wrap my head around his being Brighid's grandchild.

Nikolas spoke near my ear. "We believe that when a star arcs through the sky, a child is being conceived. A star may become a human, or a tree, or a cat. Or a dragon."

Or a dragon.

The thought of Eirian made my blood sing, reaching into the realm of destiny.

That night, as the ship slipped through the fjords, a tremor of urgency ripped through the darkness, rocking the boat and shaking me awake. I gripped the bedrail, checking for Brendan, who was still strapped in his cradle, bolted to the floor.

Nikolas launched out of bed and grabbed his boots, which were across the room from where he'd left them. "Ola calls." His voice scraped low. "Raiders were sighted on their way to the village. Stay here."

I nodded, watching him leave, the ship already turning as he called the elements to his need. Seer that she was, it didn't surprise me that Ola could reach her brother telepathically, but what a wake-up call. My stomach churned, thinking of the village with its steep-roofed homes and central tree, of Ola and the children Nikolas had left in her care. Of all the families who lived along the sheltered bay.

Would the raider's ships sail past the cliff carved with the World Tree?

The deck rang with the crew's footsteps. Water rose beneath the ship, and a gust of wind came up behind us. The boat tore through the ocean. We sailed away from the dragons, away from my chance at seeing Eirian.

If a ship could fly, that is what the *LófiDanu* did. We emerged from the fjords into the open sea and a frenzy of waves. Wood groaned as Nikolas drove the ship to its edge, and anxiety gripped me in a storm of its own. Forcing myself to breathe slowly, I closed my eyes and prayed.

The baby inside kicked hard, making me wince. Pushing back with the flat of my hand, I sang quietly to myself, to Brendan, to my unborn child. Nothing like a lullaby in the midst of complete chaos.

Eventually, I got dressed, and sat in the chair beside Brendan to wait out the storm.

Through the wood, past the wind and pounding water, I heard Nikolas bellow to the crew. The ship slowed. I peered out the cabin's small window, daggers heavy in my boots.

From what I could tell through a sheet of rain, we were coming into the harbor. Long before we reached the docks, Nikolas dropped anchor. The force of the ship dragging to a stop threw me to the floorboards next to Brendan's cradle. Heavy steps sounded on deck, and the rowboat splashed into the water.

I got to the window in time to watch the rowboat surfing a swell. Nikolas stood with one foot on the bow, sword and hammer drawn, the crew behind him.

Lightning crackled. Then, they blurred out of view.

I could see nothing more than moving shadows through streaks of rain and the splash of seawater. I stepped back from the window, retrieved my dragon sword, and sat down in the cabin's chair.

Brendan slept fitfully while I paced the small space, sat again, and paced some more. The ship rolled in the raging sea. Occasionally, the sound of screaming carried over the water with the distant clang of metal on metal. It was hard to tell if my nausea was from being pregnant, deep-set dread, or seasickness.

Just keep breathing.

Footsteps on the deck made my skin crawl. Nikolas wouldn't be back already. Had someone come to pillage?

I squeezed the grip of my sword, swaying with the ship. Heavy steps thudded on the stairs. Then the cabin door flew open.

Lightning flashed, shining on the whites of a man's eyes. He didn't expect me.

Not about to waste my chance, I lunged forward. He brought his sword up, and I hustled to keep him from entering the cabin, steel ringing against steel in the small space. The boat tipped, and I stumbled, arms rattling as I blocked the brute strength of his strikes.

Drops of water flew off his hair, splashing on my face. He roared, pushing forward, forcing me to give way. Bracing myself, I put all my focus on my sword, and it came alive in my hand, sparking as it collided with my attacker's.

Seeing an opening, I ducked, drew my dagger, and plunged it into his ribs. The sickly sound of blade meeting flesh slid beneath his garbled cry. As he fell, I pushed him back, onto the stairs. Blood ran warm over my hand.

Another raider strode toward the cabin, with two more behind. I pulled the dirk free from the man at my feet, slammed the door closed to hide my son, and clambered up to the main deck, where I had room to let loose the full fury of my sword.

Lightning crackled along my blade in tune with the roar of the storm. I let it direct my movements, putting all my energy into the deadly dance. With a slash, a bolt jumped from my sword to one of the men, who fell in convulsions. His comrade, a large man with shaggy hair, snickered as my coat came open, exposing the cleavage of a nursing mother.

My attacker's sword slammed against mine, and a sharp pull in my abdomen made me cry out. My arms shook as the blade carried itself through the air.

The weapon was the leader. I just held on.

When the man came close enough, I drove my dagger into his belly. He fell to the deck with gut-wrenching moans. I gripped the sword's hilt with both hands. The last man rushed forward, growling.

Thoughts dissolved. There was only the blade singing. Clanging. Clashing. It was in its glory, electrical current running through every movement. My opponent lunged, slashing through the leather of my coat, drawing blood from my right shoulder and a yelp of pain from my throat.

A sudden flare from my sword blinded us both. Trusting the dragon blade, I swung out. A muddled moan and thick thud made me stagger back, squinting. I'd slit his throat.

He died slowly, and it hit me like a fall from a great height. I'd killed. Again. This time it was up close and personal, not with a rifle at a removed distance. Blood on the deck. Blood on my hands. My right coat sleeve was soaked in red. Rain splattered my face.

Thunder roared, and flashes from the clouds illuminated the fighting on shore.

Lightheaded, I stumbled across the tilting deck and grabbed the rail, over which I lost whatever food was left in my stomach.

My sword glowed dull at my feet, as if waiting for the next fight. I turned my gaze toward land and pressed a hand to my shoulder to try to stem the bleeding.

I wasn't that far from land. The faint light of dawn grew steadily brighter, and I was able to pick out Nikolas among the figures in the fray. He lifted his hammer to call a bolt of lightning, which he sent through the five men in front of him. They fell, only to be replaced by ten more raiders. The villagers were severely outnumbered.

Nikolas swung his hammer and hurled it into the closest man, creating a shockwave that crumpled those nearby. His hammer never stopped moving, and the thunder rolled on. I leaned on the rail, unable to tear my eyes away.

Adrenaline kept me standing when I needed to sit down. Badly. My breath came shallow. The fighting was desperate, villagers and elements pitted against a small army. Another wave of sickness came, and I retched over the rail though there was nothing left inside.

What could have been a lifetime or only moments later, the rain stopped, the wind calmed, and the waves receded to a gentle roll as the sun rose over the mountains to the east.

Nikolas strode, tall and swift, through the bodies in the street toward his home, only now able to check on his children. I sank to the bench beside me, wrecked.

Vision blurring, I tried to get back to the cabin, back to Brendan, but I only made it halfway. I fell to my knees in slow motion, catching my weight in my hands to protect my aching belly, and rolled to my side.

As I joined the corpses that lay on the deck, the suddenly-bright morning faded to black.

CHAPTER 2
SEEKING SHELTER WITH THE GODS

SOMEONE WAS CALLING my name. Not for the first time. A man's voice. There was urgency in it.

Killian? No, that wasn't right, but I knew this man, knew his touch.

Why did he sound so far away?

It was a long moment before I recognized Nikolas. His eyes were red, fatigue pulling at his face, blood drying dark on his clothes and hair.

"Shelta." He crushed me gently, smelling of sweat and brimstone.

Things came back to me in jagged pieces. "The children?"

"They're fine." A half-truth. Concern strained his words.

"Brendan?" I asked.

He pulled back to look at me. "All of my children are safe. You need to get somewhere to recover."

I nodded, feeling like a child myself. My body wasn't working right. My arm throbbed, my stomach was too tight, and everything hurt.

When Nikolas lifted me to my feet, a sharp pain shot through my abdomen. Reason returned in a hurry. I was having contractions—three months early. "The baby."

His eyes widened with a hint of panic. He helped me to the bed in the cabin, past someone on deck dealing with the bodies.

"My sword." I reached a cold hand out. "My dagger."

"They will be returned to you," he promised.

"Ola?" I asked, hoping she would know what to do. My breath came sharp.

"She has many wounded to tend." His words scraped with frustration.

"Of course." I had no energy to hide my disappointment.

I nursed Brendan, whimpering when another contraction caught me off guard. Nikolas cleaned and bound the cut on my shoulder. He looked awful.

"Are you okay?" My question earned me a tired smile.

"Don't worry about me." He kissed my forehead. "Everything will be alright."

Such a brave thing to say. "How?" I labored through another round. The rushes weren't too close together, but they were intense. Brendan kept drinking, hungry after so many hours alone.

"We will seek shelter with the gods."

"What?" I coughed, throat dry, his words not making sense.

Nikolas shook his head, and retrieved my flask of water. "You need broth, but all I have is bread and cheese."

Brendan finished, and I took the water, trying not to drink too fast. We shared a simple meal between cycles of alarming discomfort. I was glad to see Nikolas eat. This was probably the first thing he'd done for himself.

"What time is it?" I asked.

"Near mid-day." He looked like there was more to say, but he didn't want to burden me.

"What happened, Nikolas?" I made my voice as even as I could.

"A tribe from the north sent three full ships—more warriors than we have with so many away on voyage." He frowned, but I motioned for him to go on. "Leifr made the rain, which saved our homes from their torches. There were many enemies. It took some time to turn the tide of the battle."

"I saw. I watched you from the deck, after…" After I'd killed four men. I didn't want to say it, and was saved from doing so by another spasm of pain. The contractions were getting closer together.

"We lost some good people." He summed up the battle in a few inadequate words. "But most are safe, and most of the wounded will survive."

Most. I didn't know these people like he did. They were his family, his responsibility. When I lifted my gaze, his eyes were dark, heavy with sorrow.

"I'm so sorry, Nikolas." I stretched a hand toward him.

"Oh, Shelta." My name sounded like a prayer. His arms came around me, and I held him as he broke down in a moment of grief.

But something was still not said. "Nikolas, how are the children?"

He closed his eyes. "Leifr has not yet woken. Frøya tends him and Dagný, who is shaken but whole."

"He hasn't woken? What does that mean?"

"He overextended his ability. I sat with him for a time. He will be fine."

Worry ate at me. Nikolas's son was mine by love, as much as I'd tried to keep my distance. We held each other in silence while I tried to keep the terror at bay. But I couldn't hold back a moan, and Nikolas put his hands to my belly.

"What do you feel?" I asked.

His voice dragged with exhaustion. "I feel a body strained from wielding power, and a child who is coming before its time."

I knew both, but it was something else to say it out loud. "Can Ola save a baby this premature?"

Nikolas shook his head. "Perhaps under normal circumstances. As it is, she has too many to care for."

I nodded, fighting tears. I might not even make it through the birth—I'd already lost a good deal of blood. But this couldn't be how I died.

A sense of rebellion welled up, and I reached out with my soul. *Goddess. Mother. Help me. I need you.*

Her presence slipped past the pain like an elixir of light, her words an otherworldly invitation. *The power of the World Tree lives within you, Shelta. Use it.*

"Shelta, look at me." Nikolas slid a hand to the side of my face. "We can go to the Realm of the Gods. They will know what to do."

I stared at him. "The Realm of the Gods?"

"To Asgard," Nikolas said, the word reverberating with the strength of his bloodline.

"How?"

"Together." His voice hardened with determination. The gems in his belt glowed as he helped me up. With my arms wrapped around Brendan, we made our way to the deck. Arnþórr was there, washing blood off the boards. He looked bone tired as he lifted his gaze.

"Tell Ola and the children that we're going to Asgard," said Nikolas.

Arnþórr's eyes widened. He took a step back, his jaw dropping.

Call your power. My mother's voice echoed in my mind.

I reached through the pain and found a blinding light within.

Asgard. I drew all my focus to it, all my will.

Nikolas lifted his ancient hammer, and wind swirled around us. Intuitively, I shaped my intent, and with the urgency of need driving us, we shot into the sky.

Chapter 3
Mother, Daughter

IN A RUSH OF SPEED, we flew through rainbow nebulas accompanied by a soundtrack like a thousand orchestras playing the same piece of music. This was unlike any wormhole I'd found before. There was no spinning, no flash of light, no cacophony of sound or searing smoke.

Nikolas held me, his fatigue seeping through my awareness. We were desperate, both of us.

As we landed on solid ground, I cried out, wet between my legs—my water breaking. All I could do was breathe, and I didn't seem to be doing a great job of that at the moment, panting with panic and pain.

Trembling, Nikolas fell to his knees, and I collapsed on the stone floor, curled in a ball around Brendan.

Two women stepped forward from shadows at the edge of the large room. The red-haired one took Brendan with great care. I knew her without words: Brighid.

My mother and her dark-skinned friend helped me up, both of them taller than Nikolas. The raven-haired goddess supported much of my weight as we made our way down a sconce-lit hallway to a nearby room, where she helped me onto a bed.

Through the blur of pain, I picked up bits of detail. Arched ceilings. Golden light. The women's gowns shimmered blue-green.

Nikolas sagged into a chair, an oversized man standing beside him.

"Brighid?" I squinted at my mother as she handed Brendan to Nikolas.

"Daughter." Her hand was cool on my cheek. "Welcome home."

Tears streaked down my face.

She handed me a drink, green like one of Ola's brews. The honeyed tea returned some of my strength, but the ache didn't let up. Nikolas was saying something, but his words slurred together in my head. Brighid's friend told him to go rest, that all would be well. The person behind him opened the door, their tone kind. Compassionate.

Nikolas carried Brendan with him, his cries fading down the hall.

I reached after him. Troy had been with me for Brendan's birth. I wanted him now. Wanted Nikolas. Wanted Killian.

Hand on my chest, Brighid settled me with her touch. "Airmid and I are here. Your beloved has done more than any mortal in an age of your time. He must rest, or we will have another patient to heal."

The next contraction came, and I didn't have the capacity to focus on anything else.

"Breathe." Her voice was clear, soothing like water.

"It's too early." I gasped as the next rush rocked through me. There wasn't enough space between them.

Brighid cupped my belly. Airmid's hands came to rest on my head. They chanted in low voices, soothing me with sound and touch.

"Your child will thrive." Brighid moved her hand in comforting circles.

For a while, there was only breathing through the rushes and resting between. When the urge came to push, a witness-like part of me wondered how far my roars echoed through the halls of the palace.

After an indeterminable hour of agony, my baby was born into Brighid's waiting hands. I collapsed in exhaustion, and my mother placed the child on my belly. She and Airmid worked without words, slowing my bleeding, cleaning up the mess. They wrapped me and my baby in a warm blanket.

"You have a daughter." Brighid's smile shone. Twice now, I'd made her a grandmother.

My eyes misted over as I gazed at the tiny infant.

Troy's mother's name had been Julia. And Killian had wanted to name our child after Brighid, if we'd had a girl. What would he think, if he knew the truth?

"Julia Brighid." I named my daughter, stroking her back with a light touch. Concern crept in, and I raised my gaze. "She's so tiny."

Fully formed, but small and fragile, I was afraid to pick her up. I didn't want to break her. I brought her to my breast, where her little mouth latched on. She drank hungrily.

"Julia," I said again, loving the sound.

Soon after she finished nursing, a man entered the room looking too much like Nikolas to be anyone but Thor. Like the women, he was larger than life. His presence was *more*, on every level. Storm-blue eyes, gold-blond hair, and sheer intensity of will were traits he'd passed down seven generations.

He acknowledged Brighid and Airmid with an incline of his head, his attention on me. "I come to bear witness for the father." The depth in his voice hinted at his power, but his smile was tender. Kind.

"I'm honored." I spoke as clear as I could manage. My vocal cords were raw. Everything hurt.

Airmid slipped out before I could even thank her. Thor stood to the side, allowing Brighid to work. My mother held her hands over Julia for several minutes, and it seemed the infant got heavier, her body plumper around delicate bones. When the goddess was finished, she wrapped Julia in blue-green swaddling similar to that of her gown, which she explained was infused with healing energy.

More magic.

When I lifted my gaze, I caught a look between Thor and Brighid.

"I will leave you now," said my mother. "When you're ready to sleep, let Thor hold the child. He has been a father many times over. There is none better to attend you in that role."

"Other than you."

Brighid bent to kiss my forehead. "We will have time together. Thor is also a healer."

The door closed behind her with a hush of air. My mother had left me again.

At least I was alive, as was my child. I blinked back tears. Julia gazed at me, her eyelids heavy.

"She's beautiful." Thor crossed a dark marble floor to the sit in the chair beside the bed.

"She is." My daughter. Born in the Realm of the Gods.

He caressed her arm. Julia closed her eyes. She would've fit in his hand. "We don't often have babies here. Most of our children live out their lives in other worlds."

Propped on pillows, tired as hell, I met the god's gaze and saw Nikolas in the depths.

"Thank you for receiving us." My throat constricted. "I don't think we would've survived, otherwise."

"We are glad to receive you, Shelta. World-weaver. What is her name?"

"Julia Brighid." I loved the sound of it; the way it sang in my chest. Even if I was still upset with my mother for deserting me most of my life.

Thor stroked the infant over the protective swaddling, barely touching her. "Julia. Daughter of Troy. Granddaughter of Brighid."

"Why did she abandon me?" The question spilled out. I'd been asking it since the first jump through time at age three. Maybe he'd tell me straight.

Thor's brow wrinkled. "Your mother?"

"Yes." I was grateful she'd saved my child, but she'd left me to stumble through life alone. How could I reconcile with that?

Thor leaned back, hands splayed over polished-wood armrests that curved in a cascade of knotwork down the chair's legs to its clawed feet. His slow-drawn breath contained an eternity.

"We aren't supposed to take mortals as lovers." His fingers tapped out a rhythm, then did a twist to expose his palms. "We do, of course, but the commandment cuts it down to perhaps a few each century, rather than worlds overrun with the potency of star-blood."

I gaped at him.

"We cannot bring our offspring to Asgard," Thor explained. "We can do little to assist our mortal sons and daughters. They can enter the Realm of the Gods only on their own, and most never make it." He tipped his head and pursed his lips. "We grieve our lovers and children, and our grief tends to have consequences."

"I know a bit about grief." I sank deeper into the pillows, the memory of being ripped away from Troy and dumped at the edge of the sea fresh in my mind. I knew I shouldn't hold my mother's actions against her, but the resentment was hard to fight. "Why the wormholes? Why pull me through time? Does that happen to a lot of your *offspring*?"

"No, it doesn't." Thor leaned forward. "But that is Brighid's story to tell. You've earned the right to ask her your questions, now that you've found your way home."

Home? I almost laughed. "This isn't home for me."

"Not yet, perhaps. It is one of your homes. You are a world-weaver, now."

Sure. "Is Nikolas okay?"

"Yes. I went to him first. He rests."

Rest sounded good. My eyes wanted to close of their own volition, so heavy.

"May I give the child my blessing?" Thor's voice made my eyelids flutter open again.

"Of course." Julia was so tiny. She needed all the help she could get. I tried to sit up, wiggling awkwardly.

Thor stood, helping me rearrange the pillows. "Will you allow me to heal you, as well?"

"Sure." If he could make the hurt go away, I was on board.

He put a hand on Julia, cupping her back. "First the father's blessing, as Troy is on Earth, and Nikolas is unable to attend. My blood runs in her veins, however distant."

"But she's Troy's daughter."

Thor smiled. "You have a habit of finding my bloodlines as you travel the Tree."

My jaw dropped. "How many mortals have you slept with?"

His laughter filled the room with warmth, and faded too soon. "Eternity is a very long time, Shelta. Now. The blessing."

Thor's voice became rhythmic, his cadence reverberating off the curved ceiling.

Blessed is this child of my seed.
Blessed will this child ever be.
Blessed be the journey of her life.
Blessed be her spirit, bold and bright.

A shimmer surrounded the infant on my chest, and magic seeped into me.

"That's beautiful," I whispered as the sound settled.

His hand moved to caress my cheek. "*You* are beautiful."

My breath caught in the look he gave me, and I had a feeling of recognition all too familiar at this point in my world-jumping career. Here he was, the god version of Killian, Troy, and Nikolas—and yet Nikolas was here as well.

How does this work?

Thor answered me inwardly, his words awash with love. *Divine masculine and feminine. God and Goddess. You are the goddess, Shelta, one of the brightest stars she has created.*

It was too much. I blinked away tears, my focus on Julia. She barely weighed anything, rising and falling with my breath. My joy. My burden. I braved the brilliance of Thor's eyes, my heart feeling like it might explode. "I love three men. I'm torn each time I leave them."

The god touched my arm. "Each time you've walked through a world, you have been given a choice. To trust and love, or to fear and resist. You've chosen to love. Your courage is legendary. This child is born of that love, which is boundless."

Boundless love.

I shook my head. Wiped tears from my face. "But there's so much loss. And now I have another child to look after. To try to keep with me through the World Tree."

Thor's smile deepened wrinkles in a face that was timeless. Ancient. "You will have help." His hand moved to my shoulder, the heel of his palm above my heart. "Are you ready for the healing?"

Would I ever be ready? "Yes."

His eyes changed, starlight dancing within the blue. I took a deep breath, and something inside locked into place. The connection between us blasted open. The god could see every part of me: every thought, feeling, dream, and doubt. He took in the whole of me in an instant.

Complete vulnerability. Laid bare.

When Thor returned the gesture, opening the vastness of himself in my mind, I couldn't venture far. Thousands of years and fathomless layers overwhelmed me. Drowning in him, breathing his essence, I closed my eyes. There he was, within me, his own private universe open to mine.

Lines blurred. Spirit overlapped with existence. Everything became one.

The god asked a question, wordless at the threshold of my soul, and my heart extended an invitation without consulting my melting mind. His presence thickened. He was in my blood, surging. His immortal strength reached into my bones. He lit up the paths of my nervous system as his consciousness danced with mine.

The torn skin on my shoulder knit into wholeness, as did the flesh of my pelvic floor, fingers of thought-touch healing tissues that were stretched and torn by the trauma of childbirth. Inflammation receded. My body mended in waves of euphoria, and glorious pleasure replaced throbbing pain. The god's essence electrified. There was no trespass. He gave me strength—fed my desire so it would burn bright.

And burn it did. Every nerve, every cell illuminated and sang together in victorious aliveness. My breath churned. My mind gave over to a soft song of bliss.

Finally, Thor withdrew. Sweat and tears mingled on my cheeks. His face was flushed, eyes bright, his hand on my shoulder hot. He pressed gently on the skin above my heart.

"Boundless love." His voice trembled the slightest bit, making him seem almost mortal, despite what we'd just shared.

Caught in a vortex of awe, I had no words to give.

CHAPTER 4
INTERTWINED

WHEN I WOKE TO Julia's cries, it was Brighid who sat beside me, sunlight streaking copper through her hair. Her eyes shone with the depth of every forest in every world.

My mother.

I brought Julia to my breast beneath the velvety blanket, an act of love and survival. Breathing in her newborn scent, I studied each miniature feature: the way her skin creased around her eyes as she closed them to drink, the pink of her lips, her eyelashes and wispy hair.

Brighid was quiet for a long while. Finally, she broke the silence. "What do you know about the power that makes you travel the World Tree?"

"Very little." I tried to hold back my sense of abandonment, but it leaked out anyway. "You loved a man and left me to find my way through time and space, right? Because you couldn't bring me here?"

Her lips thinned, pressing together. "Your father was murdered and I couldn't save him. Avenging him brought no comfort. I used the remains of his body and a shard of his spirit to grow an incarnation of the World Tree." She raised an eyebrow. "The oak where you met your beloved."

"Killian." I could see it clear in my mind. The sacred spring. He'd been kneeling, praying to the goddess before me.

She tilted her head. "You were born in the spring by the Tree, but I couldn't leave you in that world, in that time. Your chances of survival would've been slim. And, as you said, I couldn't bring you here. I sent you into the future and bound you to the World Tree in the hope that you would find your way home."

"Which I did. By falling through the past." All the way to my Viking.

"Your journey touches the fabric of each realm you enter," said Brighid. "Your music ripples through time and space—this is one of the ways you weave your will into existence."

My throat tightened, all the hurts of the past piling up in my chest.

Brighid smiled at Julia. "You, little star-child, bring *your* life into the Tapestry." Her voice dropped, bringing a sense of eternity. "Each individual adds to the radiance of the whole. Each choice illuminates or diminishes the essence of that being. For most humans, life is a wavering dance between wanting to shine, brief bursts of brilliance, and the dimness of fear. And yet you're made of the purest light. You are so much more powerful than you comprehend."

"But I'm not entirely human, am I?"

"No." She tipped her head. "You have a high concentration of god blood, but humans with the merest trace of stardust are still powerful. Your choices, your thoughts and words, your spirit leaves an imprint of energy on the landscape of the cosmos. This is how it is for every being, but the impact of *your* life is magnified. You have more influence on the Tapestry."

"Why?"

"Because you're a world-weaver. This is your purpose."

"Because you chose for me." A lifelong rage over lacking control of my destiny singed the edges of my words and stung my eyes.

Brighid frowned. "Not only me. The gods have chosen you, in hopes that you will turn the tide of oppression and violence that destroys the world you knew before you found my spring and your father's Tree. You can change things you yearned to change when you were there."

My gaze dropped to Julia, tendrils of dread scraping at my ribs. "What is required of me?"

"To navigate the World Tree and weave more light into the Tapestry of all that is." Her hand stroked the blue silk of her skirts. "Each time you sing, you do this. Each time you turn toward love. Each thought you have ripples out."

"I haven't been navigating anything. I've been blindsided time and again."

"You will learn. You've already begun a new thread: you chose the destination and initiated the crossing to come here."

Out of desperation. But she was right.

"You have only to believe yourself capable," she said after a while. "Can you believe it of your children, that they could weave worlds together? Do you see how intertwined your life is with theirs? How—simply by being—their lives brighten your own?"

My head dipped in a sideways nod. "Of course, but they're my children."

"It's no different as you follow the spiral out," she insisted. "Nikolas has bent his will to be with you. You wove your soul together with Killian's through your song.

Troy found his way to my spring, seeking the path that brought you to him. Those threads span worlds, and you wove them. You and your beloveds."

Memories washed in like waves, along with a yearning to see Killian and Troy again. To visit them, and be able to return to Nikolas. That was all I wanted in life.

But Brighid wanted more from me.

"You've even laced a thread in Thor's heart." One side of her mouth curled up.

"That wasn't planned." Not that the others were.

Brighid laughed, soft and low. "He wove it himself. He's watched you closer than many, almost as closely as I." She swept her hand over my hair, then returned it to her lap. Her forest eyes were shadowed, and I got a glimpse of her grief. It made me think of my father, who would've lived hundreds of years before Killian and his clan. A father I'd never know.

"What was his name?" Hot tears streaked down my cheeks. "My father."

"Gillean." The name escaped her lips in the hush of a guarded secret.

The weight of time plummeted through me. No way. "Gillean of the Battle Axe? The Celtic king who founded clan Maclean? The legend behind the dragon?" An image of the statue in the gardens at Duart flashed through my mind.

"The same." Her hands moved in slow-motion, the fingers of one tracing the palm of the other, like she was comforting herself.

Something in my belly twisted. "Wait—does that mean I'm related to Killian?"

Brighid gave a throaty laugh, head tilting back on her long, sinewy neck. "No." She shook her head, hair shining like fire. "You're separated by five centuries and a different bloodline. Gillean's wife had a lover. It is from his seed that Killian's clan was born, though Gillean was given credit for siring them. He was away too often to take proper care of his queen."

"Who was her lover?"

"Thor."

"Of course." My brain hurt like I'd dropped through a wormhole. "So, did Gillean ride into the afterlife on his dragon?" Had Charlie told me that, or Killian? I missed them.

She smiled. "I do like that legend. I spun it myself. Your father was a dragon rider, but he was slain by a confidant. I wanted him remembered for his deeds, not his death."

"So, you crafted a legend."

She nodded.

That was about as much as I could take. I pushed back, sitting higher against the pillows on the overlarge bed. "I'd like to see my son."

Her mirth faded. "I'm sure Nikolas would like to see you as well."

Without another word, she rose from the chair, and glided out of the room.

A few minutes later, the door swished open and Nikolas stepped through, carrying Brendan. His beard was trimmed and his clothes were clean. His hammer hung from the jeweled belt at his waist—gifts from the gods worn in their presence, signifying his belonging in this strange, glittering world.

Brendan waved his hands like he could grab me from across the room. "Mama!"

He was talking now? "Hi, baby!"

Nikolas beamed at the infant in my arms. Brendan reached out with a sound halfway between wonder and indignation.

"Brendan, this is your sister, Julia." I guided him to touch her small hand. Her fingers wrapped around his, and Brendan let out a squeal.

"How are you feeling?" Nikolas traced the curve of my face.

"I could ask you the same." I took hold of his hand. "You look refreshed."

"I am. And you look radiant. How do you feel?" The question again.

"Mind-blown, but good."

He kissed me, his mouth warm on mine. Then Brendan pawed my chest with a cry, and we traded babies. Brendan gazed at Julia as he nursed. With her three-months premature, the two of them were only nine months apart. I hoped they'd be best friends.

It wasn't long before Brighid returned, asking, "Would you like to bathe?"

"Definitely." I swung my feet over the side of the bed.

Nikolas left with Brendan. Brighid took Julia, and I stood naked in the chamber, but for a blanket draped around me. My feet touched cool marble. Thanks to Thor, I felt stronger than I'd been since before I was pregnant with Brendan.

We walked across an arched corridor and into a cavernous room. Steam closed around me like fog as we entered a bathhouse straight out of a fairytale. Pools waited, sunken into white floors, the room quiet. Brighid guided me past counters laden with flowers, crystals, salts, herbs and honey, all the way to a pool in the back corner of the room. A trinity knot gleamed on the wall above.

Milky water swirled at my feet. "What's in it?" I asked.

"Rose-light and lavender, silver-essence and spring water, six different crystals, and cream taken from the first milking after a calf is birthed." She rocked Julia in her arms.

"Oh." So that's what gods bathed in. I hung my blanket on a hook and submerged myself in the pool, skin tingling as layers of sweat, blood, tears, fear, and elation washed away. The grime of battle dissolved, as did the remains of childbirth.

Dunking down, I ran fingers through my hair. A gentle current slid past, and I floated in warm, dreamlike bliss.

When I finally emerged, the towel covered me from shoulders to toes. In a dressing area around the corner, I found a pile of underclothes and a shimmery, blue-purple gown. The skirts brushed my ankles, sleeves loose. Flowing.

Brighid helped me wrap Julia to my chest with thick, stretchy fabric. The whole outfit tingled with magic.

"Are you hungry?" she asked with a knowing smile.

I groaned, ravenous.

As we neared the dining hall, it smelled like a steakhouse in Chicago that I used to treat myself to if I'd had a particularly good day busking. Except when we approached the doors, I realized this was at least fifty times as big. The din of people talking and eating made me want to shrink back.

I held Julia to my chest. "Isn't it too loud for her?"

Brighid shook her head, running a hand over the swaddling. "This shields her. It's best to keep her with you. She needs her mother."

I put a hand on her arm, stalling. "How long was I with you before you sent me through the Tree?"

"I birthed you through the Tree." Her lips drew tight. "I didn't even get to hold you."

I saw her grief, but she was a goddess. She could've taken some time with me if she'd wanted to. "Was that your choice?"

"It was my choice to set you free." Brighid picked up the pace. End of discussion.

I scrambled to keep up with her strides, anxiety rising as we plunged into the dining hall.

Maybe I wasn't adapting well. I was a world-weaver. The daughter of a goddess and an ancient king. I'd traveled the World Tree at will for the first time. And, apparently, I'd been chosen by the gods—the people eating in this very hall—for a task that seemed impossible.

They wanted me to turn the tide of greed that destroyed the world I grew up in. As if one person could do that.

I'd always wanted change, for the earth to be respected and all people to thrive, but how was I going change the course of an entire planet?

CHAPTER 5
FEASTING WITH LEGENDS

THE CLATTER OF CUTLERY and celebrating made me hug Julia closer to my chest. Towering pillars held arched ceilings over the massive hall. I sat at a round table between Brighid and Nikolas, with Thor and a handful others, most of them larger than life. Thor was a head taller than Nikolas, but otherwise they looked remarkably similar. Seven generations between.

The dark-haired goddess who'd been at Julia's birth joined us, sitting next to Brighid, who held Brendan on her lap.

"Thank you," I said to them both. "For helping with... everything." I dropped my gaze to Julia, words jumbling together. My mother and Airmid had saved us. Saved me.

When I glanced back up, Airmid's smile was like sunshine. "It was my honor."

My mother wrapped her hand around my shoulder, gave a soft squeeze, and let go.

Airmid slipped her hand into Brighid's, and I leaned back in my chair, considering the two of them. Pride shone in my mother's eyes, with a shadow of sorrow beneath. Did I remind her of her grief, dredging up memories she'd rather avoid?

The shock hadn't worn off. After a lifetime of not knowing where I came from, I was sitting next to my mother, eating at the same table. The green in her eyes was darker than mine, but the more I looked at her, the more I saw myself in her features. She laughed at something Thor said, and my brain flashed to a photo taken of me, published in a local newspaper as part of a series on street musicians. I'd given a false name, declined their offer for an interview, my hat and hair covering part of my face, but they'd captured my smile in the picture. It was the same as Brighid's.

I looked away, making eye contact across the table with a man who was shorter than the gods who surrounded him, a touch slighter than Nikolas. He tipped his head, and I dropped my gaze with a shy smile.

In the middle of the table, platters of food and pitchers of liquid made slow circles on a rotating centerpiece. Nikolas heaped my plate with roasted meat and colorful veggies. Fresh breads ranging from dark and sweet to crusty sourdough were followed by dishes of butter and honey, jams and tea, milk and cream... I wanted to sample it all.

There was a diverse selection of wine, ale, mead, and—to my surprise—aged Scotch whisky, apparently imported from Scotland on a regular basis.

"How does that work?" I asked Thor once he finished listing off the drink choices and Nikolas was pouring me a glass of mead.

His mouth made a secretive curl that reminded me of Killian. "We have a supplier."

"Of course, you do."

I took a look around the room, studying the table on a raised dais. A bear-like man sat beside a golden-haired woman, who caught my gaze with wise eyes.

"That's Frigga," said Thor in an undertone. "And Odin."

I looked away from the goddess queen, my mind spinning with so much grandeur.

Julia was a warm weight at my chest, Nikolas a comfort beside me. Brendan leaned against Brighid, staring at the center of the mini-buffet where a small fountain poured water over clear gems.

"What kind of crystal is that?" I asked.

"It's diamant from Edenverdi," answered Brighid, "an island in the sky where crystals grow. There, you can watch a bed of diamant shine in the sunlight. Or the moonlight."

As I imagined being surrounded by growing gemstones, I remembered that *my* crystals were on a ship in medieval Norway, where a village was picking up the pieces after battle. And they were doing it without their chieftain.

Nikolas sat next to me, when he should've been with his people, and his children. Leifr hadn't even been awake when we'd whisked off to Asgard.

"Nikolas," I whispered. "The village."

He brought his hand to my face, leaning forward to kiss my cheek. "Our people will be fine, Shelta. They have seen this before."

"But your children, Nikolas. They need you."

"They know I am with them." Conflict darkened his gaze. "These are my children as well." He looked to Brendan and Julia. "And you are my wife. You needed me more."

"Your *wife*?" He'd never called me that before.

"What do you think we did at the standing stones?"

My cheeks tingled. "We never said husband or wife. No ring or formal vows, I mean."

Nikolas threw his head back and laughed, drawing the gaze of Thor and several others. But when he spoke, his words were only for me, his breath warm on my neck. "I vowed to find you in other worlds. Is that not formal enough?"

I blushed. "I guess I meant 'traditional' vows."

"Do you want a ceremony? A ring? You are my wife without these things, but I can give them."

My eyes clouded and I shook my head, wordless, proposed to by a soul I'd already married, surrounded by feasting gods.

Nikolas kissed my knuckles, and leaned back. "Enjoy this, Shelta. You deserve it."

Enjoy it while it's here.

I took a sip of crisp, cool, honey-wine. The mortal-sized man across the table raised his glass to me, saying, "Enjoying the Middle-Earth mead?"

"Middle Earth?"

He met my gaze with bright eyes. "I believe there's a book about it in your original world?"

"A number of books, yes." I'd read them all.

"Those books were an account of its history by someone who traveled to Middle Earth, and then returned to your world." He smiled, light brown hair framing his face. "Ah, but it is not your world any longer, is it Weaver?"

I shook my head, feeling the truth of what he said. "No, I don't think it is."

A knowing grin. A charming bow. "Lancelot du Lac, at your service."

Legends upon legends. "Lovely to meet you." I breathed the words out, struggling to process everything. Nikolas eyed me. Then Julia woke with a cry, little hands searching, her mouth making sucking motions.

Brighid leaned toward me, pointing with her gaze toward the far corner of the hall. "There's a quiet room where you can feed her."

I sighed as we entered the relative silence of a red-curtained lounge. The room was empty but for a woman who disappeared through the door on the far side. Collapsing into a plush, bronze-colored couch, I tried not to drown in my thoughts. I'd reached overload, unable to process anything more.

Brighid sat in a tall chair, gazing at a painting as I nursed Julia.

Finally, the infant cuddled into my neck. I adjusted my gown, putting myself back together as best I could.

"You are a mystery to me," said Brighid.

"How's that?" I asked. "Don't you see everything?"

"No." Her eyes sparkled in the light. "Your path weaves a pattern the Tapestry has never seen. Your gifts—the possibilities you can create with music, your heart, your soul, the way you love—Shelta, no one knows what you will do, but we know it will be great."

I nodded, wondering how I was supposed to live up to the expectations of gods.

Brighid stood, extending her hands. "King Odin has requested a song, if you're feeling up to it. I can hold Julia."

A bard to the gods? I almost laughed at the absurdity of singing for my supper in a hall of legends. A grander audience I'd never had.

I passed my daughter to her grandmother, and we reentered the hall. My cheeks flushed as we walked to the dais, heads turning. Brighid hung back as I got to the head table, where King Odin raised his glass.

"Will you give us a song, Weaver?"

"I'd be honored." I bowed at the shoulder, sliding my gaze to the queen at his side, her hair braided with ribbons and flowers.

Odin pointed me to the side of the dais, and my heart leapt. The guitar Killian had given me rested in a stand beside the chair. I knew the dark wood, the dragon at the top.

"How did this get here?" My voice wavered. I didn't think I'd see it again.

"We borrowed it from a time when it would not be missed." Odin smiled, one eye surrounded by wrinkles, the other covered with a golden patch adorned in copper-colored knotwork.

I picked the strings, and found someone had already tuned the guitar. Looking out over the room, my belly flip-flopped. A hall full of gods watched me. Not from the stars, this time, but in the flesh.

Closing my eyes, I evened out my breathing, willing my heart to calm as I attuned to the instrument. Slow and steady, I began a trance-like song in a minor key. It carried through the chamber and echoed off arched ceilings.

Perhaps my music would prove I belonged here.

When the song came to a close, I opened my eyes, braving a glimpse at my audience. Nikolas stood near the dais with Brendan in his arms, face shining as if he'd seen me anew. Which made sense, really. He'd never seen me play. I'd hidden my music after losing my guitar.

Thunderous applause tore my gaze from Nikolas. I curtseyed, smiling as I straightened, and faced Odin.

The god sat, tall and regal, his queen glittering at his side. He lifted a hand in subtle acknowledgement. "Well done, Weaver. Perhaps you'll give us a few more?"

I sat back down, and launched into a lively tune I'd played in countless places. It worked its charm, the aisles filling with twirling couples and people dancing on their own. Clapping hands added to the rhythm of the song, making me grin.

Men danced with men and women with women as often as not. Thor's remark about boundless love warmed me as I strummed the strings. Nikolas stood nearby, his foot pounding the beat into the marble floor.

I merged two dancing tunes back-to-back. Then, because I could, because I didn't have to hide where I'd come from, I played Joplin's *Me and Bobby McGee*, which triggered much hooting and whistling.

When I finally finished, I stood and bowed, first to the room, then to the king and queen. Odin nodded once, slowly. A man appeared with the guitar's case, took the instrument from my hands, and placed it within.

"It will be taken to your rooms for you," he told me with a reassuring smile.

I thanked him. That was fine, I was ready to retreat from the hall as fast as possible.

Nikolas led me down a long corridor littered with statues and paintings I was too tired to appreciate. "Our chambers are this way," he said, aiming us toward a wide set of stairs. When we reached the bedroom, the door swung quietly closed behind us.

On one side of the room were two cradles, into which we lowered two sleeping children, Julia snug in her swaddling. A big bed sat on a plush carpet opposite a roaring fireplace and luxurious furniture. As beautiful as it was, none of it held my attention.

I turned into Nikolas, instantly enveloped. He lifted me up, brought me to one of the chairs, sat me in his lap and held me close. I put my head on his shoulder, and he stroked my hair, comforting my soul.

"It feels like we've been here for a week," I murmured. "It's only been a day."

"Time is a poor measurement for the fullness of life." His lips brushed my cheek. "There are days and nights, seasons and ages, but their cycles are only the parchment upon which we write our stories. The moments cannot be measured."

"Here and now." The theme of my life.

But even in his arms, I couldn't help but wonder what would come next. How would I transform from a girl lost in time to a goddess-born world-weaver?

CHAPTER 6
RIDDLES

NIKOLAS SLIPPED OUT of the room at dawn, leaving a kiss on my lips and kindling a fire in my heart. I got up to nurse my babies, then snuggled them back to sleep.

Hours later, I sat to breakfast with Brighid and Airmid, the dining hall quiet compared to the night before. The goddesses helped me with the children. Airmid laughed easy and smiled often, diffusing the tension between my mother and me.

When Brighid looked at Julia and Brendan, she lit up, but when she looked at me, there was grief in her eyes. Maybe I didn't make her happy, but my children did. That was something.

"She's doing wonderfully," Brighid said as she handed Julia over at the end of the meal. She'd grown already from the delicate child that emerged yesterday. "Will you walk with me?"

"Sure." I pushed back and stood. She carried Brendan, I carried Julia, and together we made our way through the corridors, and went out a door that opened onto lush green grounds.

Trees provided shade as we walked a path dotted with magnificent statues, riotous displays of flowers, and fountains that towered into the sky. The palace of Asgard glittered behind us, a sculpture of stone and metal that shone rose-gold in the sunlight. A creek ran along the trail, cooling the air and adding its soothing song to that of the birds.

"The World Tree. The Cosmic Tree. The Tree of Life." Brighid's voice added a layer of ancient knowledge to the music of the moment. "By any name, it is the matrix into which life is woven. All things are imprinted on the field of energy permeating this map of the universe—what we call the Tapestry."

I imagined threads of energy weaving existence together; the Tree like a nexus that everything plugged into. My steps were a drumbeat beneath the whir of my mind trying to absorb what she was saying.

"When you travel the World Tree, you pass from one possibility to another. To you, they are different timelines and outcomes of planet Earth."

"How do I control my destination?" I'd only wanted to understand this my entire life.

"You will learn." She nodded; her face serene.

"Will you teach me how?" *Please? Now?*

Brighid took several strides before answering. "There is another better suited for that task." Her gaze landed on a roundish door set in the trunk of a massive tree.

When we reached it, she lifted a hand to knock on the gnarled wood. The knock echoed as if a large chamber lay behind.

The door creaked inwards, opened by an old man wearing green-and-blue robes dotted with patches and pockets. "Ah, Brighid. You've brought me the weaver. Lovely."

"Merlin," she replied with a nod of her head.

Merlin? My life just kept getting stranger.

He was taller than me, but not as tall as the goddess, with silver hair and a thick beard. Round glasses sat on a hooked nose beneath overlarge eyebrows. His posture showed no bend of age. Square shoulders. Sharp grey eyes.

"You wish the wisdom of the Weaving?" he asked, his gaze like a laser.

"Yes."

He looked me up and down, took in the sight of my children, and stepped to the side with an open palm toward the shadowy entry. "You'd better come in."

"See you later." Brighid handed Brendan to Merlin, who chuckled.

He led me inside as he chatted to my son. "I say, young one, you've landed yourself in an adventure, haven't you?"

The round door shut of its own accord, leaving us in light that filtered through windows set in thick walls. Plants grew in every corner of the room from earthen pots: on top of wardrobes, racks of shoes and boots, mosaic tables, and shelves that held collections of shells, rocks, and all manner of curious things. I followed the wizard through his treehouse, swaying Julia as I went.

"The oak grows around the rooms," Merlin explained. "I negotiate the layout with the dryad—the tree's spirit—but sometimes I hear a groan in the night, and the next morning I find a room turned around or moved to a different level." He grinned, like he enjoyed this game the tree played with him.

The rooms were roundish, with circular windows, and a great deal larger than what the tree trunk showed from outside. A sitting room graced the level above the entrance, with a kitchen above the sitting room, a map room above that, and a library on every level, it seemed. The main library began two floors above the kitchen, which is where we spent most of our time. Julia napped in a wooden box padded by a blanket, while Brendan crawled around getting into whatever he could find.

"Pick something that interests you," said Merlin, who meandered a few shelves away, mumbling in a pleasant tone, like he was speaking to the books.

But it was hard to focus on browsing when Brendan kept dislodging things from the lower shelves. Finally, Merlin brought a book over and sat next to Brendan on the floor, murmuring with a storyteller's cadence and capturing my son's attention entirely.

Free from my child's distractions, I stood back and blurred my gaze. A shelf to the right drew me, and I made my way over to pull out a book bound in soft leather, dyed crimson red. The title on the spine read *Dragons in the Tapestry*. Illustrations covered the front and inside pages, including one that looked remarkably like Eirian.

Leaning against the wall, I flipped through the book, reading random pages. Tactical instructions for dragon flight. Combat maneuvers. Strategies for staying hidden. How to communicate between worlds and navigate the World Tree.

This was the kind of book I'd hoped to find in the libraries of my past.

As Merlin told his story, he taught Brendan the fine art of turning pages without ripping them in half. The wizard's persistence made me smile.

When I looked up, my gaze caught on a piece of metal that shone on its own shelf amidst the overflowing collection of books. I went over to study it, finding an intricately engraved flowering vine that framed a short poem.

Merlin.
Master Shaman. Priest of the Natural World.
Wisdom Keeper. First and Last of the Druids.
World-Weaver. Prophet. Bard. Tutor. Advisor.
Riddle Maker. Entertainer of the Finest Order.

"Ah, yes." Merlin came up behind me as I read the plaque. "One of the elven-children made that for me when he was learning his metal craft."

"You're a world-weaver?" I asked.

"I am." He frowned. "I've retired, however, as have the others that remain. You're the first in a long time. The gods have been waiting for you."

A headache started at the base of my temples. "I'm sorry. I'm supposed to go out there and be the only weaver in the World Tree? That seems like—a lot."

"It is." He smiled beneath his beard, then strode over to the table and chairs that sat before the window. With a flick of his hand, food appeared. "Lunchtime. Come now, Brendan."

At the wizard's words, my son crawled over to the foot of the table, where Merlin picked him up and settled him into a wide seat. He gestured for me to sit, which I did, flabbergasted. My child had not only understood, but obeyed.

Hunger overtook my astonishment, and even Brendan was quiet as he alternated nibbling the cheese clutched in his left hand with the bit of bread in his right, crumbs littering his dark-blue clothes.

After we finished eating, Merlin gazed across the table, his eyes clear and serious. "A weaver is more than a traveler of worlds," he said, "and a dragon is more than a magical beast. A wish is more than a passing thought, and fate is more than a whim. The question is, what is the will, and what is the weaving?"

Riddle maker, the plaque had said. Indeed.

Pleased with himself, the wizard raised his considerable eyebrows and offered me a plate of cookies. "Ginger snap?"

Later that afternoon, Nikolas and I walked the garden promenade away from Merlin's tree. Julia slept in her wrap at my chest, while Brendan rested his head on Nikolas's shoulder.

He smiled beneath his beard. "So, a wizard. How was that?"

I giggled. "Weird and lovely. Like having a visit with an eccentric grandfather. And where have you been?"

"At council."

"Council? With whom?"

"Odin, Brighid, and others."

"What did you discuss there?"

"Mostly, the turning of the tides. There are concerns regarding some of the realms, particularly your original world."

"Concerns?"

He frowned. "It appears there is so much unrest, so much manipulation by people in power, that it's pulling other branches of the World Tree out of balance. Nature spirits are dying, dissolving into other realms, and they take their trauma with them."

They take their trauma... "How do you define 'nature spirits?'"

"Elementals. Fairies. Dryads." He gestured toward a nearby grove with the hand that wasn't holding Brendan. "The consciousness of the forests, the mountains, the waters. They've fled the world where you were born, taking shelter in others. And it's causing a chain reaction."

"The more they leave, the worse that world gets?" I guessed.

"Exactly. And some of the worlds they're running to aren't doing well either."

As we passed a bench, Nikolas turned his palm up, inviting me to sit. He settled beside me, took my hand, and met my gaze with wary eyes. Like he was about to drop a bomb.

"What?"

"The council thinks you're the solution."

Images of the world I'd left behind bombarded my mind: impoverished populations, clear-cut forests, mountains of plastic, decades of propaganda and lies.

Corrupt governments ruled every corner of the globe.

"The gods have sworn not to intervene," said Nikolas. "As a weaver, especially one who lived in that particular world, you're the only one who can do something to change what's happening."

I threw my hands out. "No pressure, just save the world."

"Our children will help."

"Our children?" I looked at Julia, wrapped snug at my chest, and Brendan, dozing against Nikolas. "They're babies."

"They will not be babies for long."

All mirth left his eyes, and a sense of doom crashed through the denial in my mind.

Nikolas changed course. "I've also arranged for our wedding ceremony."

I cleared my throat, off-kilter. "Oh? And when will that be?"

"Tonight, if it pleases you."

"Of course." No time like the present.

Chapter 7
Vows Before Gods

SUNSET COLORS SHONE on the clouds outside the window, the sky a gradient of twilight blues. I stood in a doorway I hadn't known existed, opening into an adjacent room beside the bedroom we'd been given. Nikolas had gone to get ready with Thor. Brighid and Airmid sat on the floor with Julia and Brendan. My mother lifted her gaze and smiled, nudging me into the dressing room with a lift of her chin.

I closed the door, and quiet enveloped me. As freeing as it was to have a moment alone, I had to push away the sense that I was doing something wrong when my babies weren't by my side. Motherhood fit me like someone else's clothes. Strange. Uncomfortable. Nine months in, and I still hadn't fully adjusted.

Would I ever?

I'd broken every rule I had for traveling through time, all the promises I'd made to myself: *Don't fall in love. Don't get attached. Don't have children.*

Killian had changed everything.

I'd charged through the World Tree to the oak that carried my father's essence. The spring where I'd been born. And found the soul that matched my own.

With these revelations swirling through my dizzy mind, I crossed the room to the wardrobe, and opened the doors. Rich colors and familiar scents hit me, making laughter hum in my throat. I buried my face in the red plaid skirts of my fighting dress.

Wood smoke. Sea air. Killian.

The smell transported me to Scotland, to the training field where I'd been accepted, surrounded by brothers. Surrounded by family.

Annelle. Cristina. Charlie. Wallace. Sir Malcolm. Remembered names and faces turned into tears on my cheeks. I'd see them again. I'd find a way back.

Beside my sassy training outfit hung my green riding dress, and the blue-and-gold gown. I'd married Killian in this gown. Grasping handfuls of silk, I pulled it down. The trinity knots embroidered in gold around the low collar echoed those in the palace, a symbol of interconnectedness.

Three men, one essence. The warp and weft of time caught at my heart and pulled.

I dressed myself, missing Annelle as I twisted my arms behind me to tighten the laces of my corset. I could've asked my mother for help, but stubbornness won out. I brushed my hair, leaving it down.

When I returned to the room where my children were, Brighid handed Julia over to Airmid. Their lingering touch made me think they might be more than friends. Airmid's thick black hair coiled around her head in a braided crown, accented with sprigs of aromatic herbs and lavender flowers. Brighid wore a flowing dress of purple. They reminded me of the pagans who worshipped them. Was there a high priestess here? Did the gods fight amongst themselves like so many myths I'd read?

Finally, we walked down the corridors to meet up with Nikolas and Thor. Airmid carried Julia, swaddled in pink so light it was nearly white. Brendan looked dapper in a blue tunic with soft breeches. He and my mother grinned at each other.

The flowers in my hand gave off a sweet scent; luscious red blooms with velvety petals. A ribbon wrapped the stems, tied in a knot around a ring that sang in my hand, brilliant white and yellow gold woven into a wide band of intricate knotwork.

I slid the tip of my finger through it, and the hum intensified. Did Nikolas hear the same music from the ring he had for me?

As my mother led me through the maze of vaulted hallways and welcoming atriums, each person we passed stared. Many tipped their heads, their attention making my skin crawl.

Who here thinks I can save the world?

I hoped none of the gods were listening in on my cynical mind.

We came to an enormous pair of doors, where Thor waited. He placed a hand on my shoulder, and said, "You look magnificent, Weaver."

"Thank you," I answered, my stomach a hive of nervousness.

Brighid and Airmid continued into the room with my children.

Thor held me back with a warning of what was to come. "This is as much an initiation as it is a wedding ceremony."

"How so?" My heartbeat kicked into double time.

"This is the Hall of Masters, Shelta. Tonight's ritual brings you into union with Nikolas. In the same ritual, you will be initiated as a weaver."

No going back. I swallowed. Nodded.

Thor offered me his arm, and in we went. The chamber ceilings soared like a cathedral, making me feel small. The last light of sunset shone golden on the walls, and on the people gathered in a circle around the space. Some of them glowed on their own, as if they were made more of light than matter.

Nikolas waited at the far side of the room, in front of the goddess queen, Frigga, who was clothed in white robes and light, her hair in long curls. Odin stood beside her, holding his staff. On the other side were Brighid and Airmid, with my children in their arms. Merlin was among those in attendance.

Thor kissed my hand and delivered me to Nikolas, then went to stand next to his father.

Seeing Frigga, Odin, Thor, and Nikolas together, the resemblance was unmistakable. Their piercing eyes and striking features were obvious, but what hit me hardest was the intensity of their will. In it I recognized Killian. And Troy.

I was the daughter of a goddess, marrying into a family of gods.

Still didn't believe it.

I gave Frigga the flowers when she reached for them. She placed the bouquet on a pedestal at her side, next to a candle, a jeweled wand, and the red flower that Nikolas handed over, tied with a ribbon that held another ring.

When the goddess queen spoke, her voice filled the room. "It begins." She picked up the wand, pointed it at the candle, and lit the wick. "Let this flame remind us that all is one, and that love is the light of creation."

The sun sank below the horizon. That single flame lit the room, as did each person attending. Everyone—including me, Brendan, and Julia—glowed in their own signature of light.

Nikolas took my hand.

"We have come together in ceremony to strengthen the bond between Shelta and Nikolas," said Frigga, "and to bring their individual awareness to an advanced level. The energy they receive and intentions they weave will be shared with their children, of which there are seven—two in attendance, four off-world, and one yet to be conceived. Their names are Julia, Brendan, Dagný, Leifr, Frøya, Charles, and the one who is to come."

The one who is to come. Really? I could do without prophecies concerning my children.

"Roots, heart, and branches, we call the World Tree." Frigga's voice dropped into a chant. "Starlight and planets, time and space, we invoke Eternity. Weave us into the Oneness."

As she called in the World Tree, my energy anchored and extended upwards. When she called the stars, there was an expansive sense of connectivity, as if rainbow colors danced in a sphere around me. When the goddess named Eternity, stillness settled. Vast, immeasurable knowing.

The hair on my neck rose.

"Is it your intention," she asked Nikolas and I, "to journey together in love, boundless in potential and binding you together?"

"It is," we answered.

She turned to Nikolas. "Nikolas Thorson, speak your heart."

He kissed my hand, and put my palm on his chest. "Shelta, my beloved, I wish you to be my wife. Will you take me as your husband, in this world and all worlds?"

"I will," I answered. He was so bright. The color of his energy intertwined with my own in an orb around us.

"Shelta," said the goddess, "speak your heart."

My words tumbled out, trying to match his simple vow. "Nikolas, my beloved. Thank you for choosing me. Will you take me as your wife, in this world and all worlds?"

"I will." A pulsing current ran through our hands.

"This bond you've created is powerful and enduring," said the goddess. "It allows for growth and change."

Pointing her wand at the flowers, the ribbons unraveled and set the rings free. Frigga handed me the larger of the two, along with a small card. With a quiet voice, she said, "You can use these words or create your own. It is the forging of the ring-bond."

I slid the ring onto the fourth finger of his left hand, and read the verse she'd provided. "With this ring, I claim you as my husband, and forever become your wife."

The word forever had weight to it here, in this palace of immortality.

Nikolas didn't need the card. He took the ring, held my left hand, and said, "This ring is a link that binds us, strengthening the infinite nature of our love." He slid it onto my finger. "This ring exists in all worlds, having been forged at the Heart of the World Tree. It will never abandon you, and it will always bring you home to me."

Tears caught in my throat as his words echoed in my soul. *It will never abandon you, and it will always bring you home.*

Gathering me in his arms, Nikolas kissed me, and I kissed him back with everything in me.

But the ceremony wasn't finished. When Nikolas and I faced Frigga again, she looked each of us in the eyes. "Shelta, daughter of Brighid, and Nikolas, son of Thor, we offer assistance in expanding your abilities. Do you accept?"

"Yes." It was the only answer. I needed all the help I could get.

"I do," said Nikolas.

The queen nodded. "Walk into the center of the circle and stand back-to-back."

As soon as we'd done so, the light from those around us grew brighter, until it was so bright, I had to close my eyes. Each cell in my body was illuminated in my inner sight. For a flash of time, I believed I *could* be the one to change the fate of worlds.

"This is a revealing of your potential," Frigga said. "This fullness is ever within your grasp. It requires practice, and will, but this is your truth."

The clarity fled as the energy ebbed, and the light faded to a gentle glow.

Nikolas took my hand. We turned together, facing each master as they spoke.

"I give you my blessings," said Brighid. Mother.

"I give you my blessings," said Frigga.

"I give you my blessings," said Odin.

"I give you my blessings," said Thor.

On it went, all the way around. Arthur. Portia. Merlin. Lakshmi. Some I didn't recognize. Two of the blessings were songs, not words. After Airmid had her turn, we'd gone full circle, and Frigga raised her wand, bringing it down in a sweeping motion.

"So it is."

Nikolas bowed to our company, and I made a curtsey, holding onto him for balance. I was buzzing, ready to get out of the room.

We retreated across the hall, to a balcony with night flowers and a sweeping view of twilight descending on the Realm of the Gods. Nikolas closed the door, giving us privacy in the nectar-sweet air, our only witnesses the distant mountains and pristine sky.

"Fresh air. Good idea."

Nikolas smiled. "How do you feel?"

"High." I laughed. "I'm pulsing with energy, and not used to wearing a corset."

"Why do you wear such a thing?" he asked.

"Because it looks good." I grinned.

"You're right." Nikolas slid his hand around my waist and drew me in. "It does."

When he released me from his kiss, I looked down at my ring. It was stunning. White, yellow, and rose-colored gold intertwined on either side of a sparkling diamond. Diamant, probably. "It's gorgeous." I shook my head. "Was it really forged in the World Tree?"

"They both were." He laced his fingers through mine, the rings not quite side-by-side. "Crafted today by the finest goldsmith in the realm. That's why I left so early this morn, so we could have something that would always connect us."

"Even when we're not together." My throat thickened, knowing that time would come very soon. He needed to get back to his people. "Thank you."

That night, Nikolas and I made love with all-encompassing awareness courtesy of our energetic upgrade. Afterwards, as we lay in each other's arms, my new ring hummed with contentment. I snuggled into his warmth, savoring the closeness.

"Shelta?" Nikolas kissed me awake. "It's time for me to go."

We couldn't have slept for more than a few hours. I squinted, propping myself up on one arm and doing my damnedest to not look disappointed. He had three children waiting for him and a village that looked to him for leadership.

Remorse weighed his words. "I do not want to leave you."

"I could go with you," I offered.

He shook his head. "There are things you need to learn here."

"I'll see you off," I said, wrapping my arms around him.

The smirk he gave me made me miss his playfulness already. "I can say goodbye to you here far better than I can with others around."

His hand traveled the length of my body, brushing breast, belly, hip, thigh. Every nerve awoke as he brought his fingers back up. I yielded to his kisses, hands roaming his skin, over scars, finding places that drew low moans from his throat.

His consciousness entered me as he did, and for a short while, there was nothing but us. Nothing but love, desire, and bliss.

But after, when he got out of bed, sorrow washed back in. My eyes followed every move as he dressed. The way he adjusted his tunic and fastened his bejeweled belt, covering the gems with their leather sheathes. The way he bent to put on his big boots. He laced wrist-guards over his finely woven shirt, using his teeth to tie the ends in a well-practiced motion. The fabric of his cloak billowed as he twisted it behind him.

Nikolas looked to the hammer that lay on a table by the window. Narrowing his eyes, he held out his hand, fingers spread. With a crackle of power so soft it tickled my skin, the weapon flew through the air, into his grip.

"An upgrade indeed." Nikolas grinned.

I smiled, forbidding myself to cry as he went to the cradles where Brendan and Julia slept, kissing Brendan gently, and brushing the back of his fingers across Julia's forehead.

Wrapped in a sheet, I slid out of bed and stood before him. His kiss carried me into deep ocean currents. It didn't last nearly long enough.

"I will come back to you, Shelta." His voice scraped low. "I will always come back to you, and you will always come back to me."

With one last kiss, he left.

I stood on the plush carpet in the sleepy light of dawn and listened to my husband's footsteps fade. The ring on my finger sang its song, pulsing as Nikolas traveled the World Tree. Then it went quiet, sending my heart sinking like a stone.

CHAPTER 8
WARRIOR-HEALER

I MANAGED TO GET a few hours of sleep before there was a knock at the door, and Brighid let herself in.

"Good morning." The goddess gestured toward the curtains, and they flew open to a bright day well underway. The sun lit her fiery hair and shimmered on her blue-green gown.

"'Morning." I rubbed my eyes.

"Today," Brighid informed me, "and in the days that follow, Thor has offered to teach you the ways of a warrior-healer. Merlin will tutor you on the World Tree, among other things. Airmid and I will tend to your children while you train."

"Okay." Sure. Training with gods. This was my life. Apparently.

When the children finished nursing, I left them with Brighid and opened the door to the dressing room. "Which should I dress for now?" I asked.

"You'll be with Thor this morning," she said. "And you'll want to bring those."

The goddess pointed to my sword and daggers, which were laid out on a table atop my green Maclean plaid. The scabbards shone with a thin layer of oil.

I put on the red-and-black dress Annelle had made, slid into my trusty boots, placed a dagger in each, and belted the sword at my hips. Braiding my hair, I reminisced about mornings spent in a courtyard full of Scottish warriors. And Killian.

Today, I'd be facing a god.

An hour later, I walked into a courtyard alone. Plants, flowers, and trees ringed the space, the soft song of a fountain coming from a sitting area near the inside wall. There stood Thor, larger-than-life. He met me in the center of the lawn. Sunlight shone over the walls, illuminating his eyes when he finally met my gaze—he first looked me over head to toe, and back again.

"Do I pass your inspection?" I asked with a measure of sarcasm. The sassy dress had always given me confidence on a field where I'd been intimidated and out-skilled. I was glad to have it here.

Thor made a sound in his throat that could have been laughter, and nodded. "You do indeed." Taking his hammer into his hand, his voice dropped low. "Draw your sword."

Right to it, then. The blade quivered with energy in my hand. Thor eyed the weapon with respect.

"Your sword has an affinity for lightning. As does my hammer. Our weapons are well matched."

"But surely your hammer would break my sword." I knew the legend of the mammoth tool he held.

"If the sword's metal was heated to a high temperature, perhaps the hammer could bend it or rend it in two. Or if you willed it with your thoughts." He paused on this, making his point. My thoughts alone could be the sword's undoing. "In truth, the weapons are equal."

"Alright." Legendary sword. Check.

"When you wield lightning," Thor went on, "remember it is a surge of power. You can direct its course, but never try to hold it in one place. No element will willingly go against its nature."

I nodded, swaying on my feet. "Got it."

"Energy can be used in attack or defense. You can make a shield from lightning as easily as a strike, so long as you allow the energy in the shield to move as it wishes. Whatever you do, it is imperative that you remain grounded; that you are always connected to the earth. You can do so through intention, in case you are not physically touching the ground."

I cocked my head. Easier said than done.

"Anything you imagine can be real, Shelta. Make it real now. Reach energetic roots into the core of the planet. See it as a bond of light that is flexible and unbreakable."

The quiet of the courtyard was suspended in time as I focused on the exercise. I'd experienced this grounding with Nikolas, so it wasn't entirely new, but it was something else to remember it while fighting. I made the link as strong and secure as I could.

"Good," came the deep voice before me. "Now, let's see what you can do."

Thor swung his hammer, and I brought my sword up to block, letting the weapon lead. It knew the dance of battle far better than I, directing my movements. Metal clashed. Sparks flew.

When Thor stepped back and held his hammer to the sky, lightning funneled from a non-existent storm into the hammer. I imagined a dome of light around me and pointed my sword at Thor as he let the bolt loose.

The charge hit the point of my sword, traveled around the dome, then went down, into the earth.

"Good!" The god's voice filled the courtyard, ringing in my ears after the crackle of lightning. "Again. This time, you form a strike."

"But I don't want to hurt you."

He laughed. "Nor I you. When we duel like this, in practice, think of it as a dance. The energy you diverted was meant only to challenge you. You can define the path of an element with precision when you're skilled enough. Until then, I'll be happy with your best try, and I will not allow either of us to be harmed."

He stepped sideways, hammer ready. My sword sung through the air and clashed with the blunt mass of Thor's legendary *Mjölnir*.

I imagined my sword as the conduit, and my next swing met the hammer with a crack of thunder and blinding light that threw my body backwards. Before I knew what happened, I'd landed on my rear twenty feet from where I'd been before.

Thor walked over and extended a hand. "Are you alright?"

"Fine." I was out of breath, shaking, and my breasts were leaking milk. But I wasn't going to tell him that. I was fine. Sure.

Thor pulled me to my feet, eyed me a moment, then raised his hammer. "Again," he said, and struck.

We went ten rounds before I could no longer hold onto my sword. I staggered to a bench near the fountain, and sheathed the weapon with as much dignity as I could muster.

Thor sat next to me in the shaded corner of the garden. "I didn't expect you to last so long. You have a lot of fight in you." He produced two crystal mugs from the depths of the fountain and handed me one, filled with cool water.

I drank half the glass, then put it down, my hand trembling so badly I had to use the other one so I didn't spill. A trace of lightning still lingered in my nervous system.

"Here." Thor reached toward me. A calming sensation radiated from his palms, up through my arms and into my heart. My breathing slowed and the tremors stopped. After another moment, he let go.

"Thank you." My voice came out even. "That's amazing."

"I can teach you." His eyes matched the sky. "But you may have worked with enough energy for now."

"Agreed." I downed the rest of the water, thinking we were finished.

"When do you think it is acceptable to do violence, Shelta?"

Apparently, the gods didn't do small talk. "Only when you have to, I suppose."

Thor smiled. "And yet, there is always a choice. Doing nothing is a choice. When you clash in battle, it is your choice to oppose another force. You bend your will to alter theirs." He paused, and I could sense that this was a tricky subject, even for him. "The actions of a warrior-healer are always done with intention. If another's actions threaten to destroy something good, or if they oppress those who are unable to defend themselves, sometimes force is necessary to bring balance. But there are repercussions. There is always a cost."

I nodded, seeing the bodies on the deck of Nikolas's ship. With a twist in my gut, I remembered pulling the trigger when Troy and I were ambushed. With the kind of power I had now, I could do a lot more damage.

"You've heard of battle rage?" Thor asked.

I thought of Nikolas taking out ten men with one stroke of his hammer. "I've seen it."

"It's not necessarily bad." Thor turned his palm up, curling his fingers into a fist. "Fierce passion comes when immersed in fighting, but a warrior can be calm in battle. A *warrior-healer* holds compassion in their heart, even as they fight."

"Which isn't easy?" I guessed.

"No." He shook his head. "It's not easy. But at the heart of each being, no matter how altered by fear they may be, lies a spark from the same light that created us all. Every being is a brother, a sister—kindred in the essence within. Some simply forget who they are, or allow themselves to be manipulated."

I took his point to heart. "It seems contradictory to be a killer and a healer."

Thor smiled. "And yet it's the highest path of the warrior. The intention is always to seek balance. You are only one player in a grand game. The results are out of your control and beyond your knowing."

I nodded, staring at scorch marks in grass that had been immaculate an hour before, damaged by our stormy duel.

Thor followed my gaze. "Imagine it whole. Envision it green and thriving. Love it."

"Love it?"

"Yes." He spoke as if it were the most natural thing in the world. "Love is the vibration of wholeness."

I thought about how perfect the lawn had been when I'd arrived. Emerald green, lush and cool. Closing my eyes, I sent love into the grass, imagining it green again, growing up from the soil. When I opened my eyes, I couldn't tell if I'd made a difference. Maybe there was a little new growth…

Thor waved his hand toward the spot. Instantly, it looked as if it had never even been walked on. "You don't have to know the process of healing," he said. "Don't complicate it. Creating the environment to help it along is enough. Each being has a blueprint, a natural state. To heal, invite the wholeness that already exists to reveal itself."

Thor's eyes went clear, like blue crystal, and I sensed him imparting information on a level my waking mind couldn't comprehend. Symbols flashed through my inner sight, surges of heat flooding my body. Hands wrapped around the bench, I breathed through dizzying pulses of knowledge. And then, abruptly, they stopped.

Thor refilled my water. "I think that's enough for today."

"Good call." I swayed, lightheaded. Despite his taking the edge off with some healing, I was sore from our sparring. I'd taken a beating, and worked with more energy than I'd ever attempted before.

My skirts swished as Thor accompanied me through the passages, black showing beneath Maclean red. The way my legs protested the walk made me think of days when Rodric had pushed me hard on the field, and memories of Killian came rushing.

Thor steered me into the dining hall with a hand on my shoulder. "You'll be hungry," he said, "and then you'll be tired. Rest as much as you can after your lessons."

Right. And take care of two babies. Of course, I didn't even know where my children were at the moment. Off somewhere with my mother and Airmid.

Thor left me at a table by myself. There weren't many people, it being well past lunchtime, and I ate alone, glad for the quiet.

I'd battled with a god today. With the energy I'd thrown around, I could've taken down an army of mortals. The gods were training me for a purpose.

I could only guess at what it would cost in the long run.

CHAPTER 9
THE MAKING OF A WEAVER

APPARENTLY, AFTERNOONS were to become my reading time. Airmid volunteered to tend Julia and Brendan for a few hours so I could study. The goddess's deep brown eyes shone in the afternoon sunshine that came through the windows of the sitting area outside the bedroom.

Children occupied, I settled into my nest of pillows on the bed and opened the book I'd chosen from Merlin's shelves.

Dragons in the Tapestry, by Aeron Ercliff

The realms of time and space have ever been intertwined with the influence of dragons and weavers. Without guidance, many worlds fall into chaos and imbalance; assistance is vital for harmony to exist.

Dragons have been peacemakers, advisors, and wisdom keepers throughout the history of the World Tree, often paired with weavers of various origins, working together for an agreed-upon purpose. Though the fruits of these alliances are unpredictable and often tragic, depending on your viewpoint, the workings of such partnerships are fascinating. It is this subject with which this tome is primarily concerned, as well as the influences of dragons individually on the World Tree and its growth.

Though dragons are considered mythological in many worlds, they are undeniably real, and uncannily present in the legends and lore of all cultures. Their ability to travel the Tree at will allows them to materialize or vanish as they please, confounding those whose understanding does not stretch to such lengths. It is this ability, along with other skills and unique traits, that puts dragons in a perfect position to influence the Weaving.

After reading for an hour, I got up and stretched. As fascinating as the book was, what I wanted most was to see Eirian. To bond with an *actual* dragon.

Julia gave a cry, and I went to nurse my children.

Airmid took a break, returning a little while after I finished feeding Brendan. "I can watch them until dinner," she offered.

"You're amazing, thank you," I said for what was probably the thirtieth time.

She returned my gratitude with kindness. "It's my pleasure, truly. The children of gods and mortals are rare, and rarer still are those who make their way here." She knelt by Brendan, who took her hand and used it to pull himself to his feet. She beamed at him. "I love this."

"Do you make them stronger?" I asked. "Brighid did, the first day."

Airmid nodded. "We've helped them along, but they're ready for it. Your children's souls came into this life knowing exactly what they were doing." Her gaze lifted to mine. "I don't think you understand how happy you've made your mother."

I tilted my head. "Hard to tell, with her."

Airmid smiled. "You don't know her yet. She tries to give you space. But you made it here. You made it home."

I swallowed. Nodded. And left a goddess to tend to my star children.

Book in hand, I sat on the chair by the window, but when I opened the red leather cover, a slip of paper waited next to the ribbon bookmark. A note that hadn't been there before.

> *Daughter of Brighid,*
>> *If you tire of theory and are ready to ride your dragon,*
>> *come to the courtyard where you trained this morn.*

As soon as I'd read the unsigned message, the words faded to nothing. Throwing caution to the wind, I stood, stretched, and told Airmid I needed to get some air, stopping to kiss Brendan and Julia on the way out.

If there was a chance to see Eirian, I was going.

Striding down the hall, it occurred to me that this could be a trap. Everyone in Asgard had been lovely so far, but it was a big place, and every legend warned of devious deities. I had my daggers, but no sword, and no one knew where I was going. Scratch that, they were gods. Brighid could probably locate me by thought. Which meant I should stop thinking about her.

My fingers traced the dragon pendant at my throat, then the ring Nikolas had slipped onto my hand only yesterday. I wondered how he was, which led to my thinking about Troy. About Killian. My dragon was the key to seeing them again.

And whoever sent the note knew it.

The corridors twisted, evening light streaming through windows and making the floors sparkle. It looked so different earlier, and I took a wrong turn, realizing it when I came to a stone serpent that stretched at least fifty feet down the hall. Definitely didn't pass *that* this morning.

I doubled back, and eventually found my way to the courtyard where I'd met Thor.

The diamond-shaped window in the door showed the green of trees and purple of a flowering vine that climbed the entrance archway. Before going in, I bent and took my dirk in hand. Just in case.

At first, the courtyard seemed deserted. The fountain sang its watery song. The grass and surrounding foliage infused the air with the freshness of growing things. Everything was shadowed by the high stone wall. Above, the deepening blue of the sky looked surreal against the palace's thick stone walls, gilded domes, and countless windows glittering with the setting sun.

Several steps in, I still saw no one, and wondered if I was in the right place. Then a man materialized by the fountain. Tall. Light-brown skin, midnight-black suit. He stared at me with narrowed eyes and a shrewd smile.

I squeezed the hilt of my dagger, hiding it from view by angling my right side away from him.

"I was hoping you'd come." His voice was smooth. Seductive. He stayed where he was, waiting on my approach.

I stopped a few paces away and gave him a once-over. This close, I could see the purple designs threaded through his suit, and his shirt, open at the neck, drew my gaze to the dip of his throat. Vibrant-green eyes shone with intellect; his face framed by blue-black hair.

"Where's Eirian?" Having my dragon here would make me feel infinitely better. The book I'd been reading talked about the number of times outside forces had tried to control world-weavers and their dragons.

He tipped his head a touch. "I'm not entirely sure. Have you tried calling him?"

No. Obvious that I should've, now that he mentioned it. "Who are you?"

His smile widened. "I'm Loki. And you can sheathe your dagger, unless you'd like a lesson in blades."

I'd answered a summons from the trickster god. I wondered what my mother would say, then hated that I cared. "Perhaps I can take you up on that another time. You promised a dragon."

"I did. But only you can summon him."

I reached out with my mind. *Eirian?*

Nothing.

"You'll have to try harder than that," said Loki.

"Can you read my thoughts?"

"If I want to, yes, but I won't invade your privacy unless you ask." He stepped closer, flashing a wicked grin with pointy incisors. "A little faerie told me you spent half the day reading about dragons instead of being with them, and I thought you might want a chance to get out from under your mother's watch. Thus, my invitation."

"Why should I trust you?" I still had my dirk in hand.

"You probably shouldn't, but I have my reasons for helping you."

"Which are?"

He tapped his fingertips together as he spoke. "Humans are on a crash course to destroy themselves. That would ruin all my fun."

"Aren't you the god of chaos?"

"Sometimes. But if chaos overtakes the balance, it self-destructs."

I could tell there was more to it than ruining his fun. "There are countless worlds, right? So, if one self-destructs, you have other places to play."

He purred a low laugh. "I have infinite places to play, but I happen to like your planet. Are you forgetting that the worlds are all connected? You connect them, you and your kind."

"What happened to the weavers?" I asked. "Have there always been so few?"

His lips pressed together, making a thin line. "They killed each other off."

"Did you have anything to do with it?"

He cocked his head. "Clever, aren't you? I like that."

He neither denied it, nor told me how he was involved. I didn't think he'd divulge that secret, but my gut told me he wasn't going to attack, either. Not that I'd stand a chance if he did. He was a god.

I bent to sheathe my dirk in my boot, then stood as tall as I could. "How do I call my dragon?"

"Ah. First, it's always good to ensure there is sufficient space for your dragon." He extended a hand toward the fountain.

I followed him to the perpetual waterfall that flowed over rounded stone. Loki stood an arm's length away, his presence like a dark, driving song I could feel in my chest. All bass. Melody hidden.

"Think of your dragon." His voice was low. Deep. "Say his name in your mind three times. See him hearing you, focusing on you."

Eirian. Eirian. Eirian. I envisioned his crimson scales, the gold flecks in his eyes. I felt the intensity of his gaze and the power that had charged through me when I flew with him above the standing stones.

A sucking pressure rocked me forward, and my eyes snapped open as Eirian appeared out of nothingness. His bulk dominated the courtyard. Loki grinned.

I moved toward the dragon's head. *Thank you for coming!*

I've been waiting. He nudged my outstretched hand, then turned his gaze to the god by the fountain. *Loki.*

"Eirian." The god tipped his head.

You know each other? I asked, hoping Loki wasn't listening in.

We do. My previous rider was one of Loki's lovers. The dragon showed me a vision of a dark-skinned man with two swords strapped to his back.

I bit the insides of my cheeks to hide my surprise. Loki had a personal stake in this. I lifted my gaze to his spring-green eyes.

"You'll have to do without a saddle, for now," said Loki. "Safer to ride with one, but better to learn without, so you're not dependent on it."

With a running start, I scrambled up the dragon's front leg to the space between his shoulders. Spikes ran atop most of his spine, but at the base of his neck was a patch of smooth, hard dragon hide stretched between rounded bumps. I settled in, the way I'd done beneath the full moon.

Are you ready?

I hung on, hooking my hands over the scaly ridge before me. *Yes. Go!*

The dragon's legs bunched up beneath us, and we shot into the sky. Enormous wings unfurled as we cleared the top of the palace. They flapped twice to stop the beginnings of descent, then kept on with slow beats that lifted us toward clouds glowing pink and orange. I gripped tighter, reaching to Eirian with my mind.

Where were you, when I called?

In the fjord, where I saw you last. Your beloved and his family are well.

The village is rebuilding?

Slowly, and with loss, but yes.

I couldn't expect anything more. Nikolas would have his hands full for a while. As we rode on, some traitorous part of me didn't want to go to him—wanted to stay here, in the glittering sanctuary of the gods, or go to Killian. To Troy.

I certainly didn't want to go back to a world that didn't believe in dragons.

Eirian soared on a current, with an invisible shield around him to dull the wind and cold that would otherwise be whipping through me. I started to get comfortable, to loosen my grip a bit.

What was his name? I asked. *Your last weaver.*

Roáve. He was a good man.

What happened to him? Sorrow seeped through our connection, and I rubbed my hand over Eirian's scales.

He let his guard down while we were separated. One of Loki's enemies slipped a knife between his ribs.

I swallowed. Eirian's anger pulsed beneath grudging acceptance. Helplessness. The feeling was all-too familiar. *Did Loki avenge him?*

Oh, yes. He sent me the image of Loki standing over a tortured figure. The god's eyes burned with malice. His lover's murderer suffered before he died.

Do you trust him? I asked.

Loki? No. But I respect him.

Fair enough.

Being with Eirian was easy. I'd flown with him in my dreams, and now we soared over the Realm of the Gods. No more getting blindsided by the World Tree. I was a dragon rider.

And I was supposed to save the world.

But not yet.

Were you my father's dragon? I asked.

My father was your father's dragon, Eirian answered.

Oh. More symmetry in the long march of time.

After a while, as the sun sank below the horizon, Eirian banked around. Slow. The palace was a distant mountain with towers and sprawling arms.

I remembered my babies, and guilt twisted my belly. I'd been gone too long.

We have to go back.

Imagine the courtyard, said Eirian. *See it clear in your mind.*

I did. The trees, the flowers, the fountain, the wall.

Hold on. We're going to jump through space-time and come to an abrupt stop.

I braced myself, hands and legs squeezing tight. *Ready.*

We traveled from our point in the sky to the courtyard in a disorienting blink that stole my breath and sucked us through silence that made me want to scream. I rocked forward as Eirian crouched, touching down with speed and rending great gashes in the grass with his claws. His wings flung forward, almost taking out the trees, then, just as fast, folded back.

I gaped at Loki, who stood beside the fountain.

He crossed his arms and smirked at me. "Fun, isn't it?"

I let out a grunt of disbelief, swung a leg over, and slid down the side of my dragon. Jarred by the impact, I stumbled forward on stinging feet, looking from Loki to Eirian and back again.

"I'd offer to give you a lesson in blades," said Loki, "but your mother is looking for you."

"Right." My mother.

Loki tipped his head. "Brighid isn't overly fond of me."

"I'm sure that's a story. Would you like to tell me, or should I ask her?" The sky grew dark, and I knew I needed to get back, but the freedom was so nice.

My little rebellion.

The corners of Loki's mouth twitched. "It's a matter of perspective. She finds violence disagreeable. I find it extremely effective, when called for."

"And you think it's called for more often than she does?" I ran my hands over my skirts.

"Indeed."

I nodded. "We can debate ethics another time, then. Thank you for the chance to see Eirian." *And thank you, Eirian, for hearing my call.*

A pleasure, Weaver.

"A pleasure, Weaver." Loki echoed.

With a sideways glance at the god, I headed out, double-timing my way through the corridors to my bedroom. When I made it through the door, panting, Airmid was gone. Brighid sat on the floor with Julia in a cradle, Brendan in her arms.

"Back from your soirée?" she asked, unimpressed.

As if on cue, Julia started crying. I loosened the top of my bodice and went to pick her up. "I was with my dragon," I said, walking to the couch.

Brighid waited until I'd gotten Julia settled before saying, "You were with Loki."

"I spent more time with Eirian than Loki." I raised my eyebrows. "He extended an invitation. I accepted."

"He's dangerous."

I laughed. "Of course, he is. So is everyone else in Asgard. But he offered me a chance to be with Eirian."

"You would've had that chance soon enough. And yes, we're all dangerous in our own ways, but he's different." She stood, rocking Brendan, a crease in the usually-smooth skin between her eyebrows. "Loki gets into your head. He has a way of wording things so even the most far-fetched of his schemes seem reasonable."

"Has he sometimes done good things with those schemes?" I asked.

She tilted her head. "Sometimes the outcome is positive. Sometimes it's catastrophic. When he was younger, he would go on rampages of destruction."

"And now?" Had time changed the trickster god?

She looked down at Brendan. "Now, he mostly collects lost souls and provides them a place to indulge in all manner of debauchery. To his credit, they seem to like it."

I chewed on that while Julia finished up. Brighid brought Brendan over and took my daughter. I switched him to the other breast, and he tugged on my dress, sucking hard. "Ow," I told him, putting my finger at the corner of his mouth to make him back off. After a little while, I lifted my gaze to my mother, and said, "Thank you for helping. I'd have a hard go of it if I was trying to care for the two of them by myself."

"You're welcome." She inclined her head. "They are to be weavers, after all."

"Don't you think that's a bit much to put on infants?" I spoke quietly, sweeping a tuft of Brendan's hair off his forehead.

"Perhaps, but that's what they've chosen." Brighid's eyes were as dark as a shadowed forest as she changed subjects. "Be careful with Loki, Shelta."

"I will." Careful, yes. Stay away, no.

Late that night, after I nursed the babies to sleep, I opened *Dragons in the Tapestry*. With Loki's slip of paper between my fingers, I read on.

> For dragons, the World Tree is always open, allowing their weavers to travel anywhere in an instant. Likewise, the Matrix of Knowing can be more accessible, enhanced through the bond of dragon and rider, which can provide significant tactical advantage over non-dragon-bonded opponents in times of conflict.
>
> The more frequently a dragon traverses time and space, the more it drains them. While perhaps five-to-ten jumps in a day might be easy enough, each subsequent crossing strains the dragon, requires longer recuperation, and increases the likelihood that mistakes will be made while navigating the World Tree.
>
> When bonded with a large dragon, rather than one of the smaller types, a weaver has the benefit of

sheer size. The hearts of these dragons are enormous, able to access energetic realms through their celestial origins. Creative power can be channeled from the star-hearts of dragons into whatever they will, and they have razor sharp focus.

A dragon-weaver partnership is one of the most powerful and unique forces in the universe. Nevertheless, there are adversaries that can lead to the demise of dragon, weaver, or both.

It is rare for a dragon to be taken unawares by any weapon; however, it can occur, particularly in instances where the odds are overwhelmingly against them. As for weavers, fledgling riders often believe themselves invincible. Mistakes in judgement are common. Beware of who you trust.

I closed the book, marking the page. *Beware of who you trust.*

Lights out, I tossed and turned, my brain taking forever to wind down. When I finally slept, the dragons in my dreams were all trying to teach me something at once, while Loki watched on with a wicked grin.

CHAPTER 10
THE MATRIX OF KNOWING

THE NEXT MORNING, I made my way across manicured grounds and entered the treehouse for lessons with Merlin. Brighid and Airmid had the babies, so I was unencumbered, and getting used to it.

I followed the wizard to one of his upper-level libraries, where we sat for tea. A ginger cat made himself comfortable in my lap, to Merlin's obvious delight.

The wizard took a raspberry scone from the plate between us, saying, "Elliott is an exceptional judge of character."

I stroked Elliott's soft fur and sipped my tea while Merlin launched into a story about the cat, who had appeared one day demanding that the wizard share his sardines and crackers. He'd been part of the household ever since.

"So, tell me," Merlin said, changing the subject, "what questions do you have about your book?"

I led with the first one that came to mind. "What is the Matrix of Knowing?"

"The Matrix of Knowing." The wizard tapped the table with his fingers. "It contains the records of reality. Everything makes an imprint on the Tapestry of the World Tree." Merlin took another scone, his third. "Rather useful, really. You can reach into the Matrix and pull out whatever information you need."

"And how do you do that?" I put my teacup down.

"Well," he said, butter knife in hand, "you tap into the essence of something, and through it, you can access everything there is to know about it. A dragon can help facilitate, of course, but you can do it on your own if you're able to clear your mind of all else."

A bitter sound that wasn't quite a laugh erupted from my throat. "That's doubtful."

He nodded. "Quite so. The mind is a busy place. This is why you meditate."

I chewed on my bottom lip. I'd mediated, sure, but rarely on a daily basis. I'd given up entirely since charging into Scotland. Now, I had two babies to care for and rather a lot to think about.

Merlin finished his scone, dabbed at his mouth with a napkin, then waved his hand over the table, making the whole meal disappear. A holographic image of the World Tree appeared in its place, with a sphere around it.

"You see the roots, the branches, the trunk. Inside are infinite worlds." He indicated points of light glittering in each limb; countless possibilities of reality decorating the Tree like leaves. "And out here," he pointed to the sphere that surrounded it, "is a collection of everything contained within." He looked to see if I was paying attention. "For the most part, these worlds exist without knowing the others are there. Parallel realities function as separate lives for those living them, with the exception of the odd weaver. But out here in the field, everything is happening at once. One consciousness holds the individuals within it, and each individual can access all the knowledge in existence if they find a way to open the Matrix of Knowing."

I pursed my lips, feeling the skin between my eyebrows pinch tight. I was getting the answers I'd sought all my life, and they were giving me wrinkles.

"It's rather a lot, isn't it?" he said. I nodded. "But it isn't as big if you only tap into small parts of the Matrix at once. Then you can possess knowledge of all the flavors of jam invented, for instance." He brightened with a satisfied smile. "Or instantly learn another language."

Had my music allowed me to tap into the Matrix of Knowing so I could communicate with Nikolas and his people? When I created music from nothingness, was I downloading from the Tapestry, or adding to it? Or both?

"There is a catch." Merlin's bushy eyebrows lowered.

Of course there was. "What would that be?"

He leaned forward, as if he were divulging a secret. "You must *believe* you already possess the understanding. To reveal the essence of something, you must trust that the knowledge is already yours; that it simply requires the act of remembering."

"I think I do that when I play music."

"Exactly, my dear. See? It's already within you."

I was going to protest that I only understood music by instinct, by feel, but Merlin launched into a discourse on the types of jam he'd collected from different worlds. He gave me a tour of his three-room pantry, then announced it was time for his nap.

I walked back to the palace alone, thoughts spinning. Could I access the Matrix to help do my hero thing? Save the world and be done with it? Cynical laughter rang through my head at the absurdity of it being that simple, not believing it for a second.

When I got back to my room, Airmid was there with Julia and Brendan. As the goddess stood to go, I held up a hand, asking, "Do you have a few minutes?"

She settled herself in a chair, gazing at me with expectation. Waiting.

I took the seat next to her, Julia on my lap. "First of all, I'm sorry for being so late yesterday. I didn't mean to disrespect your time."

"Thank you for the apology." Her mouth showed the hint of a smile. "That's not why you asked me to stay, though, is it?"

My hands played, fingers interlacing then coming apart. I'd meant to ask Merlin. Maybe I could ask my mother, but Airmid seemed more approachable. "Can you tell me about the battle that turned the weavers against each other? What did each side want? Why couldn't they work things out?"

She took a slow, deliberate breath. "Brighid said you were with Loki last night."

"I met with him, and my dragon."

She nodded. "What did he tell you?"

"Not much." I shrugged. "He told me the weavers were involved in an argument and killed each other over it. No details."

"That war changed him. I've never heard him speak of it, but then, I don't spend much time with Loki." She gave a little shake of her head. "The weaver's guild was divided by an idea. Some wanted to interfere directly with humans, to appeal to them through negotiation and, if that didn't work, lead their armies. They wanted to make more weavers, to raise dragons and train humans to ride."

I could see the benefit, the lure of an army of dragon riders in control of the militaries of the world. It was also easy to see how that could self-destruct.

"Other weavers were vehemently opposed to recruiting," she went on. "They thought weavers should work in secret, keeping dragons and the World Tree hidden."

"Which side did Loki back?"

"Those who wanted to grow their force and reveal themselves."

"And my mother chose secrecy." Because of course she did.

Airmid nodded. "Most of the gods thought weavers should remain unseen. Gods are forbidden to interfere with humans. Weavers are a bridge between gods and humanity, but they quickly become gods in the eyes of people who don't know any different."

"And sometimes it went to their heads?" I guessed.

"Sometimes," she agreed. "Most of them did a lot of good, though. Loki argued that gods letting humans worship them went to their heads, too."

I laughed. "The gods are not without egos, then?"

She smiled. "A rare few."

"How old are you? Are all of you immortals?" I gestured around vaguely.

"It depends how you measure time. Some of us are as old as your oldest books. Some are as old as your world."

"Brighid?" I asked.

Airmid's eyes softened. "Brighid is as old as the earth she loves."

"And Loki?"

Her lips pursed. "Loki is one of the younger gods. But even he has matured. Time keeps marching on."

I lifted my gaze from Julia to the goddess. "I'd imagine it's hard to remain unseen as a weaver. To work entirely in secret."

"Indeed." She clasped her hands together. "It's unrealistic. However, imagine the impact it would make for your modern world to learn of world-weavers? It would change the course of everyone's lives to know that dragons are real, that gods exist. If you can do your work in secret, it will leave a smaller footprint, so to speak."

"But aren't I supposed to be changing the world? Why not tell them the truth? Maybe if they saw Eirian more people would be willing to believe in nature spirits."

"Some would make you into a savior," she warned. "Some would call you the devil."

"I see your point." I nodded. "Thanks for the talk." I didn't want a public relations campaign, I wanted humans to make better choices and peacefully coexist with elementals and each other, rather than wreck the planet.

Airmid saw herself out with quiet footsteps, leaving me wondering how I could encourage people to change their ways without showing myself. Giving them a massive wake-up call made the most sense, but I didn't have a clue how to start, and the more I thought about it, the more I liked the idea of staying hidden.

Secret.

Safe.

CHAPTER 11
RAIN AND STARS

IN THE MORNING, water streaked the windows of my bedroom, dampening the incoming breeze. The rain made me think of Scotland, which made me long for Killian.

As fascinating as it was to learn from gods and keep company with legends, I was no goddess. There was something to be said for a simple life. I missed Annelle's cheerful voice, the clash of swords and camaraderie on the practice field, and the commanding, caring presence of Sir Malcolm.

While I nursed Julia and Brendan, I told them about their fathers. Killian, my spymaster husband, and Troy, with his mountain sanctuary. The stories were meant to give them a sense of their lineage, but I was really trying to soothe myself.

By the time the babies were finished, my eyes had misted over. Brendan looked at me as if he'd heard every word. He seemed to understand far more than a child of nine months ought to. Perhaps it was something in the water. More likely it had to do with the amount of time spent with Brighid and Airmid. Julia showed signs of this as well, growing exceptionally fast.

When I got out of bed, I found a one-sentence note on the table. *Thor will meet you on the lawn this morning.*

With a small groan at the thought of training in the rain, I dressed in a pair of leather pants with a thick tunic. I pulled my long green coat out of the wardrobe, and smoothed it with my hands. On went the sword. Daggers in my boots.

When Brighid came to collect Brendan and Julia, I left with barely a thank you. I was polite, but I had too many questions for her, none of which I was prepared to ask. They tumbled through my thoughts as I stalked down the corridors, but every time I asked myself why—why hadn't she left me in Scotland with Killian, why did everything have to be so complicated—I answered myself. If my path had been different, I wouldn't have met Troy. Wouldn't have met Nikolas. Wouldn't have come here.

And the gods would've been deprived of tasking me with saving the world. Had Brighid pulled me through the World Tree herself, setting me on a path to do her bidding?

I shook myself, remembering to be grateful. I owed her my life. Julia's life. And there was nothing I could do to change things.

Thor stood before the exit to the courtyard, dressed for combat. When I reached him, he opened the door and followed me through. When we didn't get wet, I turned to question him.

"Rain provides an excellent opportunity to practice holding a shield," he said, amiably strolling to the center of the field in a dome of dryness.

"And how, exactly, do I create said shield?" I anticipated being drenched as soon as he tested me.

"If failure is what you focus on," he frowned, "you will create it."

"Fair enough." I wrestled with my confidence. "You're reading my thoughts?"

"I'm reading your energy." He crossed his arms at his chest. "It isn't yet real to you, is it—that you're a weaver?"

I laughed. "None of this feels real. I'm a pawn on a gameboard I can't see."

"Then let me reveal it." He flung his arms out, and static built between us. His voice carried the rumble of thunder. "You've asked for answers, for power. Both have been granted. The elements and energies that create what you would call magic are at your command, accessible within you."

I struggled to accept the truth, standing in a dome of dryness beneath a torrent of rain.

"You've wished for the ability to create change where you see imbalance. It has been granted. You are being taught the skills you'll need in order to take on this task, to which you have formally agreed."

I'd just have to fake it.

Act as if it was real until I fooled myself.

I reached my roots into the earth, my crown into the sky, and willed my heart to brighten. Opening my awareness to the rain, I thanked it for its nourishing moisture and asked it to kindly respect the dome of energy I erected.

Without taking my gaze from Thor's, I backed away, and promptly got wet. Rain splattered on my skin, running down my neck.

Closing my eyes, I imagined a shield of dryness surrounding me. But I didn't believe it.

Water soaked through my shirt.

Fighting the frustration, I hummed a quiet song, imagining the resonance surrounding me. Sheltering me.

The rain stopped.

I stood in my own dome of dryness. Music merged with elemental power, I shifted my quiet song inward, letting it continue in my mind, embedding it in my memory.

"That's it, Shelta." Thor's voice rang triumphant off the stone wall. "Now, we can begin."

He stepped forward, drawing his sword rather than his hammer. I drew my own, and the duel was on.

Though my days were anything but predictable, they had a pattern. I would wake to the cries of my children and spend the early morning with them. It seemed I fell further in love each time I looked at Brendan and Julia, and I cherished the time we had together.

Brighid and Airmid took the babies in the morning. I would train with Thor or visit Merlin in his tree. Loki had yet to contact me on the slip of paper I kept between the pages of whatever book I borrowed from the wizard's library, and no one on my scheduled rounds offered me time with my dragon.

With Thor, I honed my combat skills to the point where I knew the dance of my sword intimately. I could handle an assortment of other weapons from the arsenal of Asgard, and often brought my daggers out to play. I became proficient in creating shields, working with different elements, and healing.

I still wanted the blades lesson from Loki.

After sparring, Thor and I discussed the dilemma of how far to go when affecting change on a massive scale. Was it for the greater good? Was it consciously sought by those involved? What were the possible outcomes of interfering? What would happen if no action were taken?

And the constant ethical quandary: when was violence acceptable?

None of the questions had definitive answers, and I found myself pondering them long into the night.

If Merlin's lessons were more light-hearted than Thor's, they were no less profound. He invited me to take a book back with me each day, which meant the stack on my table grew steadily.

When I told him I had too many books, he scoffed. "You can never have too many books!" He pressed another into my hands. "Even if all you do is open it to a random page, read a few words and close it again, you will have received something of value."

Which turned out to be true. It became my new way of reading most of the titles he gave me, though one or two were interesting enough that I read them cover-to-cover.

Navigating the World Tree by Hasthi Dimini was one I devoured in its entirety, learning various strategies to get from world to world. It all boiled down to setting a strong intention, having the way open to you (i.e., being a weaver, working with a dragon, possessing a key, accessing a portal, or being of an immortal race), and more-or-less hoping for the best.

The last page closed with this less-than-encouraging thought:

> Although accounts of successful navigation utilizing the techniques detailed herein are numerous, the possibility of random repositioning always exists. Therefore, it is prudent to travel as prepared as possible for any situation. Enjoy your explorations!

I'd had enough random repositioning for a lifetime.

The next day, over tea, I asked Merlin, "How accurately can you choose a specific time when traveling?"

The wizard hummed as he spread jam on top of a cherry scone. "It's best not to meddle too specifically in the workings of time. It can be done, to some degree, but the World Tree will pull you to where and when you need to be." He smiled fondly at his edible creation.

I was trying to understand the subject that would have the greatest impact on my life moving forward, and he was enamored with his snack. "Let me get this straight. In order to travel the World Tree, I'm to focus completely on a single time and place, but I could just as well turn up somewhere entirely different. And I'm supposed to be okay with whatever happens?"

"Exactly!" Merlin beamed at me. "Now you're getting it!"

Late that afternoon, I paced the corridors of the palace. The children were with Airmid, and I couldn't sit still to read. I had an irresistible urge to talk to Loki.

The courtyard was abandoned when I got there. The fountain sang its watery song, dewdrop flowers and duskberry trees scenting the air, the wall shadowing the lawn.

I walked to the center of the space and narrowed my thoughts to the image of Loki appearing beside the fountain as he had the first time. *Loki, if you can hear me, would you please join me in the courtyard?*

The space beside the fountain shimmered, sounding like melted-blues, as if space-time had bent through a bar I'd frequented in my twenties. Loki stepped out of thin air and strode toward me, smelling of booze, smoke, and sex. One corner of his mouth curled up.

"Hello, Shelta." My name slipped from his tongue with a seductive slur. "Are you ready for a game of knives?"

"Are you sober enough for it?" I asked. He'd lost his tailored jacket, and his shirt hung unbuttoned. "I honestly just wanted to talk."

"Really?" He let his head fall to one side. "What about?"

"I was wondering if you could tell me about some of the other weavers." My words tumbled out, and I realized how much I'd been holding back, afraid to ask Merlin, afraid to ask Thor, afraid to ask my mother or Airmid.

I didn't think they'd give me the perspective I was after.

"I've read about some of the weavers," I said, "but the books only tell one side of the story. They don't say what the repercussions were for the people living with the changes."

Loki rested one finger against his lips. "You might not like the endings of those threads." He spread his arms wide, and his shirt fell open, showing a scar that stretched diagonally from one shoulder to the opposite hip. "But I'll be your storyteller for the evening, if you wish."

"I'd appreciate it." I gave him an uneasy smile.

"I'd like something in return."

"What do you want?"

"A song." The whites of his eyes went from bloodshot to clear.

"I sing most nights at dinner." Odin made a habit of calling me up to perform. Still singing for my food, even in Asgard.

"I'd like a private concert," said Loki. "If you don't mind."

I shook my head. "I don't mind."

He frowned at the bench by the fountain. "Shall we go somewhere more comfortable?"

"As long as you put more clothes on," I said, unable to keep my gaze from straying over his skin. At least his pants were done up.

Loki's laughter shivered through me. He stepped close, shadows in his eyes. When he took my hand, the world blinked into black.

A breath later, I stood before a wall of windows looking out on a courtyard dominated by an ancient oak tree. Several of its limbs rested on the ground.

The soft brush of fabric made me turn to Loki, who was now fully dressed in a black suit with a shirt of silver. He gestured to a wrap-around couch. I took one side of the grey horseshoe-shaped sofa, and he took the other. The trickster god narrowed his eyes as if considering something weighty.

Finally, he said, "None of the stories you've read tell you the repercussions of a specific weaver's actions, because every action ripples out. Everything is interconnected, and where world-weavers are concerned, the Tapestry gets thicker. A war diverted in one world tips the scales of a conflict in another. As time plays out, so does the ongoing dance of cause and effect. A weaver-influenced government might change the world in a good way for ten years, then the whole plan backfires for three generations. Humans revert to their games of greed and power."

I shifted uncomfortably on the immaculate couch. "How much have the gods influenced weavers in the past?"

His mouth twitched with something darker than amusement. "Even when we try not to meddle, it's inevitable."

"Are you trying to meddle now?"

A grin split his face. "You called me."

"Not the first time." Even thinking about Loki's note made my cheeks warm. "You extended an invitation to ride Eirian. You did me a favor."

He stared at me, unblinking. "I did."

"Why?" I doubted this god did anything without a motive.

"I wanted you to know you could leave, if you desired. You're a weaver. You should be with your dragon." Loki's head tipped the slightest degree. "Your well-intentioned mother wants to prepare you for your task. She's probably afraid you'll jump through space-time and never come back if she gives you the chance. That you'll choose freedom."

I frowned. "I have two babies. Freedom isn't really a thing for me anymore. I can't take off and leave them here."

"You could. But you can just as easily take them with you."

"Sure." Sarcasm edged my words. "How can I do what I need to do with babies along for the ride?"

"Shields," he said. "And an enchanted saddle. But that's not your biggest fear, is it?"

My gaze locked with his, and I blew a slow breath through rounded lips. "I'm afraid I'm going to muck it up. That whatever I do, it will never be enough. What if I make a mistake and it ends up costing lives?"

"That's likely." He leaned back, the words light, as if it didn't matter either way. "Your fears are the same as any leader who isn't delusional. Any choice a queen makes has repercussions. A general must send soldiers into battle knowing some may not return. Mistakes are made. Often."

"You're not making me feel better." I tried to laugh but it didn't come out right.

He leaned forward, elbows on his knees, the silver of his shirt making his eyes shine. "Shelta, you don't have to do anything you don't want to do."

"I agreed to this." I sagged into the couch. "When Brighid first gave me power, at the standing stones, I agreed to be a weaver."

"Well. You don't have to run off and play savior right away."

"Why are you trying to give me an out?" I asked. "Not that I'm complaining."

"Because you've lived some of the greatest love stories the Tapestry has seen, and every one of them has been cut short. You deserve to control your destiny."

A stillness settled over me. "You've watched me?"

"I have." He frowned. "Visit your lovers. Get to know your dragon. Let the lifetimes of knowledge you've processed here settle before you go off and save the world."

He was right. I needed to see Killian and Troy before I did anything else. "I should come up with a plan, at least."

"And lots of backup plans."

"I honestly don't have the first clue where to start." I thought of the weaver he'd loved, Eirian's last rider, and wondered if Loki was trying to shelter me, or if the trickster god was playing at something else. "The longer I take, the more people suffer, and Brighid said that the more out of balance the worlds become, the harder it will be to create harmony again."

"No matter what you do, people will suffer. They will suffer in every conceivable way on countless worlds, and that isn't your responsibility." Loki's tone turned sharp. "If you carry that weight, it will crush you."

I swallowed. "Noted."

He looked at me hard for another long moment. "Any more questions?"

My mouth dropped open. The only thing I could think to ask was, "What do I do? How would you change the corruption of Earth if you had the chance?"

He grinned. "Widespread, simultaneous coups. And redistribute the world's wealth."

My head made a slow circle. "What would you do with the people you'd be replacing?"

"Probably kill them." His eyebrows rose as my lips pulled to one side. "No? Put them all on an island together, then."

I laughed. What did I expect, asking the trickster for advice?

Loki stood and lifted a hand. "I have something to show you."

I followed him up a short flight of stairs, past a lavish dining room, spacious kitchen, and shadowy library, to an ornate door. He paused, hand on the handle, then turned it.

When we entered, I nearly forgot he was there. My eyes blurred with tears as I crossed to the piano that waited beneath vaulted ceilings, atop a dark wood floor.

"How is this here?" My words rasped, hands touching the faded wood of an instrument given to me by a prince. Time had tarnished it, but couldn't steal its beauty.

"This is its resting place," he said. "I took it when it was no longer needed. In the future of the world where you were conceived, this piano was destined to meet an untimely end. I added it to my collection."

I ran my fingers over the keys, sliding onto the bench.

"I tuned it for you." Loki came close, leaning against the piano, one elbow on the edge of its open mouth. There was hunger in the silver-green glow of his eyes.

"For me?" I asked. "Have you not played it?"

His head swiveled. "It's been waiting for you."

I started into the first movement of Moonlight Sonata. Loki had been candid with me, I'd be open with him. My fingers danced over the keys, pouring memories of the scandalous things I'd done into the music. When it was finished, I twisted the notes into a different song. Just as seductive, with the addition of my voice.

I played Loki things I could never play in the halls of Duart castle. Not for an audience. Not these bluesy lyrics of messy love and reckless choices. Each time I chanced a glance at him, his eyes were closed. Enraptured.

I reached for songs I'd only ever sung to myself, raw emotion sewn into lyrics that applied just as well to the problems I faced now. Grief, confusion, fear, despair. I never seemed to shake the sense of being an anomaly, an outsider. An enigma without a home.

Loki wanted a private concert. I gave him one full of honesty.

Finally, I rested my hands on the keys. I didn't remember spotlights coming on, but a pair of them illuminated me in a bath of gold and white light. Sweat coated my skin, damp between my breasts, damp between my legs.

I pushed back and stood up.

Loki faced me, still touching the piano. "You're magnificent." He took a step closer, his gaze darker than joy and brighter than longing.

"Thank you." I stood my ground. Trusting him. Hoping I wasn't wrong to do so. "This was a gift for me, too."

"Speaking of gifts." He flipped a hand over, revealing two knives. The blades shone dark green, like a metal version of jade. The hilts were black threaded with sliver. Like Loki's suit. "Would you care for that lesson?"

"I'd love to, but my mother is probably wondering where I am." I shook my head, not daring to accept the blades. Very badly wanting to. "Another time?"

"Another time, yes. But these are yours."

My lips twitched in a cautious smile. "I feel like I haven't earned them. I should have that lesson first."

The tip of his tongue glided along the edge of his teeth. "You just sang your soul, to me alone." His voice made me think of a velvet-black night, glittering with stars. "I am a connoisseur of musicians, Shelta, and you… You are among the greatest. Take the blades."

I took them. Their song thrummed through my palms with sharp readiness. Waiting.

Loki produced a pair of leather cuffs with built-in sheaths. They fit my forearms, a layer of armor beneath my sleeves.

"All it takes is your thought to trigger the release," Loki flung his arms forward and grabbed the hilts of his own daggers as they shot out of his shirt cuffs. He slid the knives home, then released them again without a move, arms at his sides.

I tried it. The grips fell silently into my hands as if that was their natural domain.

"May they serve you well."

"Thank you."

"It takes nearly an hour to walk from this side of the palace to where you're staying," said Loki. "I'll send you through. Are you ready?"

I took a deep breath, and nodded.

A blurred blink later, I found myself in an atrium near my room. The weight of Loki's knives on my forearms was a strange comfort. Something real in a world full of magic.

Chapter 12
A Calling

IN THE MIDDLE of the night, I paced my room, rocking my son. Brendan wouldn't stop crying. Nothing I tried calmed him. To top it off, my ring was buzzing a warning through my nervous system, which put me on edge.

Ears filled with the screams of my son, I turned my focus inward, into the discomfort.

An image of Killian fighting for his life hit me so hard I fell to my knees. I saw Charlie wielding a sword, the grit of battle aging him before my eyes. Killian needed me. I knew it in my bones.

This was the power of a ring forged in the Heart of the World Tree.

Did gods sleep? Could I wake them? *Thor! Brighid!*

Shelta, came my mother's answer. Alert. Calm.

I need to leave, now.

Ready yourself for travel. Thor's voice came through.

I put Brendan in his cradle and got myself together. Fighting dress, boots, sword, knives, and daggers. Purse and water. Baby necessities stuffed into another bag.

As I wrapped Julia in a blanket, my mother walked through the door.

"Thor will meet us on the dragon fields," she said, holding her hands out to take my daughter.

"There are dragon fields?" What the hell? Why hadn't that been part of my training?

I kept such questions to myself, and she didn't reply. She was intent on Julia, her hands glowing blue, then gold, then pink in waves of energy. With Brendan in my arms, we headed out the door.

Somehow, it didn't surprise me that the entrance to the dragon fields was closer than the courtyard where I'd trained with Thor. Immortal warriors held the doors open, and Thor was there to usher us into the crisp night.

The stars shone as bright as they had at the standing stones with Nikolas. Like each pinpoint of light was a deity, and they were all watching me.

Eirian. I called him once. Clear.

My dragon appeared in a burst of wind, with a huge saddle strapped to his back.

Weaver. He lowered his head, gold burning in his eyes. *I'm ready.*

Brighid nodded to Eirian, whose gaze followed her as she climbed up to the saddle. Large, hard-shelled carriers hung to either side behind a padded seat. There were straps for my legs, and I itched to get up there. My mother secured Julia on one side. Thor handed Brendan up, and she strapped him into a nest of fur.

As Brighid said goodbye to the children, Thor snuck me into his arms. His hands covered my back with warmth and strength, his voice a rumble of love. "You've learned much in your time here. You will find the rest along your way, but should you need us, we're your family. You can always come home."

Throat tight with tears, I hugged him for all I was worth.

He stepped back when Brighid jumped down. She stood before me, outwardly composed, but her eyes were glassy. I stepped forward, into her embrace.

There was so much between us. She'd abandoned me, even if she didn't have a choice. She'd also saved my life, and Julia's. And she clearly loved me, even if she didn't say the words.

A fresh cry of need came through the channel of my ring, and I pushed away. "I need to go."

I ran up Eirian's leg and slid into my seat. Julia and Brendan looked at me from shells lined with fur, bindings crossing them, securing the babies in place. I imagined the dragon flying loops as Brendan and Julia slept peacefully, upside-down without a care.

The strap system that went around my legs could be undone with a quick tug. As I sat up, Airmid came across the field with long, brisk strides. Holding my guitar.

She handed it up, saying, "Blessings, Weaver."

"Thank you." Those words would never be enough, but her smile told me she saw the gratitude in my eyes. The tears that wanted to fall.

Thor instructed me to put my guitar into a saddlebag half its size. Dubious, I did, impressed when the bag swallowed the instrument.

The gods stepped back, and I turned my attention to Eirian.

You know where we're going?

I do. He showed me a picture of Duart castle from above. *It is clear in your mind.*

My ring vibrated with urgency and imagery. Killian fighting. Duart in turmoil. We'd be drawn to that time and place. *Let's go.*

Instead of taking flight, we dropped through the earth.

One moment we were on the dragon field, the stars' light glinting off Eirian's scales. The next moment we soared through daytime sky, surrounded by clouds, rocketing over the water. My heart howled with the rush of Eirian's dive even as my gut clenched at the sight of the battle below.

No less than ten ships crowded the waters around the castle, cannons booming and warriors swarming the ground. The space outside the walls crawled with men. It looked like the gate had just been breached, a surge of soldiers rushing inside. The Macleans were outrageously outnumbered.

You take the ships, I told Eirian. *I'll take the men.* Apparently swooping in on a dragon had done something for my confidence.

His laughter rumbled beneath and within me. *Be wary, Weaver. Remember you are yet mortal.*

Right. I'll take some of the men, I amended. *The ones inside the walls.* The dragon gave his assent by tipping a wing to bank toward the castle.

As we sped over the ships, Eirian roared—a primal sound that sent chills down my spine. He spewed fire from his jaws, setting three masts alight. Sails erupted in sheets of flame.

I shouted my own roar. I had a dragon! Those ships were so screwed. Eirian's power rushed through me as he went in for another round.

The soldiers panicked, half of them running into each other in their haste to abandon ship. Some got roasted. I wanted to have compassion for them like Thor taught me, to be a warrior-healer, not a heartless weaver with battle rage. I felt bad, sure, but only a little. Not shook like I'd been when I'd shot my first men while defending Troy's cabin.

Maybe hanging out with immortals had given me a skewed perspective. Maybe Loki's attitude was rubbing off on me. Either way, all I cared about was defending Duart Castle, and if I left a trail of destruction in my wake, so be it.

Can you get me to the wall? I asked Eirian.

Gladly. With a turn, we flew over the mass of swarming men. *Are you ready?*

Yes. I pulled the straps from around my legs. *Keep my babies safe.*

I will.

Eirian banked low, and I leapt from the saddle, landing in a run on the stone path atop the wall. Sprinting past the shocked faces of warriors I knew, I launched down the stairs.

Like a ship through a wave, I pushed through the crunch of battle, the flash and swing of my sword cutting my way. The air was rank with sweat, blood, and gunpowder. The soundtrack of war set a choppy, desperate rhythm. Grunts and curses, cannons and muskets, iron cutting into flesh and bone. It sickened me, even as I rode a rush of adrenaline into the heart of the fight.

I knew the enemy from their lack of Maclean plaid and the difference in their intent. They came to conquer. My clan fought to defend their home.

With a humming undertone, I maintained an invisible shield to deflect any bullets that came my way. I was a whirlwind of motion, sending bodies falling to the ground. Even the best fighters were no match for my sword and newly-honed skills.

Outside the walls, Eirian was wreaking havoc, and, according to the sensations coming through our bond, rather enjoying himself. A shield protected my children from physical attack, muting the sounds of battle. Beyond their sheltered world, my dragon was stomping, tearing, roasting, and otherwise terrorizing the enemy force. He showed me an image of men fleeing with unrestrained fear. Those were the smart ones. The others were the dead ones, or soon to be dead.

I hacked, stabbed, and swung my way through the melee, drawing my dirk to fight with two blades. Three enemies rushed me. I ducked and took one out at the legs, came up and stabbed one man through the heart with my dagger. The last held my sword off for about three seconds before he found it through his throat.

I carried on, no body count possible. I'd become a force of nature.

Thor had instructed me to keep things in perspective as I fought, one element of my awareness aloof, a witness to the mayhem. I tried, but when I caught a glimpse of Killian and Sir Malcolm fighting back-to-back, my last vestige of calm frayed.

They moved as one, father and son. Killian fought savagely, bodies splayed around him, his face splattered with blood. He and Sir Malcolm slashed through their attackers even as I advanced on mine. Five men came charging at me. My shout overtook their battle-cries as I whipped lightning from my sword.

Grimacing with rage, Killian fought two enemies. Behind him, a hulk of a man ran at Sir Malcolm. Busy fighting someone else, the chief didn't get his sword up in time to block the giant's downstroke.

In a ragged thread of doom, Sir Malcolm crumpled. I felt him fall. A shockwave of loss rippled through the land.

As if from afar, I heard my own scream. A bolt of lightning shot from my sword to strike the chief's attacker down. Grunting and cursing, killing with electricity as much as steel, I cut through the army that separated me from Killian, leaving a trail of destruction.

His eyes widened when he glanced at me. With a nod, I pushed forward, until I fought at his back with the chief's body between us. Already dead. Eyes open to the sky.

Time warped, Killian always in my periphery. He was bleeding, struggling, but still holding his own. Fatigue dragged at me, as well, the battle wearing me down. Every swing required effort. My teeth rattled when my sword collided with another. My nervous system was fried from too much lightning, but my blade didn't tire, and I kept swinging.

Finally, Eirian perched on the outer wall and roared. What few enemies remained tried to retreat, and were quickly captured. Slain if they put up a fight.

Just like that, it was over.

I turned to my husband with my heart in my throat.

"Shelta?" Killian's voice was ragged.

"Yes." I wanted to say more, but too many things needed attention before we could possibly have time for each other. "How badly are you hurt?"

"I—it's fine. I'll be fine." He put a hand on my blood-covered sleeve, his warmth seeping into my arm. "Ye're here."

"I'm here—but your father." I dropped to my knees and put my hands on the chief, searching for life, seeking out any wisp of hope. There was none. He was gone.

Anger flamed through me, as if I should've been able to stop his death. If I'd come just a little sooner. Timed our arrival differently.

Best not to follow that thread of thought, Weaver. Eirian hopped down, occupying a corner of the courtyard. Around him, bodies bled into the earth.

Killian shook his head, his gaze bouncing from his father's body, to me, to the red-gold shine of the dragon.

"Gillean's Treasure!" The awe in Charlie's voice made me whip my head toward him. "Shelta, you found him."

"Something like that." I shook my head. "A tale for another time." I dropped my eyes to Sir Malcolm. Charlie hadn't yet seen.

"Oh, Da." His face twisted from the joy of discovery to the horror of war. He disappeared into Killian's arms.

It hurt so much I had to look away.

So, this is your family, came the dragon's voice inside my head.

One of them. "Where's Wallace?" I asked nobody in particular. I was sure he'd have something to say to me, appearing out of nowhere as I'd done. I wanted to know if he was okay.

A tortured cry made me whip my head around to Wallace, who held a limp body in his arms. Bruce, his son.

"No!" I took off running, jumping over debris as I went. "Wallace." I dropped down next to him. "If he's alive I can help."

My heart broke. Wallace was usually a pillar of invulnerability, but the despair contorting his face told me he thought his son dead.

I was unwilling to accept that possibility. I put my hands on Bruce, seeking life.

There. A pulse. Weak with blood loss, but present all the same. I found the source of the wound with my mind, called upon the wholeness that was his true state, and brought energy through my hands. I asked the tissues to knit back together, and they obeyed, supplied with the life-force I provided, drawn from the roots of the world and assisted by my dragon.

I stopped when Wallace sucked a quick breath. Bruce's eyes fluttered, cradled in his father's arms as if he were a small child, not a strong boy of twelve who'd nearly died in a war.

Wallace wept. He'd lost his father, but he got to keep his son.

I stood in a daze, trying to assess where I was most needed. Seeing a warrior I knew lying on the ground bleeding, I knelt and began again, shifting into a timeless, almost weightless state.

It went on like that for a long while, man by man beneath my hands, sometimes women, sometimes children who shouldn't have been fighting at all, each healed to the point where their body could do the rest.

Increasingly, I relied on Eirian to supplement the energy I needed, beyond exhausted.

Tears made tracks through the filth on my face.

At some point, I looked up to see Killian standing near, covered in blood and grime, staring at me. Then Eirian spoke in my head, and reminded me of something that had, astoundingly, slipped my mind: I had children.

Chapter 13

The Aftermath

WEAVER, YOUR BABIES are frantic with hunger. Eirian's calm clashed with the sound of screaming children. *You might tend to them before you deplete yourself completely.*

How many women had to breastfeed after doing battle? I was in no state to touch my children, let alone nurse them—I wasn't going to pick them up with the gore of who-knew-how-many on my hands.

"Annelle?" I called loudly, searching near the castle.

She was helping with the wounded. She waved, ran over, and greeted me with a breathless, "Milady." Her eyebrows shot up as she looked at Eirian. Brendan and Julia's cries were drawing quite a bit of attention to the nests on the dragon's saddle.

I managed an awkward smile. "I need to nurse my children. Can you find someone who isn't covered in blood to help me bring them inside so I can get cleaned up?"

"Of course," she said, and went into action, heading off to recruit a friend.

I turned to Killian. He looked haggard, but my heart still leapt as I met his eyes.

"Children?" he asked.

My mouth opened, but a full breath came and left before I had the presence of mind to answer. "Two, yes. One is named Brendan." How was I going to explain Julia? Would he understand? Would he accept the fact that I loved him in three different worlds?

"A son?" A spark of joy kindled beneath the hardship.

I smiled, even if it was a shaky thing. "Yes. And a daughter, but I'll explain another time. For now, just know that she is, in a way, yours as well."

"What's her name?"

"Julia Brighid."

Killian clasped my shoulder. "It's so very good to see ye, Shelta."

"And you." I put my hand on his chest, throat tight. "I missed you."

"Aye." His voice caught, and he shook his head.

Annelle returned with another maid, clean hands both, and I assured them that they would not be eaten if they approached the dragon. I introduced them to Eirian, and Annelle climbed up. She unstrapped Brendan and handed him down to her friend, whose eyes couldn't have gone any wider.

Killian stepped close, looking at his son. When Annelle brought Julia down, he murmured at how tiny she was. Both children stopped crying, surprised by new faces and momentarily pacified by the movement, but their calm didn't last long.

They started screeching in unison. Demanding. Angry. Helpless.

I shared a last glance with Killian, then high-stepped my way to the castle, Annelle and her friend carrying my children.

"There's a bath being readied, milady," said Annelle.

I shook my head. How long had I been gone? How strange was this for her?

To me, it was surreal.

She led me to the room that was mine when I first arrived in Scotland, before Killian and I were married. The other woman tended the babies as best she could while Annelle took me into the bath chamber and stripped me down. My beloved red-and-black dress became a pile of mess in the corner, destined to be burned.

"It wasn't my choice to leave, Annelle." I spilled my confession into the relative quiet of the bathroom. "I didn't want to go."

"Ye don't need to explain yerself to me, milady." She acted like it was no big deal, but her eyes shone.

"How long has it been?" I asked.

She shrugged. "Not quite a year."

It had been about the same for me. And here I was, back again. Annelle had been my friend, my maid of honor when I married Killian. I'd missed her every day. I wanted to hug her, but I was filthy. It would've done me wonders to soak in the bath, but that wasn't in the cards. The babies called. Loudly.

"I loved that dress," I told her, looking at the remains of it on the floor.

She scrubbed blood from my hair. "It's the strangest thing, but that same dress is hanging in the wardrobe."

I groaned, cleaning the grit from beneath my fingernails. The tricks of time struck again. I guessed my dresses would be taken by the gods sometime in the future, so they were still here for me to use. How did that work?

"Milady?"

"Oh, Annelle." I was so tired. "Trying to figure it out makes my head hurt. Suffice it to say that you've just witnessed the demise of that dress," I indicated the heap in the corner, "yet it still has some life to live before it ends here and now."

She looked about as confused as I felt.

I dunked down to rinse out my hair, then surfaced. "It has to do with the workings of time and the whims of gods, which are two of the most convoluted subjects in existence."

"I'll take yer word on that, milady." She stood and got the towel.

A few minutes later, I had a child on each breast and the room was suddenly quiet. The second maid left with my thanks. Annelle stayed, sitting in a chair near the bed in case I needed her. She was too respectful to ask what had happened, and too kind to hold it against me.

"How did Killian explain it when I went away, Annelle?"

"He didn't. He said ye'd been forced to leave unexpectedly, and would answer no questions about it. Perhaps he said more to his family, but it was a subject that wouldna be tolerated—no one dared speak of it."

I rode the current of another sigh and looked down at my nursing babies. She deserved to know. Showing up with a dragon would go a long way toward helping people accept the truth about me, at least, but Annelle deserved it first-hand.

I launched into an abridged version of my adventures, starting in a forest far in the future and travelling deep into the past—and to the Realm of the Gods—to finally arrive back in Scotland atop a dragon.

I left my parents' names out of the story. Brighid and Gillean.

"It sounds crazy," I said, finishing.

"It's quite the tale, 'tis true," Annelle agreed. "But ye do have the dragon, and everyone is talking about the way ye fight with a sword made of lightning." Her smile made her glow, one eyetooth adorably crooked. "And if ye came through at Brighid's spring... I remember how ye looked at the tapestry. I suppose ye really didn't mean to leave us."

"I most definitely did not." Relief laced my words.

"Well." She rose from the chair next to the bed, dropping the subject and speaking as if I'd never left. "What dress would ye like to wear?"

Annelle called her friend in again to care for the babies while she got me sorted. I chose the green dress, the one I'd worn the first time I set eyes on Duart Castle and met my family of Macleans. The wool and velvet felt like home. Boots, daggers, and Loki's knives completed the outfit. I strapped my sword on, wanting to keep it safe in case there were any spies lurking in the castle. What had happened that Duart had been attacked like this?

I showed Annelle how I used the stretchy blue fabric from the Realm of the Gods to wrap Brendan on my back, and the green plaid to make a sling for Julia at my front. Then I walked alone through the castle.

When I stepped outside, I second-guessed my choice of the green dress. I'd have to cross through the mire of the battlefield to get to my dragon and my husband. I saw Killian among the bodies, one warrior of many checking to see who was dead and who was wounded.

Hiking up my skirts, dizzy with fatigue, I picked my way across to Eirian. *I wonder if Annelle can shorten the skirts on this dress*, I thought, then remembered the green dress had been long in Asgard. Could I go and change history by my actions in the present?

Dragon laughter rumbled through me. *You like to wrestle with the subject of time, don't you, Weaver.*

I answered with an inward smile. *It's a valid contemplation in my new line of work.*

You forget that time is multi-layered, and every possible reality exists within the Tapestry.

You're telling me I shouldn't worry about it so much. I made my way toward Eirian's massive presence near the wall.

Indeed. And, should you decide to ponder the subject, let your mind not cling to one outcome only.

Easy for you to say. I looked up into his fiery eyes. *Now, my dear dragon, what can we do for you, seeing as you've done so much for us?*

His mighty sigh blew my hair back, the air hot as he exhaled through his nostrils. *A bath would be nice. Perhaps someone could remove the saddle so I can swim in the sea that reaches toward the mountains in the distance. It looked ever so nice from the air.*

Consider it done, I said, having no idea how to undo the saddle.

My gaze darted around, wondering who I could get to help me. On the way over, every warrior I'd passed bowed to me. Formally. I wanted to be their comrade, not their queen, but I was married to Killian, who'd just inherited the role of Chief Maclean.

As I scanned the field for someone who wouldn't be intimidated by the task of unsaddling a dragon, Rodric came over, wiry and graceful as ever. He'd do nicely.

He met my eyes and tipped his head. "Shelta."

"Rodric." I gave him a smile.

"That was some of the finest fighting I've ever seen." A high compliment, coming from him.

"Thank you. I must admit, a good deal of it comes from the sword itself." He raised his eyebrows, and I tried to explain in a way he'd understand. "It leads the dance, much of the time."

"May I see it?" He reached out, palm down. I drew the well-cleaned blade without getting Julia involved, and handed it to the master of arms. Though it had a glow when I held it, in Rodric's hands it was simply a fine sword. "What do the runes say?" he asked.

"The one who wields this sword is a dragon-friend, and exists outside of time." I recited from memory, the words making me shiver.

He raised his eyebrows at the dragon behind me and handed back my sword.

"Rodric, might I ask a favor?"

"Anything, my lady." He bowed. "Ye're a heroine, ye ken."

I smiled, awkward at playing superhero. "Would you be so kind as to unsaddle Eirian here."

Rodric turned to Eirian and bowed much lower than he had to me. "Anything we can do for ye will be done, Dragon. Many thanks."

"Indeed," said Killian, coming over with Charlie. "We owe ye a debt."

You owe me nothing, Eirian said, and I knew the three men could hear him. *This was a deed of my choosing, my first act in partnership with the Weaver.*

"Eirian, this is Killian, Charlie, and Rodric." I held a hand out, indicating who was who, though I expected he could read it in my mind.

The Charlie I'd known before would've been overjoyed at meeting a dragon, but he was too much of a man now. His boyish enthusiasm had been tempered by hard loss.

Rodric took command. "Charlie, give me a hand with this saddle."

"Aye," said the lad, and the two of them started working out how to unsaddle a dragon.

Killian and I watched, side by side.

"Are there any wounded in bad shape?" I asked.

"Not ours." He shook his head. "Ye already got to the ones who needed it. I won't have ye exhausting yourself for the scum who came to conquer."

"What happened? Where did they come from?" Duart had been attacked before, but not like this. Not that I knew of, anyway.

Killian slid his gaze to mine. "Usurpers sent a fleet across the channel. Unloaded most of their men up-island in the dead of night, and were upon us before dawn." His eyes narrowed. "They planned to take the isle, to make this their stronghold before invading the mainland."

"They'll be down quite a few ships and what looks like a small army." I glanced around at the carnage. "Was that the bulk of their force?"

His frown deepened. "Sadly, no. There's a sect of fanatics funded by slavers. They've been trying to claim a single throne since King James negotiated the accords."

I remembered. A crown for Scotland, one for England, another for Ireland. And slavery abolished. I loved that about this timeline, this parallel world. Why did someone always have to mess with a good thing?

Power corrupted. I'd seen it in every place I'd been. And it was my job to figure out how to shift that power. To weave a new thread.

If I dealt a blow to those who intended evil in one world, did it harm them in other places? Other times? Would it ripple through the Tapestry?

It must. Everything I did was a weaving. Such was the nature of my life.

No pressure.

Rodric and Charlie climbed to Eirian's back, and pulled on massive buckles tucked just behind the nests on the saddle.

Killian's voice shook me out of my thoughts. "Ye have a dragon now."

"I do." We'd done it, Eirian and I. Traveled the Tree at will.

Killian looked at the children at my back and belly. His voice was a quiet scrape of love. "They're beautiful."

"They are." I swayed as I stood, keeping them content.

"*Ye're* beautiful," he said, making my heart trip over itself. "The men who were on the wall tell of a fearless beast who dove from the sky, set afire the ships and devoured the enemy host. They say a goddess of war leapt from its back and cut through every unsavory man in her path, that she can hold lightning in her bare hands." He leaned closer, not quite touching me; he was still covered in the grime of war. "I saw a fierce woman wielding a weapon made of light. One who worked magic with her hands when it was over to save my bravest warriors and friends."

My throat was so tight, all I could do was look at him.

His eyes shone. "Then I realized that woman was my wife. That she had returned from beyond my reach, powerfully changed—and with two children."

I tilted my head, needing to say something to make him understand.

Killian cut me off with a smile before I got a word out. "Not now, lass."

I took a step back. No. Not yet. But soon.

Would he understand?

Killian helped Charlie and Rodric carry the awkward weight of the saddle to a covered area near the stables, where they'd presumably find a non-gory spot to put it down. Somehow, the saddle was clean. The rest of the dragon was definitely not.

Are you hurt? I asked. He looked unscathed, but there was so much blood on him I wanted to be sure. *Would I have felt it if you'd been injured?*

You'd have known. One corner of the dragon's mouth curled. *Thank you for asking.*

Thank you for everything. The tears I'd been holding back broke through. He'd brought me here, back to Killian.

Eirian flooded me with love. It seeped through our connection like summer sunshine, warming me to my bones. Then he took to the skies with a great leap. His wings caught the light, glowing. Sunfire in flight.

A short while later, he sent me an image of himself diving in and out of the water, playing like a dolphin in the waves.

Wiping my eyes, I joined Killian, Charlie, and Rodric by the stables. When I told them there was a dragon swimming in the sea, they grinned, basking in a rare ray of happiness amidst the wreckage of the day.

It didn't last long. Rodric recruited Charlie to help him clean weapons, leaving me alone with Killian. But as he started to speak, Julia began to fuss. Three cries later, Brendan joined her.

I tipped my head up with a pained smile. "I should probably go tend them."

"Aye. I'll be inside in a bit." A shadow crept through Killian's gaze as we said goodbye. As if I'd become a stranger to him.

CHAPTER 14
OTHERNESS

ANNELLE INSISTED ON watching Brendan and Julia while I went to dinner with the family. Killian knocked on my door, clean, in a black jacket and forest-green kilt.

He pulled me into his arms, letting loose a sigh. I hugged him hard. Goddess, was it good to be here, to see him again.

Killian glanced toward the carpet, where Annelle played with Brendan. Julia watched from a blanket nearby. I licked my lips, and said, "I have a lot to tell you."

"We can talk after dinner," he said. "I'm just glad ye're here."

Another kiss, and we were out the door. On the way down, I stopped to stare at the tapestry. That was my mother in the reflection of the spring. A piece of my father in the oak.

Killian pulled out a chair for me when we got to the table. We held hands while Cristina said a somber blessing, all heads bowed, the chair at the end of the table decidedly empty. Sir Malcolm had sat there last night. Now, he lay lifeless beneath a shroud in the chapel.

It was hard to find an appetite, and though the food was as good as I remembered, it was quite a change from dining in the company of gods. Thor and Brighid and the rest of the immortals I'd been living with for the past weeks knew who

I was. They accepted me. They might entertain impossible expectations of me, but I didn't have to hide who I was.

Unsurprisingly, everyone wanted to know about Eirian, and where I'd been. I gave them an abridged version of the story I'd told Annelle, describing a great deal about living in the mountains of Wyoming and Norway, and very little about Troy or Nikolas. Nothing at all about my parents, and only the briefest mention of the Realm of the Gods.

Nothing about that dinner was comfortable. I tried not to squirm, not to sweat under their attention and the heat of the fire at my back.

The subject of Julia was tricky. I couldn't hide the fact that she wasn't Killian's daughter, and I didn't think they'd understand that Troy and Killian shared the same soul. But I needed to say something. I didn't want my daughter to be a child born of betrayal in their eyes.

"Had it not been for Julia," I said, "I'd never have gone to the Realm of the Gods, and I wouldn't have had the power to be here today, when you needed me most."

I lifted my gaze to scattered smiles and raised eyebrows. Cristina nodded to me, looking like she was about to thank me again for saving her son, which she'd done twice already.

They were wonderful people, but I was an enigma. A stranger. A savior.

I would never again feel the way I'd once felt here. Part of the family. Sheltered. I'd changed forever in their eyes.

When I was dressed for bed, the babies asleep in cradles, there came a knock at the door. Killian entered, and stood in the doorway of the bedchamber. Waiting.

"Please come in." I padded toward him in bare feet.

He stopped a few paces from me. Like he didn't want to touch me for fear I'd disappear. "I'm sorry lass. Ye're like a dream, though I am awake."

"I'm here." My voice caught.

The sheen of his eyes spoke volumes. "Would ye come to bed with me this night?"

A few notes of laughter bubbled up. "Of course." I stepped into him, arms wide. When he wrapped himself around me, it was like a blanket of comfort. Love. Recognition.

Killian, whose soul had shown up for me again and again.

We gathered my sleeping babies and walked the empty hall to what used to be our bedchamber. The sheets were clean, covers turned down.

"I missed you." I tackled him with a hug as soon as the children were settled in a corner of the room. I couldn't hold back. All I'd wanted for so long was to return to him.

A slow inhale echoed in my ears. Like he was breathing in the scent of me. "Aye." He pulled me closer, one hand in my hair. "I've prayed for this. Every day."

I tipped my face up to kiss him, but he leaned back. Out of reach. He lifted my left hand, where the diamant sparkled on the wedding band Nikolas had given me in Asgard.

"I canna help but notice ye wear a ring." Such sorrow in his eyes.

I swallowed. "This ring led me back to you."

He cocked his head.

"I'll try to explain it all." I paced to the bed, exhausted, and sat on the pillow that had once been mine. "You may as well get comfortable. It's a long story."

He undressed with his back to me, keeping his undershirt on, and slid beneath the covers. His silence scared me. Or maybe he was scared. I'd never seen him like this.

"Killian." I reached for the right words to help him understand. "Your soul has found mine three times now. Julia's father, Troy, shares your soul. And Nikolas—" I tripped on my words as I remembered him in the circle of stones, swearing to find me across the worlds. "You have vowed in more than one lifetime to find me, and you have."

"As other men?" He shook his head again.

I took his hands. He had Thor's blood in his veins; he had to be able to receive energy. "Will you allow me into your mind? I want to show you?"

"Into my mind?"

"The same way you heard my dragon speak. I can send you pictures. Show you memories." Would he let me in? He was grieving. Confused. Was this how Nikolas felt when I'd had my walls up?

Reluctantly, Killian nodded.

"I love you," I whispered.

"I love ye, Shelta." He squeezed my fingers gently. "Whatever happened, I'm glad ye've come back."

A tear tracked down my cheek, and I closed my eyes, calling memories. I reached into Killian's mind, and offered the images with as much clarity as I could. I wanted to show him who he was in other worlds. How his soul stretched through the World Tree.

I sat with Troy in a green valley, looking toward the lake as he told me what the seer had said. *Apparently, my spirit has more than one incarnation in more than one world. B'alam said I've already married you once.*

Later that night, before Brendan had been born, Troy's voice had been raw with emotion. *I feel as if your child is my own—I want to care for you as my own.*

Killian's breath came out in a rush, but I didn't open my eyes. Fragments of memories flooded me. Troy fighting, killing a man in the street. Me shooting a rifle from beneath our mountain cabin. Bodies burning in the dark.

Focusing, I chose a different image. Sent the moment to Killian.

Nikolas and I stood atop a hill ringed in standing stones, in the place where two valleys crossed. There, he wove his will into existence. *I am yours as you are mine. I will my soul to find you, to love you, anywhere we meet in the branches of the World Tree. This love knows its way through time and eternity.*

Trembling, I pulled away, separating my awareness from Killian's and erecting a shield for fear of spilling a torrent of images into his brain. He didn't need to see it all. Judging by the sheen over his eyes and the way he reached his hand to my face, it was enough.

Tears spilling down, I said, "This ring was forged at the Heart of the World Tree. It connects me to you."

He brought my hand to his lips. Kissed my fingers beside the ring. "Then I am grateful for it."

He moved to kiss me, but this time, I leaned back. "There's more, Killian." I looked to the ceiling, then back to his dark-brown eyes. I'd broken all my rules for him, he deserved to know the truth. "I'm Brighid's daughter. The goddess. She birthed me at the spring before sending me through the Tree, into another world."

His jaw dropped. Before I lost my courage, I told him how Julia had been delivered, and how Brendan had been tended in the Realm of the Gods. Then I bit my lip… Did I tell him about Thor? About Gillean?

"I always said ye were the gift of the goddess."

"You did. And the goddess, my mother, told me what I'm about to tell you." I blew a breath out. Looked at him. Couldn't bring myself to say it.

"What is it, lass? What did she tell ye?"

"Gillean was my father." The words tumbled out. "Your clan has his name, but not his blood. Your line was sired by the god Thor."

He blinked. "Wha—what?"

"That's what the goddess said." Maybe I should've kept that part to myself. "It's not something I'd tell anyone else, I just—thought you should know. I didn't mean to overwhelm you."

His eyebrows shot up. "It's been that kind of day."

"Every day made my mind spin in Asgard. It was like living in a constant state of disbelief. At least you feel real." I leaned toward him, and he caught me in his arms.

"Aye." He pulled me closer. "This is real."

I tilted my head up. His cheek grazed my temple. Lips near my ear. Still, he didn't kiss me.

"Will ye wear the ring I gave ye?" he asked.

"Of course," I whispered back.

He took my ring from where it rested in a seashell on the bedside table. I gave him my right hand, and he slid it on my finger, golden knotwork set with a blue sapphire.

"Ye're mine in three worlds?"

"I am."

He kissed me, gently at first, then with fire. Like he was making up for the time we'd lost. We made love in the candlelight, without words, bodies entangled. It reconnected us as nothing else could.

After, as I caught my breath, snuggled against Killian's warmth, it hit me how different everything felt. It was good, yes, but it wasn't the same.

Nothing would ever be the same.

Chapter 15
Singing the Souls to Peace

THE SERVICE FOR Sir Malcolm and the other fallen took place the following evening on a hill above the castle grounds. Eirian stayed out of sight, explaining by saying, *It confuses people to see a dragon when they don't expect one, and there is no dire need.*

A chill wind seeped through my clothing as clouds dimmed the early-summer sun. At least Annelle had the children inside. I pulled my cloak closer, drained from the day before. A little fragile.

I stood at Killian's side, not quite touching. Looking around, I was certain there were more people in attendance than lived on the island. Prince Charles had even made the journey. He made a slow nod as our gazes met, and I echoed the motion. If the royal was surprised by my presence, he didn't show it. I wondered how much Killian had told him in his message.

The priest who'd married us led the service, naming each warrior who'd fallen with a poetic summary of their lives and virtues. He gave blessings for their souls and the families they left behind. Although his speech on Sir Malcolm was longer than the rest, it was clear that the chief and the men who'd fallen with him were on even ground, just as they would lie together beneath the earth.

A long while later, after everyone had left, Killian stood near his father's grave. I waited, off to the side; there in case he needed me.

His gaze finally shifted my way, the weight of it settling in my already aching heart. Killian raised a hand toward the mountain in the distance, where a rough trail climbed the wide ridge that rose to the moody clouds. "Follow that path early in the morn." He dropped his arm. "Ye'll find me on the edge of land, sky, and sea. Will ye come?"

"Of course." I could see how much it meant to him.

"I take the oath at dawn." The marriage to the land. The ritual that would make him chief of Clan Maclean.

Killian took my hand, brought it to his mouth and kissed my wrist, then my palm. When he curled my fingers in and brushed his lips against them, a single tear trickled down his face. Then he turned and walked across the wet grass to the path that climbed the hill.

Where I couldn't follow.

Arms wrapped around myself, I watched him ascend, cloak billowing around him, until he disappeared beyond the crest of the rise. The sky loomed heavy with the scent of rain, as if the land itself mourned the passing of so many that had called this place home.

Fingers stiff with cold, I returned to the castle, my hair coming undone as the gale grew in strength, whispering of a storm to come.

I could smell the food before I got inside. Hearing the clamor of so many guests, I changed routes and entered through a servants' entrance. Everyone was busy, and I made it through the back corridors without much notice, returning to the bedroom where Annelle waited with Brendan and Julia, who were hungry for milk and attention.

A bit later, when the babies were full and content, I got ready to go downstairs. As much as I wanted to hide in my room with them all night, it was my duty as Killian's wife to at least make an appearance. Annelle brushed stray bits of grass from my skirts and re-did my hair, her patience a balm.

I stood in front of the mirror, wrapped in green plaid. Stayed there too long.

"Ye look lovely, milady," said Annelle.

"Thank you, my friend." I turned to face her. "Sometimes, I feel like a stranger to myself. I suppose I should go down. You're okay with Brendan and Julia?"

"Aye." Her hands swished through the air like taking care of two babies was nothing. "I'd much prefer being with the bairns over serving the guests below, if ye don't mind my honesty."

I laughed. "I love your honesty." I hugged Annelle, and headed out.

As I made my way through the halls, the din of conversations rose. I was grateful not to have the babies along. There'd be questions enough without two sudden children.

You think overmuch on the approval of others. Eirian hummed in my mind. *Remember who you are.*

Right. I blew out a breath. *Daughter of a goddess and a legend.*

I chose you for your worthiness, for the beauty and ferocity of your song.

You chose me. Warmth spread through me as my dragon sent his strength. It brought a glow to my skin, and it was thus that I walked past the tapestry of Brighid's spring: alight in power. I reached out a hand to graze it. The weave was soft beneath my fingertips. Would the gods take this from Duart in the future, too? Would my mother hang the tapestry on the wall in her chambers? She'd never invited me to her room; she had always come to mine.

My mother was a goddess, and I barely knew her.

Down the steps. Away from the tapestry. I tucked my existential problems into a corner of my mind and put on my game face for socializing with Scots.

Wallace found me as soon as I entered the hall.

"Wallace." I tipped my head in greeting.

"Shelta." His smile pinched his nose. "Have ye any idea where Killian's gone to?"

"He went up the hill." To prepare. Alone. My heart twisted, knowing he needed this time, but wishing he was here, beside me.

"Damn." Wallace frowned but didn't look a bit surprised.

He composed himself—chin up, chest high—to face the duty of playing host for the remainder of the evening, leaving me with a moment's unguarded look that made me hold back a laugh. He cared, though. I watched as he spoke patiently with someone's grandmother, wrapped a consoling arm around a fallen man's brother, comforted a new widow, and otherwise made a connection with each person as he went through the room.

Prince Charles approached, greeting me with a bow. "Lady Shelta."

"My dear prince." I made a curtsy.

"No need to curtsy to me," he replied, a hint of mischief in his eyes. "You're a dragon rider, I've learned. Surely that puts you on level with royalty."

"Perhaps, but there is grace in a curtsy, and my honor is gladly given."

"Well said." He offered his arm.

I'd been standing near the doorway, reluctant to enter the room. "You must've ridden hard to get here today," I said as the prince led me through the throng. It had taken Killian and me from dawn to dark in a coach when we'd made the trip from Stirling Castle.

"Aye." His face went hard, circles beneath his eyes. "We left in the black of night, as soon as the message arrived. Malcolm was a friend, and many great men were lost."

I swallowed, wishing I'd come sooner, knowing I couldn't cast my thoughts down tunnels of what-ifs. Not now. "I killed the man who took Sir Malcolm down." I said it quietly, for his ears only.

"Good." The prince's gaze sliced to mine as we navigated the crowd. "Thank you for coming, Shelta." He took my hand and gave it a squeeze. "These are my people, and you saved them."

I opened my mouth but no words came out. He looked away, waving as a man raised his glass toward us. We were stopped several times by people in various states of sobriety, or lack thereof. A few were at my wedding with Killian, and didn't even know I'd been gone, which made for strangely normal, awkward conversations with well-meaning visitors whose names I didn't remember.

But our aim wasn't socializing. Prince Charles had been steering me toward the piano since he'd met me at the door. The piano I'd last played for a private audience of one trickster god. A thrill shivered through me as I slid a hand along the polished wood top.

With the prince watching, I sat on the bench and placed my hands on the keys, tuning into the instrument. My breath came slow and even as I opened to whatever music the moment wanted to offer. The room fell into a hush.

My fingers moved without thought, bringing the piano to life. The notes began high and light, in a minor key that hinted of what was to come. My left hand traveled down the octaves to add the rumble of bass.

The song expanded, growing. It became an entity that took up space in the room, telling a story. The soaring strength of my dragon. The battle that called me here. Grief. Victory. Reunion. It cried for our losses, for the chief who had fallen on the field. Deep notes signified the way the earth received them. Mourned them.

And then came sanctuary. The melody shifted into a resonance of peace, of sleep that knew no pain or suffering. I thought of Killian, alone in the night, and willed the music to him, hoping it would bring him solace.

The hair on my neck rose as I realized the people in the hall weren't the only ones listening. The dead were present; the spirits of those we'd buried had come to hear me sing. I opened my voice, which rose over the sound of the piano, weaving ancient words into lyrics.

Sleep now, rest now,
Brave souls, brave hearts,
Know, now, all is well.
You lived and died with dignity.
Grieve, yes, but worry not,
Those who yet live on,
The ones you loved lie peacefully
Beneath the blessed moor.

Their souls fly freely,
Bodies left in rest.
Sleep, be at peace now,
Know, now, all is well.

The last words repeated as the piano notes faded away, declaring one final time that all was well. A collective sigh filled the silence that followed, as if the souls of the dead dispersed in a barely-there breeze.

Well done, Weaver, Eirian spoke in my head.

I opened my eyes to look around. The first face I saw was Charlie, Killian's son. He and Wallace gazed at me through layers of emotion.

The music didn't ask for applause, and none was given. Instead, there were murmurs of thanks. Smiles. Tears.

Lightheaded, I curtsied, and allowed Prince Charles to lead me through the crowd.

As we made our way past a window, I looked out into the darkness. Rain beat against the glass and wind gusted in the branches of a tree. "Where are all these people staying?" I asked. "Surely they aren't going anywhere tonight."

"No. It is not a night for travel. Some of us have rooms, but most will lie wherever they can in the shelter of the hall." As I imagined the magnitude of an eighty-person slumber party, Prince Charles winked. "They will be tended by kind-hearted guards."

I supposed that would keep the place in good shape.

It took a while to get through the crowd. I retreated as graciously as I could, creeping back upstairs. Back to my sleeping children and my circling thoughts. As tired as I was, I couldn't stop thinking about the man I loved, out in the storm alone.

Eirian?

Weaver? I could see him, comfortably tucked beneath an outcropping of rocks.

Have you seen where Killian is—is he all right? I knew I should trust him, that Killian sought privacy that night. But I needed to know he was safe.

He sits in a cave. He has been sitting there, still and silent, for some time. He attunes to the elements.

Thank you. A layer of tension melted.

I didn't ask if he'd allowed himself to grieve, but I hoped.

CHAPTER 16
THE MACLEAN

MORNING CAME DARK and soon. Rodric and Charlie wrestled the saddle onto Eirian before mounting horses to make their own journey up the hill. Heavy from lack of sleep, I strapped Julia and Brendan into their protective cocoons, then sat on my dragon, breathing in the potency of the dawn. The air was damp and cool, clouds layered in a swirl of dark greys and blues.

You feel it, Weaver? Eirian helped me connect to the sentience of nature. Land, sky, and sea were alert. Aware. The birds were watchful. Trees leaned their consciousness toward what was to come. Even the grasses were listening.

Oh, yes. I felt it.

Eirian spread his wings, took a mighty leap, and we were airborne. I used a shield to keep dry as we rose through the clouds. Above, the sun was reaching tendrils of light into the sky over Scotland.

I squinted at my babies, secure in their nests, bright eyes open in wonder at the wide blue sky.

Eirian sent an image of Killian below us, and I swept my arms open, forming a hole in the cloud cover. The top of the mountain hosted a small group of people, their horses tied off to the side. Killian stood atop a massive rock, the others in a semi-circle before him. He looked much like he had when I first met him, but larger than life. Full of power. The rock sat above the rest of the land, worn smooth by the wind and rain.

Killian and his guests turned our way, and I imagined what Eirian must look like, wings alight with the glow of dawn as we glided to a landing away from the horses. I tucked my children into their wraps, slid down the side of my dragon, and strode to the peak that overlooked the rolling island and dark blue water that surrounded it.

When I reached the rocky apex of the hill, I claimed the empty space at the center of the semi-circle, opposite Killian. To my right stood Prince Charles and two clan chiefs I'd met briefly the night before. To my left, Wallace, Charlie, and Rodric.

Julia was wrapped on one side of my chest, and settled into a nap as I swayed side to side, over and over, in a mother's simplest dance. Brendan's head swiveled, wide-awake and curious as ever, his weight supported by a second wrap that sat him on my opposite hip. I curled one arm around him, smiling as he looked at his father. A father I'd prayed he'd one day meet.

And here we were.

Eirian sat tall and splendid in the light behind me. As the dragon settled, it felt like time shifted. A new era. A new beginning.

I willed the break in the clouds to widen, and the sun shone full, warming my back and illuminating Killian in a glow that was more than daylight. Amber surfaced in his dark brown eyes, and turned to fire. Thor's presence sparked in my awareness like a lick of lightning.

Killian's voice rang clear and rich, his words an invocation that carried clear across the island and out to the sea.

Elements all, be welcome here.
Earth, Fire, Water, Air,
Land, Sea, and Sky.
Those who swim, those who run, those who fly.
Those who slither and crawl, those who grow.
I call you now. Hear my vow.

By blood and duty, on this rock I stand,
And give my oath to be Lord of the Land.
With full awareness of my responsibility,
I claim the right and power of Chief,
Protector and guide of my clan.
Guardian of my people.
Guardian of the land.

The clouds behind Killian swirled, rumbling with a brilliant flash of light. It surrounded him and obscured all else, bringing me sharply back to my courtyard lessons with the god that had seeded Killian's clan.

The ocean crashed so loudly that its salt-seasoned air reached us atop the mountain. Eirian gave a bone-shaking roar and blast of fire directed to the sky. The horses reared and whinnied in answer.

In the light that surrounded Killian, I saw Nikolas and Troy.

Same soul. Different man. A trinity knot etched in my heart.

The light faded to glittering sunshine, but Thor's presence remained. My mother was there as well, her consciousness a familiar thread. The gods watched.

We stood, all of us still, for a long time. Listening to the land. Local elementals made themselves known, their whispers and croons filling the air and rumbling beneath our feet.

According to my mother, this was missing from the world I'd promised to save. Nature's consciousness had faded in my previous future, which was hard to envision when I was surrounded by such aliveness.

The wind died down as the nature spirits retreated, and Brendan broke the silence with a shriek of laughter. He clapped his hands, giggling, and looked at his father as if he wanted Killian to make it all happen again.

Hard faces softened into grins. Killian smiled at Brendan and me, then threw his arm around his eldest son.

"Did ye get all that, Charlie?" he asked, only half joking. "Ye be the heir, now."

"Aye, Da." Charlie looked star-struck as he gazed at his father.

Killian shook hands with each of the other witnesses, clasped his brother in a strong embrace, and finally came to me. His eyes still glowed, amber and gold in deepest brown.

He kissed me full on the mouth, then rubbed Brendan's back and looked over my shoulder at Eirian. "Nice touch, Dragon."

Eirian gave a pointy-toothed grin.

Eventually, we headed down the hill, me with my children in the sky, the others on horseback. I floated above them, savoring the infinite blue space above the clouds, holding on with my strapped-in legs and reaching my arms out. I was unshielded, and the chilly air made my face and fingers tingle. I loved it. All of it.

The impact of Killian's ritual gave me an inkling of hope. Maybe I could do something similar to awaken the elementals in the modern world I knew.

It was impossible to forget my mission from the gods, looming in my future. A responsibility too heavy even for this freedom to overtake. I'd stay with Killian for a while, then go see Troy. A month with each? Was that too long?

Eirian's voice snuck into my head. *Weaver, enjoy the moment. You'll know when it's time to move on.*

Right. Here and now. I cast another look around at the sky, a floor of clouds beneath my dragon, whose scales lit up like a fiery opal.

When Killian and the others were on a rise above the castle, we dropped down to meet them. I left the children in their little nests, to be collected by Annelle in the courtyard as I joined Killian for his grand entrance. My husband, the chief. Eirian was more than happy to guard the babies, humming contentedly as I strode away from him.

Killian trotted over on his horse, which Charlie had brought along. I swung up behind him, and we rode bareback, just a cloth pad beneath us. No saddle to get in the way. I held him, savoring the closeness, the way he put his hand on mine, over his heart.

"Your eyes are still glowing," I whispered into his ear.

Killian slid his hand up my thigh, his voice a rumble that spiked my blood with desire. "I have the power of the ocean in me, Shelta. I feel strong as the earth; I feel as if I could take to the skies."

"I completely understand." The same energy thrummed through me. Its potency rippled through the Tapestry of the World Tree.

A crowd of people waited outside the castle, watching us ride in. The splendid white horse Prince Charles rode was taller than our black, but all eyes were on Killian.

As we reached the open gate, a man stepped forward and called out, "Chief Killian Lachlan Maclean!"

"Maclean!" answered the rest in a loud chorus. Cheers bounced off the castle and swept toward the sea. Petals of wild flowers fluttered down from those on the walls above.

A blush of heat flamed across my skin. My father was the man who'd given the clan their name, while Thor had seeded their lineage. My mother was their patron goddess, and I was wife to the chief. Their dragon-riding queen.

Familiar faces from the night before formed lines on either side as we rode through. I waved, one hand on Killian's side, the gold of the ring he'd given me glinting in the sun.

When we reached the castle, Killian helped me dismount with grace, but I didn't walk at his side as we approached the doors. I stood a pace behind, even with Prince Charles. This was Killian's domain.

He stopped in the archway of the castle's entrance and filled the courtyard with his voice. "Thank ye for being here, for what each of ye mean to this family." He looked around, making eye contact with so many whose lives were woven with his. "By the power of blood, I am chief of this clan. By the power of nature, I am lord of this land. By the power of duty, I serve and guard this realm."

A cheer swept through the crowd, but they quieted when Killian raised his hand.

"May our hospitality please ye this morn. There is food for all. When yer bellies are full and the day is yet long, may ye have an easy path and blessings on yer way."

More cheers. Killian led us inside, and everyone followed. Scents of breakfast hit me, making my stomach rumble as so many people parted to make way. Abundant buffets and drink tables lined one side of the hall, where people poured whisky in their cups an hour past dawn.

Gavin played a lively tune on his violin, another minstrel accompanying him on lute. Several people brought out drums and joined in an impromptu jam that some of my old friends would've given anything to see.

Memories of my summer working at a Renaissance Faire in Wisconsin flooded through me. People there had longed for escape in their costumes; playing lords, ladies, and rogues. I'd been a roving bard, playing little stages and shady corners beneath the trees. Here I was, living the kind of life they'd tried to reenact.

I smiled through a blur of greetings, with Killian's hand strong around mine.

The food disappeared quickly. The musicians played one set, and the drinks weren't offered for long, so the sun was still low in the sky when people started trickling out the door. Each new widow was given a bag of coins. Benevolent guards watched as everyone said farewell, making certain nothing that belonged to the castle accidentally wandered off.

Killian leaned close and spoke in my ear. "Go up now. I'll be right behind ye."

Glad to be dismissed, I wove a meandering path to the stairs. I didn't hurry, but he did, showing up as I reached the door to his rooms.

Killian drew me inside, kicked the door closed, and had me up against the heavy wood of it in one motion, kissing me so hard my breath rushed out. His fingers wasted no time at the fastenings of my dress. Annelle would have some mending to do before I could wear it again. My shift ripped as he pulled it off.

In a blur, I was on the bed beneath Killian, enmeshed in the intensity of power that coursed through him, electric and unstoppable. Primal. He moved with the ocean's strength, surging in waves, skin hot against mine.

Afterward, in a tangle of limbs, Killian held me as if he'd never let go. The children would need me, but I didn't want this to end. My husband, mine once more.

Crying woke me. Disoriented, I squinted, looking around. The sound was coming from the bathroom, along with a knocking at the closed door.

I pushed Killian's heavy arm over my head, grabbed a blanket, and crossed the room, shutting the door behind me. Annelle was there with Julia, holding the screaming child.

Instant quiet enveloped us when I put the baby to my breast, but for Annelle's soft apology. "I'm so sorry to disturb ye."

"Thanks for bringing her. I didn't mean to fall asleep." I tried to shake my mid-morning grogginess.

Annelle helped me get comfortable, placing a towel on the floor for me to sit before she went to check on Brendan, who she'd left with a friend.

"I'll need a new dress," I told her before she slipped into the passageway, "but I'd love a bath first. Can I sneak through the back corridor without being seen?"

"Aye, but wouldn't ye rather return to yer rest?"

I looked down at the baby at my breast, sighed deeply, and shook my head. "Brendan will need me."

She nodded, and left. I leaned against the wall. All I wanted was to crawl back into Killian's arms and the comfort of his bed. But I was a mother, now, above all else.

After a bite to eat, I brought the babies out to the gardens. Eirian was sprawled across the lawn and watched us in the peekaboo sunshine. Brendan crawled around putting leaves and sticks in his mouth. Julia was belly down on a mossy piece of ground, lifting her head and pushing into her arms while I chased after Brendan and tried to keep him out of trouble.

Eirian found all of this extremely amusing, which came through our connection in a wash of bubbly mirth. He also had a keen interest in the dragon statue that stood proudly near the castle. When I asked him what he thought of the sculpture, he replied, *The dragon is handsome, well crafted, and well-armed. It could be bigger, of course.*

I laughed. *If it were as big as you, there would be less space for people to admire it.* Brendan giggled, and I wondered how much he heard of the dragon's thoughts.

I include Brendan in most things, said Eirian. *He will be a rider when he is quite young, Weaver.*

The comment stopped me from reaching out to steady my son, letting him stand on his own with his hands on a stone bench. I watched, wary. He'd fallen so many times, and it was a particularly hard place to land.

How much do you know about his future? I asked. *How much do you know about my own?*

I see the most likely paths. I can follow threads of your essence in the Tapestry, but I cannot see the whole weaving.

Brendan toppled over, and I caught him, banging my knee in the process. Eirian laughed at the string of profanity that went through my head and the effort it took to keep from swearing out loud.

I was rubbing my knee with a scowl on my face when Killian came out of the castle. Julia had begun to fuss, and Brendan was scampering off on all fours to get into more trouble. The dragon who took up most of the courtyard's space was laughing. We made quite a scene.

"Enjoying the fine afternoon?" Killian asked with a hint of sarcasm as he eyed me.

"For the most part." I cleared the pain with a wash of energy—something I should have remembered as soon as I banged it.

Killian grinned at how agile his son was. "Mother said I was more than a wee bit of work at this age. Charlie was, too."

I gathered Julia up and rocked her, sending Killian a smile.

"I didn't want ye to go," he said, sitting next to me on the bench.

I looked at Brendan. "The babies needed me."

"Aye." His voice was soft. "I heard yer song last night."

"I hoped you would. Did it bring you peace?"

"It did." He brushed the backs of his fingers across my cheek.

The skin around Killian's eyes crinkled as he watched his son, the crescent-shaped scar near his temple curving tighter. He stood, and in two paces reached Brendan, who had gotten to his feet with the use of a tree trunk, then tumbled down on its roots. He looked like he wanted to cry, but his father picked him up, and tossed him gently into the air. Brendan's face shifted from surprise to elation as Killian caught him in sure hands.

Such a perfect moment. It made me think of the wish I'd made when Brendan was born, that he and Killian could know each other. My heart swelled with gratitude as I watched them play. Brendan's cascading laughter rang through the courtyard. Pure, unbridled joy let loose into the world. Even the guards' faces lit up on the edge of the gardens, but those on the high wall kept a keen eye outward, the recent battle fresh in everyone's minds.

Killian approached Eirian, stretched out across one side of the courtyard, and placed Brendan down. I crept closer, rocking Julia.

For a while, Brendan sat in rapture, drooling as he gazed up at the crimson dragon, whose eyes were as big as he was. Eirian waited, patient as an age of time.

The boy said, "Ha!" and followed it up with, "Dra! Dra dra ga ga na na na na na. Ha!"

He kept on with that line of speech while he clambered up to stand between two of Eirian's sharp claws, which seemed to me a perfectly safe place for my son. For the first time since we'd come out to the garden, I relaxed.

Eirian sent a wordless invitation into my mind as he upturned his other front paw. I studied the pads of his foot, tough as stone, but the smooth hollow in the center didn't look like it would scratch a baby's delicate skin. I laid Julia there on her back, and the infant gaped at the dragon, her mouth a circle of amazement.

Killian slipped an arm around my waist. "They're beautiful, Shelta. Ye've turned into a remarkable mother. It can't have been easy."

I shook my head, throat tight. No, nothing about the last year had been easy, but at least I'd had help along the way. I tipped my face to Killian's and answered with a kiss.

CHAPTER 17
STUBBORN SCOT

A FEW DAYS AFTER I'd dropped from the sky on a fire-breathing dragon, weapons practice resumed. I joined the men, leaving Brendan and Julia with Annelle. I'd taken to calling her "Aunt Annelle" around the children, which made her blush with pride.

On the training field, I sparred with a sword from the armory rather than my own, holding back the urge to use magic. Every day for a week I faced up against Rodric, Wallace, and Killian. Most of the time I lost, but my skills still sharpened.

One misty morning, Rodric persuaded me to bring my elven-made sword to the field, insisting on having a go against the legendary blade. Against my better judgment, I agreed.

Surrounded by warriors, with Eirian's crimson bulk adding to the audience, I stood in the center of the field and eyed the arms master warily. The sword hummed in my hand, ready.

I focused my intention on a dance, not a duel. Rodric wouldn't be able to shield himself if the blade brought its lightning to play. It would take as much skill to keep the sword's energy in check as it would to keep up with Rodric's swordsmanship.

"Dinna worry, lass," he said with his sly smile. "I've no plans to die today."

With that, he bowed, then lunged.

Our onlookers became a blur of color as we moved, swords clanging, a storm darkening the sky and adding to my unease. Rodric was a master, but my sword had a mind of its own. Sparks flew as it clashed against Rodric's blade again and again.

"Ye're holding back." Rodric was only slightly winded. Cheeky bastard.

"Aye." I was about to tell him why, but he cut me off.

"Don't," he said, and lashed out.

He came on with such ferocity, my sword knew only that it was being attacked. It took over my movements, and the ringing of blades became a jarring song.

Despite my efforts to contain it, to deny it, to push it back and hold it in, the lightning came through. With a deafening crack of thunder and a blinding flash, we both went flying in opposite directions, electricity sizzling the damp air.

I hit the ground hard. Ears ringing. Head spinning. Terrified I'd killed Rodric.

Up and moving before I'd even begun to recover, I staggered over to him, panic rising. He was sprawled at an awkward angle, body limp.

Tapping into the energy of the earth, I called the power of healing through my hands and pushed it into his body. "Breathe!" I ordered.

To my relief, he did as he was told, moaning and rolling onto his side. He sat up like he'd only pretended to die moments before. The crowd of warriors, some with singed hair, gathered in.

"Are ye alright, lass?" asked Rodric in a strained voice.

"I'm fine," I lied. My breath came in gasps and my whole left side ached. "Why?" I asked, the only word I could get out.

Rodric shrugged. "I needed to know."

I shook my head, gulping misty air and wincing at the sharp pain each inhale caused. Clinging to my pride, I drew on reserves of energy and stood as tall as I could. I didn't want Rodric to feel like an idiot, even though he deserved it. And I surely didn't want them to know how hurt I actually was. So, instead of collapsing on the spot, I turned toward the garden on the other side of the stone archway, and set off.

Eirian, I pleaded, *help.*

Breathe, Shelta. You'll be fine. The dragon jumped over the wall to the other courtyard, where I was headed.

Don't let me fall. As I was about to stumble, a surge of strength kept me up.

I couldn't see straight. Everything was a blur. I was vaguely aware of Killian next to me, saying my name. He sounded so far away.

I made it across the field, through the archway, and staggered two paces to the right so I was out of sight from the men on the field. Killian caught me as I fell, lowering me to the grass gently.

Bring her here. Eirian's voice brushed my mind, his words for Killian.

My husband carried me to my dragon, and the morning light tinted red-gold as Eirian brought his wing over us, creating a shelter of privacy. I began to shake uncontrollably.

"Shelta!" Killian's voice was sharp with concern.

Eirian remained calm. *She must release the energy. She took most of the current that came through the sword, and healed your arms master before tending to herself.*

Killian's anger rose, coming off him in hot waves.

Eirian sent him a warning. *Hold your temper, Maclean. She needs to ground.*

Grounding was exactly what I was doing, reaching into the earth for stability, letting go of the electric current from the sword. After a moment, Killian's newly-enhanced awareness seeped in, much like Nikolas had done, helping me connect to the healing current of nature.

My nervous system was fried, emotions on the edge of breakdown, but at least I'd stopped convulsing. I breathed slow and deep. Calling on the elements of water and earth, I channeled energy through each part of my body.

When I'd recovered, more or less, I turned my thoughts to Eirian. *Why didn't you help me?* He could've prevented the whole thing from getting out of control.

If dragons could shrug, that's what he did. *You needed to know.* An echo of Rodric. *I allowed it to play out as an opportunity to learn from your abilities. You will heal yourself first next time, I believe.*

A cool surge came through our connection; the dragon was completing my recovery. I was tired and sore, but whole. My nerves mostly settled. *Next time I think I'd redirect the current,* I told him, *rather than hold it back.*

The dragon hummed his agreement.

As I pushed myself up, Killian helped me sit, his expression more than a little dangerous.

"I'm okay now," I said.

He didn't look convinced.

I smiled, took his hand, and played with his ring; its intertwining designs a match to mine. "I didn't want Rodric's pride damaged in front of all the men."

"Damn his pride." Killian's face reddened. "I've half a mind to whip him for endangering ye both."

"Killian, he wasn't breathing. Even if it seemed like he was only down for a minute, I'm pretty sure Rodric knows he'd be dead if I hadn't been able to heal him."

The fight faded from his eyes. With a sigh, he helped me to my feet and held me close. "Ye're a mystery, Shelta. And ye, dragon." He looked over my shoulder at Eirian.

Killian helped me straighten my bodice, tidy my hair, and brush grass from my red plaid skirt. Ready to face the warriors waiting in the field, he held himself tall, as if we'd been having a picnic beneath the dragon's wing. "They'll be watching," he said, placing my hand on his arm.

Eirian withdrew his wing, and we walked to the castle. God-blooded chief, and goddess-born weaver.

CHAPTER 18
BITTER UNDERSTANDING

THE RODRIC INCIDENT did nothing to help me fit in. Everyone treated me with respect, but I was an outsider now more than ever. Feared as much as loved.

Even with Killian, there was a distance I couldn't remedy.

In an attempt to make people comfortable around me, I hid the powers I possessed, but the need to keep evolving tugged at me. No matter how much I enjoyed being with Killian, the sense of being a stranger in a familiar place only grew. I'd changed too much to belong.

I began to spend more time outside with Eirian, and less time inside the castle walls. When I gave myself over to the piano's music, songs came from other worlds, tugging at my consciousness.

Each time we flew, the call to cross to another realm grew stronger. One day, as Eirian banked in a wide turn, I looked at the castle sprawled on its rise, surrounded by sea. The mainland stretched majestic, mountains and lochs in the distance.

Killian was down there, sequestered in his office. Letters and summons demanded his attention each afternoon. I lived for nights spent in his arms, the only time the distance between us didn't exist.

I'd been here less than three weeks, and I already felt it was time to move on. Troy still hadn't met Julia, and Nikolas waited. How was I supposed to save worlds when I had three husbands and a family connected by the World Tree?

Have other weavers been tasked to better an entire world on their own? I asked Eirian.

Not without mass casualties, he answered. *Most weavers altered the course of history by choosing sides in a war, overthrowing governments, or infiltrating the circles of power. Doing things peacefully tends to take longer, and is often the more difficult approach.*

Difficult. Yeah. Sarcasm oozed through our inner conversation, and dragon laughter rumbled through me like a wave. Maybe if I focused on the elementals, it would be enough. But, no, it wouldn't. It couldn't. Even if I healed great swaths of forest, humans would cut the trees down again. They needed to *want* to change. On a mass scale.

As the sun sank in the sky, Eirian descended into the empty practice field, drawing the eyes of guards on the wall as he landed. One waved as I looked up. I freed my legs from the straps, but stayed in my seat on the padded saddle, trying to breathe through the heaviness in my chest.

I had to leave Killian. Again. I'd get to say goodbye this time, but the thought cracked through the brief joy we'd shared like a jagged rip through a masterpiece of art. I hung my head, rising and falling with the dragon's breathing.

The promise I'd made to the gods scared me silly. It was too big. I understood why the last weavers wanted to recruit others. Pretty sure Loki chose the right side on that one.

How could they ask me to do this alone?

I shook myself from my thoughts when Charlie approached, brow furrowed. His voice had gotten deeper since I'd been here last. "Shelta? Are ye alright?"

"Aye, Charlie." My words fell flat with fatigue and sorrow.

He reached up. I handed Brendan down, stowed Julia in a wrap at my chest, and slid off the dragon. With a caress of my hand, I said goodbye to Eirian and walked with Charlie toward the castle. "What is it?" he asked before we'd reached the entrance.

I stopped, swaying to comfort Julia as I faced my stepson. "I have to leave." I pressed my lips together, shaking my head. "I don't want to go, but I have obligations, and a family that extends beyond the borders of this world."

He nodded, holding my gaze with eyes that were so like his father's. Like Brendan's. "I understand," he said. "Ye ride a dragon. I don't imagine ye'll ever stay in one place for long."

I blinked, trying to stop tears that threatened to spill over. The truth of his words hit me with savage understanding. "No, I suppose I won't."

Charlie hugged me, half friend and half son. I pulled myself together, and stepped back with a forced smile. He put his hand on my back, and we continued up the stone steps, through the huge wooden doors, and into the castle.

Late that night, as Killian and I lay in bed, I gathered the courage to tell him. The babies slept in cradles on the floor, the firelight giving off a glow of false comfort.

"Killian?"

"Shelta." Acceptance sighed in the depth of his voice.

"I have to go," I whispered, already crying.

Killian held my face in his hands and kissed me soft, then drew me into his arms. "Ye cannot fight the nature of who ye are, lass. Soon as I saw ye with the dragon, I knew ye'd never be held to one world." He touched the diamant ring on my left hand.

I gave him a weak smile.

"Will ye return?" he asked, and my heart broke a little bit more.

"Of course." I had to. "I'll do everything in my power to see you again."

His response was a kiss so deep the love between us flooded my senses. He tasted of wine and mint. The salty scent of his skin mingled with the sweetness of the candle beside the bed. His breath and moan were the sounds of home.

This was world-weaving, this dance of boundless love, anchoring my presence in Killian's heart. Tonight would keep us entwined, even when we were worlds apart.

I don't know if either of us slept.

We held each other through the night, until dawn bled into the sky.

When the babies woke, I nursed them, then gathered my things and asked Killian to say my goodbyes. It would be too much to have to explain myself again. I'd told Charlie and Annelle. That was enough.

Killian carried Brendan as we walked into the courtyard, where Eirian waited. I breathed the crisp morning air, willing my eyes to stay dry. When Killian had kissed each child and whispered his blessings, I tucked them into their fur-lined nests.

And then it was time.

"I love you." I stood on my tiptoes to kiss him.

"I love ye, Shelta, with all my heart." He squeezed my hand. "When ye think of me, of this place, let it be with joy, not sorrow. Agreed?"

I smiled past the tears; my throat crammed full of emotion. "Agreed." One more kiss, and I climbed up to the saddle, securing my legs with a tug on the straps.

Killian raised his hand. In a whoosh of wings and wind, Eirian rose into the sky. He circled once around the castle, and I waved to the guards, drowning in tears as every warrior saluted us.

Then, we glided toward the sea. *Where to, Weaver?*

I sent Eirian an image of Troy's cabin in its meadow on the side of a mountain, silvery-blue lake below, surrounded by forest, with a teepee behind, and Brighid's spring beyond. I could see Troy's face. My heart called for him, for his hideout in the Tetons of Wyoming, in the year 1888, in a world where California and much of the southwest still belonged to Mexico.

The dragon hummed beneath me.

Clouds swirled, everything went dark, and the worlds shifted.

PART II

~

CHAPTER 19
RETREATING ON BORROWED TIME

AS SOON AS EIRIAN and I materialized above Troy's homestead, the horses neighed a warning and went galloping behind the stable. Damien the wolf-dog launched himself off the porch, barking an alert.

It's me, Troy. I reached for him, heart and mind.

Shelta? A flood of affection came through our connection, as clear as ever.

I'm here. The dragon isn't a threat, though I doubt Sundance and the others would believe me if I tried to tell them. I'd let Troy communicate with the horses, calm them as only he could.

We flew a wide circle, with a view of the forest and its hidden spring not far from the cabin. The sun cast a golden glow on the trees. Smoke curled up from the chimney, as did the scent of rabbit stew. Dinner time.

Eirian landed in the corner of the field farthest from the stables. Troy strode across the meadow, guns at each hip. Damien came with him, crouched, padding at Troy's side.

I pulled my legs free, slid down, and ran smack into his chest.

His strength surrounded me, pulling me into the familiar scent of horse, pine, and fresh herbs from the garden. "Shelta. You're here."

"Hi." I leaned back, looking up into hazel eyes that matched the trees.

"Hello." He kissed my temple. "Where's Brendan?"

"On the dragon. This is Eirian."

Troy lifted a hand. "Hello, Eirian."

The dragon tilted his head in greeting. Damien whimpered, and sank belly down by Troy's feet.

Bittersweet words tumbled off my tongue. "I can't stay that long, but I needed to see you. And give you some time with your daughter."

His eyes brightened, widening as he caught sight of the cradles hanging off the saddle. "I have a daughter?"

"Her name is Julia."

His gaze swung back to me. "My mother's name."

I nodded. "Julia Brighid. After your mother, and mine."

His jaw dropped. Last I'd seen him, I hadn't known who either of my parents were. "Did you meet your mother?"

"Yes." My voice broke, and I shook my head. "It's a long story." I cleared my throat and gave him a tight-lipped smile. "Let me get the children."

Perched on the saddle, I unbuckled the babies. *Will it always be this hard, Eirian?*

You will adapt, Weaver. He hummed a note that vibrated through my feet.

I handed Julia down to Troy, whose face shone. He greeted her with quiet words filled with so much love I had to swallow tears as I tucked Brendan into my wrap.

Thick leather moved reluctantly under my fingers as I unlaced the straps that secured the saddle onto Eirian. By the time we'd stowed it in the lean-to by the stable, it was nearly dark.

Eirian went hunting in the forest while Troy served me rabbit stew in the cabin. The herb-rich broth brought back memories. Of my multitude of temporary homes, this one was the coziest. The intimacy I shared with Troy wrapped me in contentment while the meal warmed me from the inside.

Kicking back by the fire afterwards, I nursed Julia and watched Troy play with Brendan. The light cast shadows across his face, silhouetting the bridge of his nose, which sported a bump that hadn't been there before.

When the children were content, I joined Troy on the sheepskins, and gently slid a finger from his forehead to the tip of his nose. "You get into a fight?" I asked.

He cocked his head. "I did. Last time I was in town, I had a drink with Tom and ended up in a brawl."

I arched an eyebrow, remembering Tom, the local sheriff. "Outlaws?"

The way his eyes narrowed was all the answer I needed. "There've been a few. None have bothered me here, but Tom's had his hands full."

I scowled. "I dare them to show up now. I've got a dragon and a sword that shoots lightning." My voice scraped over dark thoughts. Murderous ones. Probably not a good look for a world-weaver, but I didn't really care. The first time I'd killed, it had been here.

To protect my family.

"A sword that shoots lightning?" Troy's question made me smile.

"Aye." I winked. "Let me tell you a story or three."

The surge of vengeance dissolved as I launched into the increasingly strange tale of what had happened since I last saw him. Troy leaned against the wall with Julia in his arms, Brendan crawling over his legs, and listened.

Late that night, the children slept, Julia in Brendan's old cradle, while he was tucked into a nest of blankets beside her. If it wasn't for Troy's thumb gently rubbing my upper arm, I'd have thought he was asleep.

Titling my head, I planted a kiss on his cheek.

He turned, lips finding mine in the darkness. When he leaned back, his voice slipped through the space between us. "I'm still convincing myself you're real."

I laughed softly. "I know what you mean."

His hand brushed my cheek, a solemn note creeping into his words. "It was hard when you were gone. I never thought I'd have a family, and then I did."

"And then it was gone in the blink of an eye?" Guilt ate at me. I'd left him behind and broke both of our hearts.

"Exactly." A heaviness seeped through our connection, like it was hitting him all over again.

I threaded my fingers through his. "You told me you knew we'd see each other again." I remembered the way he'd reassured me, long before I'd found Eirian and realized I was the daughter of a goddess.

"I didn't want you to worry. It was harder to trust when you were gone," he admitted. "I was never so lonely as the first months after you disappeared. And then I went into town to commiserate with Tom—"

"And found some trouble to distract you?" I guessed.

He made a quiet snicker. "Indeed."

"Was it bad?" I resisted the urge to touch his nose again.

His shoulders lifted in a shrug I felt rather than saw. "No worse than any other brawl I've been in. Five lowlifes against Tom and me. We handled it."

With casualties, I was sure, but I didn't push. I knew his past haunted him.

I sighed, shaking my head at how much my life had changed in a couple of years. "You never thought you'd have a family, and I once promised myself I'd never have children. Then I fell in love with you. Three times."

His kiss was a kindness I'd dreamed of tasting again. "How lucky am I?" he whispered. "In love with the daughter of Brighid, and a descendant of Thor, no less."

At the mention of his ancestor, tenson crept back into my jaw. "So say the gods."

"The gods who've tasked you with saving the world?"

"Yes." The word came out flat. "I still have no idea what I'm going to do."

He hummed a thoughtful note. "Let me get this straight. The gods aren't supposed to interfere, but they've trained you and set you this task. Isn't that interfering?"

I snorted a laugh. "Pretty much, yeah."

He tipped his forehead to mine. "Well, Shelta my love, how about we not worry about it tonight. There's enough time tomorrow to contemplate grand adventures."

"Agreed." I pressed closer to him, my body coming alive as he slid his hand over my hip.

His touch was all I wanted. I'd have to face my fate soon, but not yet.

CHAPTER 20
TARGET PRACTICE

THE NEXT MORNING, just after dawn, Eirian checked in with me before slipping between worlds. He said he was off doing dragon things. Whatever that meant. I'd call him when I needed him. Until then, it was me and my little family, alone in the glorious wilds of the Tetons.

To the side of the cabin was a woodshed made of log beams and rough planks. To the left, under its own roof, Troy had a woodshop. He set to making a little bed for Brendan while I rocked Julia, swaying from foot to foot beside the teepee that stood at the center of the backyard. Brendan wandered in the grass between the fenced gardens.

"That's new," I said, lifting my chin toward the extension he'd built since I was last here.

He squinted with a crooked smile. "Brogan helped."

The draft horse. I'd seen him pull logs out of the forest. The big brown horse loved the work—a lot more than he'd liked clearing dead bodies from the field after Troy and I killed a dozen men intent on murdering him.

I shook myself from the memory and forced a smile. "Have you seen Sarina and Diego?"

Troy set a wide board on his workbench. He brushed his hand over the wood and tipped his gaze up to mine. "I've been out their way a few times."

I looked down at the child we'd made together, and willed myself not to let old grief rise. Losing him had shattered me. The Tree had taken me from him after a mere handful of months, newly pregnant. He'd gone from recluse to father to all alone again. Of course, he'd go to the Nwetaka for comfort. They were his family—had been his family longer than I.

A woman wandering time.

Troy selected a long, narrow board, saying, "They've had some trouble lately. The army has been staking claim to land that isn't theirs, trying to force the Nwetaka into reservations like they've done to other tribes in the east." He laid the board on the table, measured a length, and grabbed his saw. "The government thinks they own all this land. They're marching across the country, taking all they can get." He shook his head.

This world was different than mine, but not that different. If I helped protect Indigenous people and their land as a weaver, could it mean a different future for this world? Could it help heal the world I'd promised to save?

A sinking realization turned my stomach as I recalled a nightmare I'd had the first time I'd been here. I'd seen Troy fight blue-coated soldiers, outnumbered, helpless to do anything about it.

"Will they fight?" I asked.

Troy nodded. "They will. I'll help, if it comes to that. Tom has tried to negotiate for them, but the army isn't interested in compromises. They want control of every natural resource, control of every person. Forcing people off ancestral land is criminal."

"Yes, it is." My mind turned with possibilities. "I'd like to help."

"You and your dragon?" His mouth turned up, drawing a smile from me.

"Me and my dragon." We could lay waste to an army, but letting Eirian be seen was risky. If the military knew there was a dragon out here, they'd want it for themselves. It would make Nwetaka territory that much more desirable.

Julia began to fuss. Swaying, I hummed a soft song, a lullaby for all of us. The music rolled, soothing. It didn't erase the sorrow and injustice, but it washed the sting of it away.

I sang the words of a poem I'd read in Merlin's library, and Brendan giggled as he walked his way along the fence of the nearest garden, one hand out, fingers barely touching the wood. Little Julia had grown fast as well, no longer the premature baby, her cheeks, arms, and legs properly plump.

She watched Troy with wide-eyed curiosity as he cut and sanded each piece of wood. By the time she'd fallen asleep, Troy had the makings of a crib.

I held Brendan's hand and brought him inside to keep me company while I put Julia in the cradle. Outside, Troy started banging, hammering nails into the wood. Brendan jumped at each hit, until I sat him on my lap and snuggled him close. "It's okay," I cooed, and started into another lullaby.

Did Brendan remember the gunshots he'd heard last fall? He'd cried at the sound when I'd learned to shoot, and screamed when we'd hidden in the room beneath the house, him wedged between fur and blankets behind a trunk, me standing on a chair, sighting targets through the window below the front porch.

Why did it haunt me now, when I'd massacred half an army at Duart Castle? Maybe because the threat was to

Troy's sanctuary. Killian had a castle, a keep designed to defend against invaders. Troy's cabin was hidden in the wilderness, the home of someone who wanted to be left alone. The fact that bandits had found us here still made me angry, as did the thought of soldiers coming to remove the Nwetaka from their land, but I kept my feelings out of my song, and settled Brendan.

He laid his head against my chest, a comforting weight. Soon, he was asleep, and the hammering had stopped.

I left the window open so I'd hear the children if they woke, and went back outside. Troy grinned when I came around the corner, mouth agape at his quick craftsmanship. The crib was simple, but well-built. Solid and smooth. The pine shone golden in the mid-day sun.

"Nicely done," I said.

"Thank you." He looked at his creation. "I planned it out while you were gone. In case you came back. I just... never finished it."

I closed my eyes. Opened them with a shake of my head.

He tipped his head toward the house. "They're asleep?"

"They are." I held his gaze as he crossed the space between us, and wrapped me in his arms. "And you have plans for me?"

"I could think of a few things." He kissed my neck.

A giggle bubbled up, and I turned my mouth into his. Soft. Warm. Seductive.

When he steered us toward the teepee, I stopped him with a hand on his chest. "I won't be able to hear the babies."

"Damien can let us know if they wake up." Troy's eyelids drooped, like he was sending the wolf-dog a message. Damien loped across the field from wherever he'd been, and met us at the back door. "Don't wake them," said Troy. "Let them sleep, but tell me if they wake up."

The dog gave a quiet woof to let us know he understood, and slipped inside.

Soon, Troy and I were tangled together atop a bed of furs, our clothing in a heap, a blanket drawn over bare skin. The teepee smelled of soil, days-old campfire, and leather. The woody scent of sawdust clung to Troy.

I sighed between kisses. At least Killian, Troy, and Nikolas all knew about each other. Maybe it was weird to jump from husband to husband, but I had three of them.

Our souls were intertwined.

"I missed this," Troy whispered into my hair.

"Me too." I ran my hand down his arm, fingers bumping over the scar from a bullet wound I'd sewn up myself. Sliding into our way of speaking mind-to-mind, heart-to-heart, I kissed him. *I want you. All of you. I want to lose the boundaries of where I end and you begin.*

Shelta. His touch turned to fire, enhanced through our bond.

Instinct took over, melding us into a flame of love and desire that burned brighter with every kiss. We became our own song, music of belonging woven into the Tapestry, every feeling amplified. His ecstasy was mine; my bliss was his.

In the thoughtless, dreamlike aftermath, I slipped toward sleep, until Troy whispered, "Damien says Julia is starting to fuss."

With a sharp inhale, I sat up and reached for my clothes. No nap for me.

Once the children were tended and we'd all had some lunch, my mind turned to future plans. Which gave me an instant headache.

"You're scowling." Troy eyed me from the kitchen, where he was washing the last plate.

"I'm trying to figure out how to save the world." I laughed, no joy in the sound. "Every idea I come up with falls flat."

"Maybe a walk will help?" he suggested.

"A walk," I agreed. "And some target practice."

His eyebrows lifted, but he asked no questions.

Outside, I drew Loki's blades and showed them to Troy, who sat on the front porch with Julia and Brendan. The green knives shone deadly in the sunlight.

Troy whistled low. "Where did you get those?"

"They were a gift." I lifted my gaze. "From Loki."

"The god of chaos?" His voice rose in disbelief.

"Yes, but the legends aren't necessarily true. I spent time with him in the Realm of the Gods. My mother didn't like him much." I frowned.

"What was her reasoning?"

I looked up, wondering if she was listening. Did I ever have a moment of privacy, or were the gods always watching? "The way I understood it, he doesn't play by the rules. He's unpredictable, and his past is messy."

"Who doesn't have a messy past?" asked Troy.

"Exactly. He seems to have come around. Eirian likes him, even if he doesn't trust him." I shrugged. "That's good enough for me. Anyway, he gave me these. I've yet to use them. Thought I should get some practice in before I try throwing them in a fight."

Troy's gaze slid toward a stump that stood on its own, halfway between the cabin and the lake, near the trail that led to the Nwetaka village. It had long been used for target practice, shot to hell by bullets. It resembled the surface of the moon more than it did the remnants of a tree.

"I'll watch these two." He smiled down at Julia, who had her hand wrapped around his thumb. He cradled her easily in one arm. Brendan had crawled down the stairs backwards while we talked, and was toddling through the grass, his progress resembling the drunken walk of a very small sailor.

I slid the knives into their sheaths, turned my back to my family, and stalked through the grass. It swished around my skirts, my boots thudding on firm ground. The sunbaked smell of pine rode a soft breeze, infusing my breath with memories of the last time I'd gone to the destroyed stump for target practice.

The gods wanted me to change the world. Every one of them stressed the importance of avoiding violence, of using the light, of creating peace. All of them but Loki.

They'd also trained me for battle, and Loki's blades were an unexplored tool, as was his advice. *Wait if you want. Do it on your own terms.*

I stopped before the stump, feet braced, and called the knives. The black-and-silver hilts dropped into my hands, the single-edged blades glinting. As I turned my thoughts to the night I'd sang for him, I felt his presence.

Loki watched me.

A shiver crept across my upper back. Did he see me from the sky? Did he stand invisible beside me? And the question I didn't dare test: if I spoke to him, would he answer?

I lifted a knife and took aim at the deep dent in the stump that served as a bullseye.

Breathe. Focus. Let fly.

Dead center.

"Ah." I smiled. "So that's how it is."

Loki's blades weren't messing around. They sang a song of cutting precision that made me tingle and triggered a grin. Eyes narrowed, I shifted my weight back, lifted my arm, and sent the other one after the first, aiming at a higher spot on the trunk.

Thunk. Direct hit.

My laughter rose like a hawk's cry and fell like a brook over stones. Inside, a current of power coursed through me. I strode to the stump, high on whatever energy Loki had put into my blades.

I threw again. And again. And again. The only time I didn't hit my mark was when one of the horses whinnied, and my focus wavered. As long as I tuned into the song of the blades and told them where to go, they flew true.

I moved back, putting more and more distance between me and the stump, but not once did a knife fall short, or under rotate. They sliced through the air to exactly where I sent them.

After countless throws, as I returned from retrieving the daggers, Troy walked across the field. He held Brendan in one arm, shadows falling across their faces. Smoke rose from the cabin's chimney.

The sun was nearly behind the mountain, evening cool creeping in. I sheathed the blades, and swiped a hand across my forehead, wiping away beads of sweat.

"You've been at it for a while," said Troy.

"Apparently." I hadn't even noticed. "Where's Julia?"

"Napping." He smiled. "Damien's on watch. I thought I'd check on you."

I stepped in beside him, heading toward the house. "Thanks. I lost track of time."

He eyed my forearms, where the knives lay hidden beneath my sleeves. "Are they magic?"

I shook my head, suddenly exhausted. "Must be. I need to lie down."

He walked beside me, not quite touching, there in case I needed him. But as we neared the cabin, the back of my neck prickled, and I stopped to gaze at the darkening forest.

"What is it?" asked Troy in an undertone.

I started walking again. "The gods watch me," I said quietly.

As if I could hide from them.

Troy shot me a narrow-eyed look of concern.

Inside, Troy put Brendan inside the new crib, which was snugged up to the wall opposite the bed. Julia slept in the cradle. Damien headed outside, mouth open in a doggy grin.

I left my boots by the door, placed the daggers on a high shelf in the bedroom, and collapsed into pillows and blankets. Troy put his guns on top of the dresser, and hung his holsters on their hook. He slid into bed beside me, eyes searching mine.

"I'm okay." Fatigue crushed me, but I didn't want him to worry. "All I need is a little rest."

He brushed strands of hair away from my face. "They give you quests, and gifts."

I grimaced. I hadn't gotten any closer to making a plan to carry out said quest. "It's an honor, and a lot of pressure, yeah."

"And they watch you."

I closed my eyes, sighing into the pillow. "They watch me. They watch us all. It's a thing immortals do, I guess. They have all of forever and insatiable minds."

He stayed quiet, which was good. I didn't have it in me to discuss existential ponderings. Sinking into the mattress, it occurred to me that Loki had just given me my knife lesson. The energy drain was similar to the times Thor included energetic transmissions of knowledge in my training as we sat beside the fountain. Loki had been with me as I'd thrown the knives. Had he helped me tap into the Matrix of Knowing?

Would Loki answer if I tried to talk to him, like I sometimes did with my mother? I almost reached out to him, common sense muddied by fatigue, but Troy stroked my hair, and kissed my forehead, gathering my attention back to where it should be.

Chapter 21
Bad Ideas

THAT NIGHT, AFTER singing the children to sleep—and Troy with them—I sat by the fire and wrestled with my thoughts. The pre-dinner nap had messed up my sleeping pattern, leaving me with a problem that had become an obsession.

I needed a plan.

I had to come up with something to tip the scales and leave the world where I grew up a better place. But how did I get in, do whatever I was going to do, and get out again, without anyone seeing my dragon or making me a public figure?

I once asked Thor if I could go way back in time and make adjustments. He'd told me I could go back only as far as my lifetime, that it was best to weave during the period of time I'd experienced, so I'd be sure to weave that exact world. That part of the Tree was starting to fracture, he'd said, and the gods thought the world I'd lived in was the crux of the destruction. It was my job to bring it back into harmony, into alignment.

Restoring nature had to be part of my plan, but what would stop people from continuing to pollute and pillage natural resources? What would make the rich share their wealth with those in need? What could possibly take down the corruption that infiltrated every government and institution?

Loki's idea of widespread coups seemed like the most effective approach, but nothing about it was peaceful. Or easy. I had mad skills and magic blades, but the idea of going up against special forces trained security to take out politicians didn't seem smart. And who would replace them? I couldn't wipe out entire political parties. How could I even know which politicians and corporate elites had sold their souls, and which ones could do something good if they weren't fighting the others?

As effective as a change in management might be, the thought of assassinating even a few rotten politicians turned my stomach. Why was it different than battle? I could think of a number of governments who perpetuated genocide through the future I'd lived in my original world. Shouldn't those people pay? Shouldn't the ones who profited off prisons and war and oppression pay for what they'd done?

The justice system had always been a joke, with as many judges bought off as politicians. Should I leave it as it was? Broken. Run mostly by men with narrow minds and thirsty pockets.

Every idea I came up with was a bad one.

In my decades of fast-forwarding from 1963 to 2035, it didn't matter if I was living in a foster home, a library, a van, or sleeping in a lover's bed, the outer world stayed the same. Wars. Oppression. The privileged few affecting the fates of the many.

How was I supposed to turn that around?

A regime change made sense, but I couldn't think of a way to pull it off without a full-on massacre. Pretty sure my mother would be disappointed if I started off my world-weaving career by turning into an assassin.

I scanned through my memories, looking for the best time to strike. When were the worst of the world's leaders most vulnerable? Eirian and I could traverse through time like ghosts and take out single targets. We'd have the element of surprise, but we'd have to spread our attacks out. Eirian could only make a handful of jumps before he'd be too fatigued to maintain a shield strong enough to keep out the arsenals that might get thrown at us. However, if we rested in between, we could make it so they never knew when we were coming.

My mind followed that thread for a while. Fifteen minutes later, I was holding my breath, caught in a theoretical dogfight between military aircraft and a dragon.

I groaned and shook myself out of it. After adding another log to the fire, I took my leather-and-fur coat down from the hook, and went outside. Damien padded through the grass beside me. I walked to the middle of the field, halfway between the cabin and the forest, and stopped. My morose mind contemplated if one of the men I'd killed had been on this spot, or if they'd been dragged over this patch of ground by Brogan and Troy as they'd cleaned up that evening.

"Come on, Shelta. Pull yourself together." And now I was talking to myself.

I told my mind to shut up, and stared at the stars.

The night sang in whispers of wind through trees and grass. An owl hooted in the distance, and frogs croaked near the lake.

This sanctuary had been Troy's escape from his life as a gunslinger. A deputy. Vigilante. Some outlaw-gangster put a price on his head, and a bunch of men had come for the bounty. The illusion of safety was broken when their blood stained this ground.

The greedy and selfish were everywhere.

Stomping them out was akin to genocide. It was definitely murder. And I didn't think that's what the gods were getting at when they asked me to be a world-weaver.

How was I supposed to make the world a better place when every peaceful option seemed like it wouldn't make enough of a difference? I didn't know how to hack into banks to redistribute money, or how to change a government without forcibly removing the corrupt.

I wasn't a goddess. Definitely not a reaper of souls. I didn't want that kind of responsibility.

Head down, I closed my eyes and swayed in the darkness. The wind chilled my cheeks, my coat wrapping me in warmth. After a while, a song rose. Quiet. Pensive.

Music swept through me, settling my nerves and stilling my thoughts. I sang to the earth, to the trees, to the mountain I stood upon. I sang to the night.

Beneath my feet, something shifted. The memory of bloodshed dropped down a layer energetically, the song washing the residue of death away like rain had long washed away the blood. I kept swaying, and singing, until there was only the field and the night.

And me standing with a dog at my side.

Empty, I made my way home on stiff legs.

My brainstorming didn't improve as the week went by, and I looked increasingly to Loki's blades for inspiration. I practiced with the sleek, green daggers until the whistle they made as they cut through the air became part of each day's music. I wore the cuffs when we went for family walks, leather wrapping my forearms in armor. I touched the hilts of Loki's knives as often as I traced the dragon pendant at my throat, or turned the rings on each hand.

Daggers at my wrists, daggers in my boots.

No matter how many times I sifted through the wisdom Merlin and Thor had imparted, nothing seemed effective enough to create lasting transformation on an entire planet.

The gods had a history of messing things up when they intervened. How was I supposed to be any different? Even the most benign change could cause a chain of events completely out of my control. I had the power of a goddess—the blood of one. Did that make me a demigod? Did that give me the right to decide who lived and who died, or which field to bless?

I could help grow food, make barren ground fertile. Heal the earth in sections. But that only worked if people nurtured their renewed planet. I knew a lot of people cared, but too many struggled to get by. If the quality of life went up for the majority of people, maybe it would ripple up the line of authority. Maybe there'd be less corruption. So how did I redistribute wealth in a way that allowed for that?

As soon as I thought of doing things on a global scale, my mind broke.

Each night, I got out my guitar and sang to my family, making the best of the time we had together, cherishing each moment with Troy. The pine and horse smell of him couldn't drown out my restless thoughts, but his kisses kept them at bay.

One afternoon, as Brendan and Julia napped, Troy brought me out to the field and took my hands. "Talk to me," he said. "I can feel your discontent."

"It's not because of you." My words tumbled out in my need to reassure him.

He leaned in to give me a kiss. "Good. But maybe if you tell me what's on your mind, I can help."

Leaves whispered in the trees, birds and insects singing with the breeze, a subtle soundtrack to my indecision. "I feel like I have to become a vigilante to make the kind of changes my old world needs."

My confession made him flinch. No surprise, considering his past.

"It's a hard road," he admitted. "I don't recommend it, but sometimes there's no justice any other way." He didn't pull back or shrink from me, which said more about our love and his courage than anything. Even as I reminded him of the killing he'd done, knowing it haunted him, he held me with his eyes, nothing but respect in his gaze.

"I don't know if it's my job to dole out justice." My voice cracked. I cleared my throat and took a breath to calm myself. "The gods trained me to fight, and to heal. They taught me the need to seek peace, to use my influence without anger. And I want to help—I do. But I can't think of the people at the top of the power pyramids without rage rising inside. I don't see a way to reason with them, a way to effectively change the world without going on a killing spree or emptying their bank accounts. Or both."

I choked on my honesty, eyes stinging.

Troy pulled me in, wrapping me with silence and saturating me with love through the bond we shared. It wasn't his way to tell me what to do. He held space, this man.

How I cherished that.

Not that I didn't need advice. I did. Desperately. But he didn't have the answers I needed. He gave me what he had: reassurance. Deep love that reached my soul.

I tipped my head up, tears on my cheeks, my mouth seeking his. Losing myself in him. Love was easy. If I stayed firmly in the moment, immersed in the wonderous current of us, I didn't worry.

Troy couldn't save me from the future, but he saved me in that moment.

He was everything I needed.

After another two weeks of banging my head against a wall of bad ideas, it got harder to pretend I was okay. I'd been here as long as I was with Killian. I could come back, but I couldn't procrastinate any longer. One way or another, I had to do something to help—nature spirits, humans, the whole timeline. I just needed to start.

Late one night, as Troy and I reclined on the sheepskins by the crackling fire, I readied myself to break the news, letting loose a massive sigh.

"You have to leave, don't you?" He couldn't quite keep the sorrow from his voice.

"You read my mind a lot, you know?" I smiled, forcing the grief to wait behind a wall of willpower. There was never enough time.

He kissed my forehead. "You're easy to read, my love."

"I'll come back," I promised.

Troy nodded, squeezing me closer. "I'll still miss you."

Loss lurked like a cloud of tears filling my chest, his emotions spilling over into mine. "I'll miss you, too, Troy. Every day. I wish it wasn't like this—no matter where I am, I'll always be torn."

I didn't say their names, but he knew. Killian. Nikolas. I missed them even when I was with him. What a fate the goddess had given me. She said I'd woven this thread, but it never would've happened if she hadn't birthed me through the World Tree.

Not that I'd change it now. They were my family. Each man had a piece of my heart. Three fathers for my children.

Didn't make it any easier. Somehow, I had to find peace with the way I loved and my role as a world-weaver. Despite this sanctuary in the mountains and Troy's constant kindness, I needed my own space to think.

I'd go somewhere with Eirian for a few days, then return to Nikolas. I could leave the children with him and Ola—surely there was another nursing mother in the village who could feed Julia for a few days while I went world-weaving. It was the best place to leave them.

"Whatever you decide," said Troy, pulling my focus back, "don't lose yourself to the duty you've been given by the gods. It's your life, not theirs."

I nodded, my head pushing against his shoulder.

The next day was painfully sweet, each moment its own treasure. The way Troy's face lit up when he played with the children, the tilt of his shoulders as he built up the fire, the resonance of his voice... They were fleeting gifts taken all too soon by the relentless march of time.

That night, lying beside him in bed, I slipped off my diamant ring. "This ties me to you," I said, handing it to him. "Will you put some love into it, so I can carry it with me?"

He brought it to his lips, then to his heart, and slid it back on my finger. "My love is always with you."

"And mine is with you." The ring sent a tremble through me.

Another layer in the weaving.

CHAPTER 22

ALL ALONE, YET NEVER ALONE

AT DAWN THE NEXT day, I called Eirian. As my dragon came in for a landing in the bit of meadow by the stables, Damien's sharp barks and the horses' objections broke the quiet of the morning.

My hair flew back at the gust of wind from Eirian's wings, which blew Troy's black hat clean off his head. He gathered it, settled it where it belonged, and faced the dragon.

"What do you say we get this saddle back on you?" Troy offered.

Eirian tipped his head, and I sensed them talking, unable to hear the words.

Fair enough. I gave Troy and Eirian mental privacy, wondering if the gods watched them as closely as they did me. Was there anywhere to hide from my mother? She wouldn't like what I was contemplating.

Eirian picked the saddle up in his teeth and placed it on his back, which solved the problem of its weight. We arranged the straps, then I climbed up and fastened them.

"I'd be hard pressed to do this myself," I said, smiling down at Troy. I'd already taken a step away from him, closing down the connection between us. It was the only way I could get through this without falling apart.

When the saddle was settled and the children were tucked in, I slid down to face Troy. I had no words left to offer. They'd all been said. Instead, I pushed up to my tiptoes and kissed him.

One last breath of pine, one last moment in the sanctuary of his arms.

Time to go. I gave him a sad smile, squeezed his hands, and stepped back.

A minute later I was high in the sky, gliding in a wide arc over the homestead. Troy watched from the field, head tipped up, wide-brimmed hat completing his signature silhouette.

Where do you want to go, Weaver?

To Nikolas, but not to the village. I needed somewhere I could collect my thoughts and do some dangerous thinking without anyone watching me. Other than the gods. *To the fjords, my friend. Take me to the fjords.*

Gladly.

We passed through the World Tree into a sky full of brooding clouds, over canyons where ocean flowed inland, mingling with freshwater from the mountains. My stomach did giddy flips as Eirian dove toward a high peak.

We landed on a wide ledge that resembled a porch for the cave beyond. Wildflowers and edible weeds grew defiantly from nooks in the rock. A sheer drop led to the water below, flowing by on its course to the sea. I peered into the cave, which reached deep into the mountain, spacious enough for Eirian to move about freely.

You've been here before? I asked.

It's a favorite of mine. His contented hum made me smile.

We were utterly secluded, the fjords stretching out in a dramatic show of nature's majesty. The perfect place to contemplate the path ahead.

CHAPTER 23
CONVERSATIONS IN THE DEEP

I WOKE IN THE deepest part of night, the faint light of an overcast sky barely reaching into the dark that surrounded me. My children slept in their saddle nests, tucked into an alcove in the cave, with Eirian stretched out nearby. Driven by an urge I'd been ignoring for weeks, I pulled back my thick blanket, sat up on my bedroll, and slipped on my boots. Enveloped in my cloak, I walked to the entrance of the cave and gazed into the night. Even the stars seemed to sleep, concealed by clouds.

I returned to my belongings, located the sleeves Loki had given me, and slipped them on. As soon as I touched the knives, a shimmer of power hummed through me. Eirian's presence waited at the edge of my mind, asking a silent question.

I want to reach out to Loki, I told him. *What do you think of that?*

The dragon thrummed a near-silent sound of consideration. *You seek his counsel?*

Yes. I don't think any of the other gods will talk me through this. I'm thinking we create a shield that blocks the other gods from knowing what's in this cave. I'd rather they didn't know I'm talking to Loki. If he even answers.

All my theorizing could be for nothing, but it was worth a shot.

Instead of replying, Eirian's magic crept up the walls, adding to the depth of darkness. I stood in the center of the cave and wove my intention with his. Hidden. Safe. Secret. Unseen.

When our shield was tight and thick, I stroked the hilts of my blades.

Loki? I sent the call out through heart and mind to one god, and one god only, but there was no response. Shrouded in darkness so close it was a living thing, I sang a low, slow chant.

"Loki, I invoke thee."

"Loki, I invoke thee."

"Loki, I invoke thee."

The shield devoured the sound, leaving me in heavy silence.

A few heartbeats later, Loki appeared with a wisp of music, standing before me in a subtle silver glow. His eyes shone green as the metal of my daggers, sharp with cunning and mischief.

"You came." I hadn't expected to see him, only to hear his voice.

"You invoked me. Quite effectively, I might add. No one's done that in an era or three." He tilted his head, taking in the shield. "Impressive. Might even work."

"Can you help me?" I asked, skipping the preamble. "I can't figure out a peaceful solution to turn the tide of my original world. I've spent weeks trying to come up with something, and I'm not getting any closer."

"Ah." He clasped his hands behind his back. "I'd love to help, but I'd be exiled. Again. Exile gets lonely and excruciatingly boring. I much prefer having a wing of the palace to myself and my friends, and being largely ignored by the high and mighty."

"Oh. I wouldn't want you exiled."

"That's kind of you." The way he smiled invited more conversation. Like he wanted me to find a loophole.

"Thank you for the daggers." With a thought, they dropped into my hands, green blades gleaming in Loki's glow. "They fly like magic."

"They do, yes." A note of satisfaction crept into his voice.

"Are they magic?" I asked.

"Everything has a bit of magic, if you know how to access it." He sidestepped the question. I could only assume that meant yes. "Do keep in mind that, like any tool, they have multiple uses. And, whether or not you include the daggers in your plans, remember that the consequences are out of your control."

"So, I've been told." I rocked on my feet. "How am I supposed to reconcile that?"

"However you can." Loki's frown deepened creases in his face, giving a hint of his age. "They call me the god of chaos, and perhaps I have been, but much of the destruction I'm blamed for came from the fallout of smaller actions. Even the noblest deeds can wreak havoc, which is why the gods vowed not to interfere with humankind."

And yet they wanted me to play god for them. "Did you take that vow?"

He dropped his chin, gazing at me from beneath lidded eyes. "Do you think I was given a choice?"

I sucked on the insides of my cheeks. Of course, he wasn't. "So, you don't think of yourself as the god of chaos?"

"Mischief, maybe. Chaos, not so much. Most of those legends miss the mark."

"What do you call yourself?"

"I am the Keeper of Lost Souls and Stories." His hands swept out to either side in a motion that was almost a bow.

The timber of his voice touched something deep, making me shiver. "Is my soul lost?" Felt like it, with all the violence I'd done and the murder I'd contemplated.

Loki's laughter was a bassline of amusement. "No, Shelta. You're not lost. But I have collected quite a few of the songs and stories you've left behind."

"You—you have my old music?" Time had stolen so many of my creations.

He turned somber, like we spoke of something sacred. "Much of it."

The Keeper of Lost Souls and Stories. That was his chosen role. The care he portrayed made me want to trust him.

"Would my soul be lost if I turned vigilante and started reconfiguring the world's leadership? I mean, I know I'm supposed to do this peacefully, but there are a lot of people who aren't going to stop causing problems as long as they have the power to do so."

His teeth shone in the faint silver light. "You're thinking of playing reaper?"

I cocked my head. "Reaper. Assassin. Eirian says it's been done before."

"It has." He drew his mouth tight, as if contemplating how much to say. "They're mortals; they're going to die anyway. Sometimes selective elimination is extremely effective. I've also seen it go horribly wrong, and it would put you directly in the line of fire."

"Right." Next question. "Not that I'd want to, but has a weaver ever tried to rule?"

"They have." Loki's mouth twisted into a cynical smile. "Many have tried to rule. *I've* tried to rule, several times, none of which went very well. Now, I run a night club. It's much more fun."

My mouth dropped open. "A night club?

"Loki's Lair. I'll take you next time you're in Asgard, if you'd like." He lit up, making me grin along with him. "But you're right to be wary of playing savior, even with the best intentions. It's considerably less enjoyable than it looks. If you're not the one making moves, moves are made at your expense."

I shook my head. "No politics, thank you."

Loki turned a palm up. "Have you tried focusing on what you want to see happen?"

"Of course." I traced the dragon on my necklace at my throat, fingertips following the comforting circular flow. "Eirian and I could restore natural areas. Grow trees and food, clean up the oceans. But what's the point if people come and bulldoze the forests down again, or keep throwing trash into the sea? We could grow community gardens, but people need so much more than that."

He held my gaze. "Do you know we call you the Song Weaver?"

The name rang through me with the low chime of a singing bowl.

Loki bowed his head. "I should go. Good luck, Shelta." He touched his brow in silent farewell, and vanished.

I stood in the darkness, enveloped in a shield of secrecy, and wrapped my arms around myself. *What do you think, Eirian?*

I think Loki has matured. He said something to me, just before he left.

What did he say?

That I'd chosen well. He respects you, Shelta, even though it's hard for him to watch the gods send you to do the job he always wanted.

Better him than me.

Eirian's mirth tingled through me. *He tried that path, and failed spectacularly.*

Well, I might fail just as badly. I walked back to my bedroll and sat down.

What comes is not up to us. Our job is to spark change, not to direct the twist of fate.

Sarcasm crept into my thoughts. *As if fate would let itself be directed.*

Was I overthinking things? Could it be as simple as singing my weaving into the world?

Eirian and I dissolved our shield of secrecy, and watched the inky darkness give way to a grey dawn.

When I walked out to the ledge, the folds of my cloak blowing in the wind, my ring began to hum. Nikolas was coming to me.

I took the day to come up with a plan. It was a little bit desperate and probably not big enough, but it was a start. As the sun began to set, I caught sight of the *LófiDanu* gliding swiftly over deep water, pale sails billowing. The dragon-winged ship was framed by jagged peaks kissed pink by the sky.

Loading Brendan and Julia into their nests, I cooed to them about how wonderful it would be to see Nikolas's children and Ola. At least my family here wouldn't be intimidated by me or the dragon I rode. They each had their own magic. Thor's blood ran strong in their veins.

Did that make Loki part of the family?

If anyone could understand me, it would be Nikolas.

Looking over the side of the cliff, I had the giddy urge to jump, and sent Eirian an image of what I planned to do. *I'll meet you down there.*

I received dragon laughter in response.

At the edge of the cliff, I sent a thread of awareness to Nikolas. *I see you.*

His presence was fathomless as the ocean, spacious as the sky. He looked up from the helm of the ship. *There you are. Welcome home, Shelta.*

On my way down. With a breath, I erected a shield, connected with the wind and water, and bent my will into the weaving of the world.

Arms opened wide.

A deep, full breath.

I leaned forward, and jumped.

Time stretched out as the mountains flew by on either side. I brought my hands together above my head, pointed myself down, and the water opened up to receive me.

It would've been an icy swim without the shield, but there was no pain, no stinging slap of water on skin. One moment I was in the air, the next I was beneath the surface, the rushing roar of air replaced by a muted submarine song that underscored the pounding of my heart.

With a splash, I broke the surface, and swam toward the ship.

Nikolas leaned over the side of the boat and lowered a rope ladder with wooden rungs. "That was miraculous. So, now you fly?"

I laughed. "Not quite, but Eirian does."

The dragon took his cue, and spiraled down to land on the shore nearby. I climbed out of the water, gathering the elements of fire and wind to dry myself off.

He met me at the rail and pulled me into his embrace, his kiss becoming its own song. For that drawn out moment there was nothing else. The children, the dragon, the sunset that lit the fjord with color—all of it was eclipsed by this man and the love that bound us together.

Nikolas pushed back, eyes bright. "I'm glad you've come. I wanted to go to you, but I was needed, and something told me you had matters of your own."

"I did." Another kiss.

I wanted to tell him everything, but the children fussed in their nests. Eirian waited on the rocky beach, patient as ever. Nikolas steered the *LófiDanu* close, then held a hand out to me. After a second, I realized he meant to go to shore without dropping anchor or launching the little boat we'd used in the past. The ship held unnaturally still as the current flowed around us.

"It stays put by your will alone?" I asked.

"It does."

"Are we about to walk on water?"

His smile grew wide. "We are."

I shook my head. Considering the relationship Nikolas had with the elements, I didn't doubt him. Maybe it was as simple as shielding myself from rain, or the dive I'd just taken from an impossible height.

I followed Nikolas down the ladder, and stepped onto perfectly solid water. My feet didn't get wet, though the water continued to do liquid-like things on either side of the rolling path we took to the shore. When we made land, I sensed a sigh as Nikolas released the water from its duty.

We approached the dragon, and each of us took a child from their egg-like carriers. Julia and Brendan were all smiles and squeals, delighted to see Nikolas. A father reunited with his children.

Nikolas said hello to Eirian, placed Brendan on the dragon's paw, and proceeded to take the saddle off with the ease of someone who'd done it before. Another layer of Nikolas. As close as we were, there was so much I didn't know about this man who'd bonded our souls across the worlds.

Take the pouches that hold your belongings, said Eirian when the saddle rested on the ground.

I picked up the big leather saddlebags and locked my gaze onto one great, gold-flecked eye. Even if I knew it was necessary, I didn't want him to leave. The dragon was my safety net. My confidence. My time-traveling friend.

Worry not, Weaver. Eirian's uncanny calm enfolded me. *Call me from your heart, and I will be there in the span of a breath. We are bonded, you and I.*

I nodded, no words coming, throat thick and eyes stinging as I swayed to keep Julia quiet. Nikolas held Brendan. I went to Eirian and wrapped one arm around as much of his neck as I could. It was like trying to hug a massive tree, my heart pressed to his scales, radiant love between us.

When I stepped back, I glimpsed a spiraling, star-strewn World Tree in the depths of the dragon's eye. It hit me with a sense of eternity. Then it was gone.

Nikolas led the way to the ship with Brendan in his arms and my magic saddlebags slung over his shoulder. I secured

Julia at my chest, and walked across water like it was no big thing.

On deck, I turned for one last look at Eirian, but he was already gone. No whoosh of wind or sound of wings. The saddle had disappeared with him, as if he was never there.

Nikolas wrapped his arms around me as I looked at the perfectly dragon-less shore. I put my hand over his, glanced down, and saw our rings together. They lit up like a star for a split-second, then faded to a glow. Tipping my head so I could see his eyes in the dimming twilight, I said, "Take me home."

"Gladly." Nikolas turned a willful gaze toward the sails, and they filled with wind. The ship moved into the center of the channel as if the current wanted nothing more than to carry us. The wheel spun on its own, the *LófiDanu* giving off a hum of contentment.

"Neat trick. I guess you don't need a crew anymore."

"No." Nikolas grinned. "We both grew in power during our visit to Asgard."

"Did you get schooled by Thor, too?"

He laughed. "Once. It was wild."

"I bet." I wished I'd seen it. "He taught me a lot." So much had happened since I'd last seen Nikolas. I didn't know how to start, so I said nothing, content to bask in his warmth.

As I looked down at Julia, an image of Loki flashed through my inner sight, and I pulled a mental shroud of secrecy around the memory of our conversation in the cave, tucking it away in a corner of my mind. The gods couldn't know Loki had helped me, so neither should Nikolas.

CHAPTER 24
STORIES IN THE NIGHT

AS TWILIGHT GAVE way to darkness, the little ones got our attention. Brendan learned how to find his balance at sea, staggering around the swaying ship with me hovering over him in case a wave rocked us and he went flying. Julia entertained herself by sucking on any bit of Nikolas's clothing she could get into her mouth. He moved to the helm and gave her a chance to feel the ship's wheel, guiding her to steer with his hand around her tiny fist, making her squawk with joy.

The stars brightened at the sound.

Finally, the children slept, tucked safely into their cradles in the cabin. I stood with Nikolas at the prow of the ship. There was no moon, but the stars were enough to light our way. The mountain walls on either side of us shone silver, the water reflecting points of light above.

Nikolas made a bed on deck out of furs and blankets, and we settled in, alternating between looking at each other and the millions of stars. I remembered a midnight lesson with Merlin, and greeted some of the stars by name.

As we sailed, we talked, the night deepening around us as if it, too, were listening. I told Nikolas about the rest of my time in Asgard: the training, the magic, the music I played each night to an audience of legends, gods, and goddesses. The way the children grew so fast.

I told him how my ring had called me back to Killian, and how Brendan had picked up on his father's danger. I told him how Thor had sired Killian's clan, and about the ritual marriage to the land.

"It was strange," I said, "being with people who knew me before, but them having to come to grips with this woman who rode a dragon and didn't belong to their world."

"You belong to every world," Nikolas insisted.

"Maybe, but that's easier for us to understand than the people who welcomed me into their family without that knowledge. Even if they were grateful for my sword and my timing. I saved them, Eirian and I... At least now, when I disappear, they know I flew off on a dragon. That I didn't abandon Killian."

My throat caught, but I recovered, and told him about my visit with Troy.

"Was it hard to leave?" Nikolas ran his hand down my arm.

"It's always hard." I gave him a sad smile.

He looked at me, eyes full of stars.

"How have things been since I saw you last?" I asked.

His voice added its resonance to the song of water swishing along the hull of the ship. "Ola had many to heal. She had help from Frøya, and there are other healers among us, but it was good that I did not stay away too long. My trip to Asgard gave me the power to save lives."

"That's good." I swallowed rising emotion. It must've been hard for him. How many friends had he lost to the raid?

"There was much to rebuild. Leifr brought the rain, but the invaders still managed to set fire to a couple of buildings, and did damage wherever they went." He gave my hand a squeeze. "It's done now, Shelta. You're holding your breath."

He was right. I breathed, and he changed the subject.

"Just as everything was more-or-less back to normal, my brothers returned."

That caught my attention. I'd only heard him mention his brothers a couple of times.

"Sefi and Siggi." The way Nikolas's mouth twisted told me there was a laugh just beneath the surface. "They were birthed at the same time."

"Twins?"

"Yes. They think with one mind. But it isn't like we talk, or the way you communicate with a dragon. My brothers' minds are linked as if their intelligence is from the same source. They work together on every endeavor more quickly than you would think possible. Made quite a bit of mischief for our mother."

"I can only imagine." Their mother must've been a force of nature in her own right. "Do I get to meet them?"

Nikolas shook his head. "They set off days ago on another voyage. But I have some wonderful stories."

"I like stories." I wiggled closer. He smelled of saltwater and wind.

"Many moons ago, my brothers took two ships full of men to the west. Not to the first island, the one you call Scotland, but the one beyond. There, they found a green land with fair people. They did some exploring, good trading, much drinking, and a bit of fighting. They gathered news of potential allies and woeful enemies. And, on the way back, somewhere between the western islands and our coast, they found a stowaway."

"Really?" It would've been hard to hide from a ship full of men.

Nikolas nodded. "They were none too happy to find a boy inside a cask that was meant to be filled with ale. Sefi kept him safe when he might've been tossed overboard, but I believe, once they got over their disappointment, most of the men admired the boy's bravery."

I shuddered at the thought of a kid surrounded by a horde of thirsty Vikings. "He must've been desperate to hide like that."

"The lad was in rough shape. Bones beneath rags of clothing. When they brought him in, Frøya put herself in charge of his recovery, which mostly meant feeding him quantities of decent food." He grinned. "She's taken quite a liking to him."

"They're the same age?" I asked.

"Near enough. The lad was orphaned from the start, it seems. He's kind. Makes himself useful as he can."

"What's his name?"

"Patrick," said Nikolas. "Ola's taken him in."

It seemed a lifetime ago that I'd left Ola's cabin, early in the morning, to journey through the fjords. Another thought hit me, making my stomach turn. "Oh, Nikolas, your children."

"What about them?" he asked.

"We married without them even knowing." What would they think of me, coming into their home with two babies, suddenly their father's wife?

"Shelta." His voice was gentle, eyes shining in the starlight. "They knew how I felt about you. They were pleased when I told them about our marriage, and about Julia. Even Leifr is excited to meet her. Dagný was overjoyed when I told her you were coming home."

"Did you know as soon as I came into this world?"

"I knew when you entered, and where you were." He paused, as if considering whether to tell me something. "I knew where you were all along, that you were safe."

My eyes asked him how he knew as my mind raced to figure it out.

"Eirian is the mate to Rúna. My dragon."

I sat up, back straight. "You have a dragon?"

"I do."

I reached out with my mind. *Eirian!*

Weaver?

You have a mate named Rúna who is bonded with Nikolas?

Yes.

You could have mentioned it.

You never asked.

How very like a dragon. I laughed, and shook my head at Nikolas. "So, you've been checking up on me?"

He returned my smile. "I have."

I almost protested the fact that I wasn't let in on it, but instead I snuggled into him and brought the blanket up over my shoulder. Eirian would keep the meeting with Loki to himself. Surely. Better not to think of it at all.

"Okay," I said, "tell me about your dragon."

"She's silvery blue and wears her horns like a crown."

I felt him smile. My eyes were closed, head on his arm, imagining the dragons. "I'd love to see her and Eirian in the sky."

"I saw them fly together once. The sun bent its rays to touch them. Their colors changed constantly—amber and garnet, sapphire and silver. The awe of it has never faded in my heart." He fell quiet.

I waited. Breathed. Listened to the water lapping at the sides of the ship, and the soft whoosh of wind in the sails.

"I have only flown with Rúna thrice," he said finally. "My duty is to my people. I am bound to my village. But when I was younger, I had the chance to roam."

"How did you meet her?" I asked. It was enough to listen to his voice, to feel the warmth of him next to me. Without looking, I knew he gazed at the stars.

"Do you remember me telling you I was once in the company of the *ljósálfar*?"

"I do." He'd world-walked to visit the elves of light, where he'd gotten my sword. It had been a turning point for me, to know I wasn't alone in my wandering. "I think you said it took three years of this time when it felt like only a fortnight there?"

"Their existence is not bound to the rules of time, nor was mine while I was with them." His voice changed, like he ventured far away even as he touched my side. "I sought them out when I was a young man. I followed the old paths, overgrown and forgotten, invisible to most."

The ropes rasped in the wind and the water flowed around the ship. My mind journeyed with him.

"Most believed the Forest of Light was a myth. My mother told me stories of the *ljósálfar* when I was young. She said that only the pure-hearted would find them: those who sought secrets for the evolution of their soul."

His voice dropped deeper, trance-like. I saw him younger, seeking, with earnestness in his gaze.

"I visited elders," he went on, "asking them to share their stories. I turned to nature to answer the questions that no book or human could. This brought me a level of affinity with the elements that went beyond what I'd known before. I lived in the forest, where trees taught me quiet patience, steady growth, and interconnectedness. I stood atop a mountain, and learned from the wind and sky how vast the world is. I felt the flow of the ocean in my blood, and knew in my bones the presence of the earth. I spent days on a stone in a river, and the water showed me images it had seen when it was held aloft in the form of clouds." He turned his mouth toward my ear, quiet. "That's how I found the stone circle."

I opened my eyes and looked at him in the starlight, sliding my hand to his chest. Nikolas made more sense, now. He'd been taught by nature herself. "What happened at the stone circle?"

"I spent a moon cycle atop that hill. Finally, the elves deemed me worthy of admittance, and I entered the Forest of Light."

Had he vanished, one moment standing on the glowing center stone, the next gone from this world into another? It seemed a private thing, so much time alone with the elements, dedicated to his quest.

"What were they like?" I asked.

"Beautiful. Some are tall, some are tiny like you'd imagine a faerie would be. They choose their own appearances. The elves are more light than flesh, more energy than matter." His eyes met mine. "Their vibration is higher than that of this world, so to meet them I had to raise my own enough to slip through the veil. When I did, I realized they'd been with me even as I sought them."

"A different dimension, but the same world?"

"Just so," said Nikolas. "The shift is slight for them, though it can be uncomfortable when they take on denser bodies in order to be seen by humans. In ancient days, our vibrations were not so different. They played in the forests and waters, and were seen frequently by people. But some feared them, and others hunted them. They withdrew beyond the veil until they became legends. Now, few people believe they were real to begin with."

I nodded. The same thing had happened to dragons. Hunted, they hid. Same with the elementals in the world I would soon be revisiting.

"They embraced me as a guest," Nikolas continued, "welcoming my infinite questions. They played joyful music and offered me delectable drinks. I learned how to speak with a tree's spirit so it could move its life force into its seeds before cutting it to use for wood in craft. Each seed was sacred, planted with reverence and ceremony; a continuance of the tree's spirit."

He shook his head, awe softening his face. "I learned so much from them. It was a wondrous part of my life. But time passed quickly here. I was missed. Ola, seer that she is, was certain I was alive, but couldn't reach me with a message. Finally, my father sailed to the dragons and asked for their assistance, offering treasure. Rúna accepted his request, but told my father to keep his coins, that she would make the journey for the sake of meeting a human who had crossed the veil." He laughed. "When she first appeared, I was half-drunk on mead. One moment I was in a meadow, dancing with an elven-lady to music that enchanted the soul, the next moment much of the meadow was occupied by a dragon."

He smiled wide beneath his beard. "Rúna caused quite a stir, even among the elves. Once they got over their surprise, the revel got even livelier. Rúna drained a barrel of mead at their insistence, but she did not forget the reason she'd come. While everyone else was merrymaking, I was shocked to stillness when her voice spoke within me. She explained the difference in time, and told me I was needed in my village, that my father had asked her to bring me home." He sighed. "What made me trust her, is that she didn't assume I would come with her. She left that choice to me."

I understood. "Eirian is like that too. I have the feeling dragons don't like to interfere with our freedom."

"Exactly. It was a difficult choice. I was learning so much, and the feeling, Shelta, the lightness of being there was magnificent! But my duty has always been to my family. The elves sent me off with three gifts, one of which was your sword."

"Why didn't you keep it yourself?" I asked.

"They told me the blade was not meant for me." He drew a breath, quiet for a moment. "I went with Rúna as far as it was safe for her to take me, and did the rest of the journey on foot. Though I do not see her often, it's enough to have the heart-link that allows us to speak with one another. This I do frequently."

"You never told me."

Nikolas tipped his head close. "It is a deep secret. I'm telling you now."

I nodded, shadow-wrapped thoughts of Loki lurking in the back of my mind.

He fell quiet, which gave me time to wonder at the perfection of life. Eirian and Rúna, Nikolas and I, all woven together.

"Have you ever been back?" I wondered.

He shook his head, sorrow creasing the corners of his eyes. "No. I became a father, then chief. I've not wanted to risk being lost in time when I have so many who depend on me."

A sacrifice made. I could hear how much he missed it.

He pulled me closer. "It's been a comfort to know you are safe—to have a way to connect with you even when we're worlds apart. For Eirian and Rúna, the World Tree is not the mystery it is for us."

Chapter 25
Home and Truly Home

SAILING TO THE VILLAGE of Thorson took two days. Nikolas could've brought us there sooner, but we wanted to enjoy our time together with only the babies to distract us.

Brendan and Julia were fun to watch together, him nearly a year old and she almost three months. Or so. It got increasingly harder to keep track of time.

On the second afternoon, as breaks in the clouds sent beams of golden light onto the island, we came around familiar cliffs to the sheltered bay and the village beyond. Julia was with Nikolas at the helm of the ship, while I held Brendan to make sure he didn't dive off the bow. I wondered how much he remembered of his time here before, of Ola and Nikolas's children. He'd recognized Troy and Nikolas easily enough.

The village had such rugged grace. Houses with steep, sloping rooftops surrounded the central tree, which boasted a resplendent crown of spring leaves. Cliffs framed the beach, forested hills rising behind it all.

I wore one of the dresses I'd been given by Ola, what felt like forever ago. The wine-red shirt and green woolen over-dress were hand-me-downs, soft and worn. Julia rested, wrapped in plaid at my chest. Loki's knives were tucked in my purse, my sword and daggers stashed in the saddlebags with the rest of my belongings. I figured my re-emergence into this small society would be easier if I appeared non-threatening. Rather opposite from my entrance to Scotland.

The brothers Agmundr and Arnþórr—who usually crewed the LófiDanu—tied the ship to the wooden dock and helped unload our belongings. It took a while to adjust to ground that didn't roll and rock. Nikolas walked with me, Brendan in his arms, steady as always.

His children were there to meet us.

Six-year-old Dagný ran full-speed into me, arms wide, one hand clutching flowers. I laughed, hugging her back, while holding Julia safe to one side. Dagný presented me with a crown of purple and yellow blossoms bound with a green ribbon. Frøya, more composed at twelve years of age, ensured the crown was well placed on my head, and that I understood she'd helped Dagný make it. I thanked them both, and let them see Julia, shifting my eyes to Leifr as they fussed over the new baby.

Leifr had changed in the time I'd been gone. He held himself different. I'd seen the same change in Charlie. They'd both fought their first real battles. Leifr held my gaze, waiting for his sisters to have their turns before stepping forward for a hug of his own.

"Hello, my friend," I said when he stepped back.

Leifr spoke formally, as if he represented the whole village though he was only ten. "We are glad you have returned. Welcome home."

I blinked back tears. "Thank you."

And so our party grew: Nikolas and I, five youngsters, and the brothers carrying our things. We walked across sand and rock to the hard ground that ran up to the settlement.

It wasn't a procession; no crowd on each side or anything, thank goodness, but people waved as we went. Neighbors gathered in groups to chat. Children played, their laughter soaring over the distant breathing of the sea.

A few buildings were recently repaired, new wood showing bright against older, darker boards and posts. There was a new house going up at the south side of the village, presumably to replace one that had been burned. And while most people gave me a smile and wave when I caught their gaze, others stood in their doorways watching, the weight of grief still visible on their faces.

Ola emerged from her cabin, wiping her hands on her apron. She caught me in a firm hug that engulfed Julia, then proceeded to inspect the new baby with her seer's eyes and the cooing voice of a happy aunt.

"Now you have five children," she said to Nikolas.

"And you have one." Nikolas nodded to a boy who stood awkwardly in the doorway. He was pale, with freckles, fiery hair, and sea-green eyes.

I glanced at Frøya, who flashed the lad a beaming grin. He returned it shyly.

"You must be Patrick," I said.

He gave me a nod, sticking to the shelter of the doorway. Nikolas spoke to the boy in Gaelic, and the magic that translated language as if it were another form of music helped me understand it as an invitation to join us for dinner. Patrick gave a half shrug and tipped his head toward Ola's cabin, making it clear he was more comfortable staying where he was. Nikolas didn't push it, and Frøya appeared content to leave him be, though she kept giving him looks of encouragement.

Ola walked the short distance to Nikolas's house with us, insisting we come by for lunch tomorrow before she strode back to her cottage. Agmundr and Arnþórr deposited our belongings in the main room of the house, then departed to their own homes for dinner.

Which left me surrounded by my new family.

"Are you to be our mother now?" Dagný looked up at me with expecting eyes.

Butterflies danced in my belly. "Would you like me to be?"

She nodded her little blonde head, eyes showing worry that I might not accept. I looked to Leifr and Frøya, seeking their thoughts. Each gave a little nod.

Trying not to make my discomfort too obvious, I said, "I'd be happy to be your mother while I'm here, and I'll always love you when I'm not, but I will have to take frequent trips away. I won't be around all the time. Do you understand?"

I received slow nods in answer, and a sad smile from Nikolas. Then, Dagný went to the kitchen to help Frøya finish the dinner preparations. When Nikolas put Brendan down, he charged toward Leifr with uneven steps.

How was I going to be a mother with all the world-walking I needed to do?

Moving behind me, Nikolas slid a hand around my waist. He spoke low, near my ear. "This is your home. We are your family."

Eyes wet, I smiled at him. I was here for now.

For now.

CHAPTER 26
THE ONE WHO IS TO COME

THE GODS HAD TOLD me I'd have three children, but I wasn't ready to be pregnant again. I'd taken herbs to prevent conception while I was with Troy, and was grateful Killian hadn't managed to get me pregnant in my short time there. My last child would be from Nikolas. But not yet.

The morning after we arrived, I went to Ola's cottage. I visited until Patrick was out doing chores, waiting for a private moment to ask Ola for an herb that would be safe to take while I was breastfeeding. She looked at me for a full minute before replying, which gave me time to wonder if I'd overstepped some cultural boundary, or if she was looking into my future to decide if fate would allow me to put off the third prophesized child. Dark lashes shadowed her blue eyes, chunks of brown hair escaping her braids to either side of her set jaw.

Finally, she went to the corner where dozens of plants hung from strings to dry. She returned with a sprig of thin stems covered with tiny leaves, and a square of cloth.

"Take one leaf in tea each day." She caught my gaze and held it. "No more."

"One leaf only," I repeated.

Another nod. "You can mix it with mint so the taste is pleasant."

There was a healthy supply of mint in Nikolas's backyard. "Sounds good."

I went to leave, but she stopped me with a hand on my arm. "Frøya will know."

My eldest step-daughter was a seer as well as an herbalist. Of course, she would. "I will talk with her," I said, the idea making me squirm.

Ola shook her head. "I will tell her. You will tell Nikolas."

Fair enough. I wanted time to feel like my body was my own—as much as it could be with two children to nurse. I didn't even want to think about a third child. Not yet.

That evening, we had a chance to walk alone together after dinner, heading toward the ocean as was our habit. Nikolas was silent, as if he knew I had something to say. I breathed the sea air, summoning my courage.

"I went to see Ola today," I began. "I asked for an herb to prevent me from becoming pregnant." I took a quick breath, and added, "Until I'm ready. After I've completed my task."

Small rocks crunched beneath our feet as we left the village behind and neared the beach. Nikolas said nothing until we reached the water. Finally, he said, "I understand."

I tipped my head to reach his gaze. There was love there, but something else. "What are you thinking?"

He continued walking along the arm of the bay, like he needed to keep moving. "It is fair for you to want to wait."

But there was more, and I knew it, so I kept my mouth shut. Several minutes went by to the steady sound of our footsteps.

"I think about the one who comes," he said finally, "and my blood races. My mind turns in colors and my heart presses hard in my chest. It is right for you to wait, and there is nothing missing in my life, and yet it takes resolve for me to have patience in this."

The weight of time pressed hard as I remembered how far back we were. Far enough that the magic of my music was needed so I could speak with Nikolas and his family, the evolution of modern English a long cry from now.

"I understand." My words whispered through the soft crashing of waves.

He wrapped an arm around my shoulder and brought me closer. *I can wait, Shelta,* he said in my mind. *For a time.*

I nodded. Decided I might as well tell him the rest. "I need to go soon. Maybe the day after tomorrow. I have to get started on this world-weaving thing, and I was hoping to leave Brendan and Julia here."

He held me tighter. Kissed the top of my head. "We'll take care of them until you return."

"Thank you." I choked the words out, wondering if my life would ever be more than a string of hellos and goodbyes.

Chapter 27
Into the Future

THREE DAYS LATER, I readied myself to leave, packing what I thought I'd need and hugging Brendan and Julia every five minutes.

Just before twilight, I snuggled my babies one last time, then said goodbye to the older children, who saw my world-weaving like going to sea on voyage.

Nikolas stood before me at the entrance of our home, his gaze swirling with unspoken sorrow and fierce love.

I squeezed his hand. "I'll be back as soon as I can."

He kissed me, then opened the door. I'd already told him I had to go alone.

The children watched through the window as I walked into the wind. I waved, eyes stinging, then turned my back to them and took long strides toward the sea. The leather strap of my guitar case pressed on one shoulder, made heavier by my sword, wrapped in cloth, hidden beneath the instrument. My plaid pouch rested on my other hip with food, water, and a few things that might be worth trading. Not that I'd need them if I could pull off the first part of my plan.

I didn't even know if I could make the crossing through the World Tree. I'd never done it this way. I wanted to go in without a dragon, without pretending to be a god. I'd revisit some old haunts, and busk my way through a few cities. Song would be my offering. If I could make music a force of healing, maybe I could shift enough energy that it would spark change. I had to make some incremental difference, to entice nature spirits to return and humans to treat the earth—and each other—better. It would be faster if I had Eirian to help, but if someone caught sight of him, it was game over.

Hopefully, I could shift the timeline toward harmony.

It was a shaky plan. A vague one. But it was the best I had.

Leaving Julia and Brendan shot a spear of guilt through me, but I couldn't bring them along. Not this time. Ola had found another nursing mother to help with Julia, but she was growing so fast, she'd already started drinking broth and nibbling fish. Brendan was eating solid food and barely nursing anymore.

My children were in good hands. Even if I didn't come back—which was a possibility, all things considered—I couldn't ask for a better family for them.

Low tide mellowed the waves, the sky a dusky blue. I turned left at the water, and reached toward Eirian with my mind. I'd discussed my plan with him, but I wanted to double check my exit strategy. *You're sure you can hear me from that world?* I asked.

I can hear you from any world. The dragon's voice washed through me with reassurance. *If you call, I will come.*

Okay. I blew out a breath. *Here I go.*

At the end of the beach, where the cliff ran into the sea, I faced the carving of the World Tree that had delivered me here what felt like a lifetime ago. Daggers in my boots, knives beneath my sleeves, I wore my long green coat, adding the kind of swagger I'd always wanted when I was younger and worked at Renaissance Faire. Which is where I was headed.

Back to 2010.

Faire folk were eccentric. If I showed up the evening my younger self disappeared, I'd be able to fit right in. I just had to time it right. Twenty-three-year-old me had wandered off Friday night before dinner, and touched the wrong tree. Thirty-four-year-old me would sneak in that same night.

My van had been parked in the field, on the edge of the forest, away from where the other players camped. My spare key would be under the roof rack, secured by several layers of duct tape. I could play a set or two on Saturday, get some food, make enough in tips to fill my gas tank a few times, then go on tour.

Chicago. Indianapolis. New York. And from there, Washington D.C., where I hoped I could influence the largest concentration of politicians and lobbyists.

I would've preferred a more solid plan than singing in the streets, but I'd failed to come up with something better, and it gave me a place to start. Once I was there, I'd improvise the rest.

Rough stone beneath my fingers, I tapped into the current of energy that led to the World Tree. I narrowed my focus to the where and when of my destination, and slid my hand over the worn indent of the carving, which buzzed beneath my palm. Eyes closed, I could still see the lines of the tree. Roots intertwined. Branches above. Light flowed in, filling the carving, seeping into my fingers and flooding my being.

The beach disappeared; the ocean's song replaced by the Tree's symphony. Music and light wove the Tapestry. Threads streamed through me.

I held tight to the strand of thought that led to the moment I sought: a warm Friday night in July, in the trees on the edge of a wide field in Wisconsin. I could see my maroon mini-van with its long roof rack. My handmade curtains would be drawn, making the windows black. Soccer-mom van. Low-profile.

The music faded and my feet hit ground. The light retreated, revealing a forest of ash and elm, and leaving me in deafening silence. As I reached for equilibrium, the chirping of crickets and croaking of frogs filled the void. Locusts sang. Fireflies glowed in the darkening dusk.

I'd traveled the tree. On purpose. Alone.

It was still rather disorienting, and I stumbled a few times as I made my way to the well-worn path that led toward sounds of people. A laugh I recognized rose above the other mingled voices in the distance. The Pirate Mistress, Melody. Who, no doubt, was the center of attention somewhere, with her tall boots and long legs.

She'd called me the Siren. And I'd liked it.

I crept to the end of the path and took a deep breath before I entered the field, just another shadow in the night. Battered grass bent beneath my feet as I crossed to where I'd parked.

What a trip, to touch the metal of a van I'd said goodbye to so many years ago. I climbed up and slid my hand beneath the hard plastic roof rack until I reached the bump of nearly-indestructible tape. I peeled it back, took the key, and opened the van's sliding door with a familiar rolling whine.

The inside smelled a little like wet dog, even with the windows cracked open, left over from the last woman who lived out of the vehicle with her rescued pup. The driver and passenger seats were the only ones left; a mattress stretched across a platform where the rear seats would've gone, covered in rumpled blankets. The platform folded back on one side, leaving space for a tiny kitchen consisting of a two-foot table, a cooler that sat below, a clear bin of dishware, and a jug of water. The camp stove was stowed; I didn't need it in a place where I could sing for breakfast, lunch, and dinner.

I reached under the platform, behind a bag of costumes, and retrieved my purse. The black leather wallet inside contained all of thirty dollars, a few small crystals, and a fake I.D. that said I was Gretta Adams. The guy I'd gotten the I.D. from told me Gretta had traded in her identity to hide from some gangsters, which probably meant Gretta was six feet under. Or deeper. I didn't much care, back when I'd bought it; I'd done anything to slip through the world.

Contemplating my next move, I unloaded my things on the bed. Better to wait until tomorrow to sing. If I went out tonight, people might notice the difference in me—over a decade of age and experience would show if someone looked close enough.

Melody would notice, with her keen eye and sharp tongue.

At least I'd made it here. It was a good start.

The next day, I emerged from my van into a muggy morning that promised a scorcher of a Saturday. According to the schedule I checked on my way back from the toilets, a.k.a. privies, it was a pirate themed day, which meant everyone who worked the Renaissance Faire would be extra roguish. Melody would be in her glory.

I rummaged through my costumes, pulling out thigh-high stockings, a frilly skirt that was short in the front and long in the back, and a shirt that fell off my shoulders. I had to lace my blue bodice looser than I'd done when younger me had worn it, my milk-filled breasts threatening to spill over. They ached, missing my babies, so I sent a tendril of magic to the mammary glands to put a pause on milk production.

Better not to think about the family I left behind. It filled me with longing I could do nothing about right now.

Unwilling to leave my treasures in the van for potential thieves, I strapped my weapons belt over my skirt, complete with sword and dirk, both of which I peace tied with strands of leather so they couldn't be easily drawn. Faire rules. I tucked my smallest dagger in my left boot, then wrapped Loki's knives in a scarf and put them in my plaid pouch with my water bottle. Not that I'd need the blades for fighting today, I just didn't want to be away from them. They'd become a comfort, like my sword and my guitar.

Eying the instrument, I decided it was time for an experiment. I got out the guitar I'd had when I'd played faire before, a beat-up beauty I'd bartered off another street musician back in the day. Sinking into stillness, I focused on the two metal pegs that allowed me to attach a strap to the guitar, and asked the molecules around them to shift. When I pulled on them, they slid out, leaving the wood behind intact.

Now, to install them in the instrument Killian and his father gave me; a piece from one world merged with another. The task required concentration, but not a great deal of energy. Soon, I had a leather strap attached to the dragon-adorned guitar. I tucked it back in its case.

My old hat waited on the driver's seat. Its dark-brown sides were folded up, a plume of black and purple feathers splashing over one side and off the back. I added finishing touches of eyeliner, mascara, and lip gloss, donned my fancy hat, and stepped out of the van.

Ready as I'd ever be, I headed across the field to one of the staff entrances. Out front, a line of patrons stretched into the parking lot, waiting for the gates to open.

The smells hit me as soon as I was within the walls: donuts frying, turkey legs roasting, and the odd vendor who hadn't bothered showering. Dust rose from the ground as I walked. At least it wasn't muddy.

I hadn't gotten far before a deep voice said, "Good morrow, Mistress Siren."

I turned to face a bearded man decked out in over-the-knee boots, hose, short, puffy pants, a long-sleeve brocade jacket, and a feathered hat. I couldn't remember his name, but he was management. I made a quick curtsey. "Good morrow, my lord. How fare thee?"

"I'm well." He frowned. "However, Master Jensen has not yet recovered from last night's festivities, so I'm short an opener on the Sphere Stage. Would you kindly perform? Now?"

"Of course, my lord." I bent my knees and bowed again, acknowledging the fact that he'd just given me a stage, which was a leg up from wandering minstrel.

The last time I'd curtsied this deep was for a king of gods.

"Grammercy," he said with a tip of his hat. "I'll see you anon."

"Fare thee well." I headed in what I hoped was the right direction, reaching for decade-old memories. What a mind fuck, coming from the actual past, into the future, playing at the past.

The gates had been open for ten minutes by the time I took the stage, my leather guitar case open at the edge of the platform. Entertainers worked for tips here. I hoped to make enough today to fund the rest of my road trip, but the point of this adventure was to make a change in the world. For that to happen, each individual had to wake up to the interconnectedness of life.

More laughter, less fear. More kindness, less hatred.

I hid my plaid bag in a gap beneath a painted cardboard and foam prop pretending to be a fountain at center stage. An elaborate façade of buildings backed the roundish platform, complete with turrets and balconies often used by actors. I could see at least four taverns from my vantage point, all of which already had lineups of people who would make a day of beer, mead, and food. A bell rang out from the nearest tavern, indicating a customer had left a tip, and the staff yelled "Huzzah!" with the energy of a new day.

Farther down the way, storefronts sold costumes of all sorts, weapons, leather goods, crafts, fairy wings, jewelry, and wizards' staffs. The benches in front of the stage were bare, other than a couple who'd sat down to look at their map, and a mother kneeling in front of a child. She appeared to be reasoning with a very small knight, telling him he could choose one toy today, not get something at every stall. I wished her luck with that.

The supervisor I'd met earlier strolled by, pausing beneath a tree and standing with his chest out importantly. I gave him a nod. Showtime.

"Good morrow, Lords and Ladies!" I stood at the front of the stage and used the tiniest touch of magic to project so the people at the taverns would be able to hear me. "Be welcome to the faire! Dance and make merry."

I beamed a smile, strummed a cord progression, and launched into a jig I'd last played in the halls of Asgard. I bounced with quick footwork and faster fingers, sending waves of joy out through the grounds.

By the time I transitioned the first song into an equally-lively second, most of the benches were full. By the third, when my voice rang out in lyrics that invoked the elements, a wall of people ringed the outside edge of the bench seating, some of them faire folk who trilled and whooped in answer to my chorus.

The song was a raw call to freedom. The stomp of my foot boomed through the stage and was answered by clapping hands. Someone had brought their drum, playing along. They were good, too. I drew it out, repeating the song twice before ending it a cappella, with half the audience singing along.

Thunderous applause and raucous yells made me laugh, and I indulged in a bow. This was so much fun, I barely thought about the magic. *Awakening. Joy. Kindness. Connection.* If these people went home with a greater sense of that, then I was doing something good.

Would it be enough?

I played until a stage hand gave me a signal to wrap it up, which I did with as much grace as I could muster. Something gentle to send them off. I didn't even have to ask for tips—as soon as I thanked the audience and bid them good day, people started tossing bills into my guitar case.

A few minutes later, I slipped out a door in the set to a staff-only area, surrounded by trees, where a trio of women whose act consisted mainly of bawdy humor waited take the stage.

I made my way past them, and turned a corner, where I found a man whose lined eyes stopped me in my tracks. "Miguel." I remembered his name intimately, and the way his smooth brown skin felt under my hands. "Good morrow to you."

"Siren." His finger brushed briefly beneath my chin. Black leather everything with this guy—hat, pants, boots, and sculpted vest atop a loose-sleeved shirt.

Melody called him a plaything, and he didn't mind. She'd called me the same. Which had been a whole lot of fun. Memories obliterated my ability to speak.

"The Pirate Mistress missed you last night," he said. "As did I."

"I was tired." My words came out stilted.

He cocked his head, eyes narrowed, curling mouth framed by his trimmed goatee. "Well, you performed like you're all charged up." He took my right hand and kissed it, running a thumb over the ring Killian had given me. "Save some spunk for this evening."

I opened my mouth in a wordless reply as he spun on his boot heel and strode away.

Melody had summoned me with the most seductive messenger she could procure. I needed to slip away before she had a chance to get me alone, or I'd have a lot of explaining to do. But first, breakfast. And a couple more sets.

Chapter 28
The Pirate Mistress

THANK THE GODS FOR fresh donuts and coffee. The taste of sweet, chewy goodness washed down with bittersweet elixir made me whimper, a quiet note that blended into the din of people feasting, day drinking, and yelling "Huzzah!"

I'd perched myself in a large tree on a partially-hidden platform, planning to play after I ate. On a bough opposite me, massive wind chimes hung. The biggest had a resonance so low it cast a spell of peace over the place all on its own. The other chimes rang a melodic tune, bringing the magic of faire to life.

This was one of my favorite spots, above a grassy area far enough from other stages that I could sing and not disturb anyone's performance. With a tavern at one end and storefronts making a semi-circle around the space, there were plenty of distractions for patrons to enjoy.

A couple sat beneath the tree, leaning against each other. One man had his eyes closed. His companion gazed at the chimes with a soft smile. They were regulars, these two, showing up in costume every weekend. Across the little clearing, a woman came out of a large, purple tent, long skirts swishing, scarf around her hair, and sauntered over to talk to the lovers. When she caught sight of me in my perch, she lifted her chin. I raised my coffee in a silent greeting. A minute later, she headed off toward the mews, where knights battled and royals sat around looking important in their finery.

The gates had been open for a couple of hours, and the crowd continued to swell as more people arrived. I blurred my vision to focus on the colors around them all, energetic imprints of auras and intentions. Some were bright and clear, some muddy. Splashes of pink mingled with lots of green and blue, with occasional flares of angry reds or anxious flickers of murky orange.

Focusing on faces again, I recognized many of the people cloaked in happy, peaceful colors from the audience at my last performance. Which meant it was working.

Having polished off the donuts, I fished one of Ola's sausage rolls out of my pouch. It wouldn't keep, and I figured spiking my blood sugar in addition to the caffeine rush wasn't super conducive to broadcasting harmony.

Halfway through my snack, I lifted my gaze toward the widest part of the road leading to the jousting arena, where a procession of pirates approached.

The Pirate Mistress led, her light-brown skin shining from the heat of the day, her generous cleavage in a shelf above a red-and-silver corset. Miguel strode to her right, a Black woman named Georgia on her left. Georgia was a fun one, I remembered. Feisty. She wore nearly as much leather as Miguel, but showed way more skin, with a dagger on one hip and a flask on her other. Behind them, a colorful crew of misfits carried on, their ranks becoming increasingly more disorderly as the group dissolved into a parade of patrons.

Melody surveyed the space like it was her personal domain. As soon as her gaze lifted, I knew she'd seen me.

She was with me the day I'd bought this hat. She'd tucked a black feather into its plume.

I wrapped what was left of my sausage roll in a napkin and shoved it back in my plaid pouch, wiped crumbs off my face and cleavage, and took a swig of water to wash it down.

Melody's entourage followed her off the road, onto the green. Straight toward my tree. The woman I'd seen earlier peeled away from the group and headed back to the purple tent, sending a wicked grin over her shoulder like she was thrilled to have instigated this mischief by telling Melody where I was. When the Pirate Mistress stopped her company before my perch, the lovers below got up and repositioned themselves off to the side, waiting for the spectacle to begin.

And it would be a spectacle, of that I was sure. Might as well face it head on.

"Good day, Mistress Melody," I called. I placed one hand on the trunk of the tree so I didn't fall out of it, and swept my hat off to bow to her.

"Good day, my Siren." She smirked, and took a step forward, away from Miguel and Georgia. "All the gossip on the glen is about you, did you know?"

I tried to look innocent, playing along. "Whatever for?"

She shifted her weight, one hand on her hip. "Apparently you bewitched half the realm with your voice. What say you to that?"

"It be truth, says I." Oh, the irony, to play at something that let me speak honestly, knowing no one would believe a word of it. A crowd had formed, the lovers who'd been beneath the tree now grinning at the forefront of a wall of spectators. These kinds of shenanigans were what faire was all about.

"Well, no one invited me," said Melody with an irritated frown.

"My apologies, Mistress."

"You owe me either a kiss or a song for the oversight."

I laughed, shaking my head. "It'll have to be a song, good Mistress. I had to ride a dragon to get up here."

Eyebrows arched, she took a step toward the tree, hand on the hilt of her sword. "If you deny me now, I will find you later." The threat had teeth, delivered in a low, sultry voice.

I picked up my guitar in answer, checked the tuning, and launched into a song I'd sung to Melody the first time we'd met that summer. The Siren's song, she called it, and the name had stuck. It spoke of wild oceans, magical creatures, and unrepressed longing.

A mixed blessing, singing to an old lover who didn't know I'd moved on. Melody's scowl turned into a smirk, and the crowd lifted their faces, mesmerized.

They wanted to be enchanted. We were all seekers of magic.

Like fairy dust, I sent glittering energy through the soundwaves. It wafted on the breeze and drifted down to those who listened.

Awakening. Awareness. Kindness.

I swayed on my perch, bringing the song to its finish. When I stopped, I touched the tree trunk again, letting the magic fade with the last note.

"You *are* an enchantress," Melody's voice cut through the dissipating spell.

"Aye, Mistress. I am." If she knew the half of it, what would she say?

Before she could comment, I launched into a drinking song that at least half the pirate crew knew, and transformed the clearing into a riot of singing, dancing, drinking, and hollering.

Melody grinned at me before hooking arms with Miguel and skipping around in a circle, joining in the hullabaloo. Georgia grabbed a woman in blue skirts by the waist, and the two of them twirled together.

After a round of lively tunes, I dropped into a hypnotic rhythm, and called on a breeze to make the wind chimes play. The leaves rustled, adding to the music I picked from my guitar. Lyrics rose, and I gave them voice. Weaving another spell.

Be ye here, may ye feel
How life's threads are woven
Into a Tapestry
That breathes us all.

What thread will you weave?
Make it kind, make it bright.
All is interwoven.
Sing shield songs of might.

Be ye here, may ye see
That life's threads dissolve
Into an eternal Tapestry
That breathes us all.

When my fingers stilled on the guitar, the tones of the chimes kept on. I sang harmonies with the wind, tapping into the roots below to connect with the magic of the World

Tree, sending my intention into time and space. I saw it rippling out, through the people, through the land, past the fields and forests and beyond. I closed my eyes, suspended in the magic I cast.

Then my body tilted, my eyes flew open, and I shot a hand out to the tree to steady myself.

Half of the crowd was laying on the grass, others sitting or standing with wistful eyes and blissed-out smiles. Had faire ever been this quiet?

Slowly, people started to stir. The woman by the purple tent sent a trill of celebration up, and the glade exploded into whoops and clapping. Melody leaned toward Miguel, speaking into his ear and drawing a crooked smile from his lips.

"Lady Siren!" Miguel swept off his hat and went down on one knee. "Should you ever need a champion, I will fight for you."

The crowd erupted in whistles and laughter, a few pirates leering in jest. Melody's teeth showed in a triumphant grin. She'd orchestrated a production that would become faire legend.

"Master Miguel," I said, "your chivalry rivals a knight's, but better. I much prefer rogues. If I need a champion, I will call."

He stood, bowed, and settled his hat back on his head.

Melody stepped in next to him. "And should I need an enchantress," she said, her voice a warning edged with lust, "I will call." She turned her shoulders, summoning her following. Time for her exit.

I tipped my head. "Fare thee well, Mistress."

"Fare thee well, Siren," called Miguel.

Melody didn't comment. True to character, she walked off without a backward glance, with all the poise of a queen. She left with about half of her original company, having lost most of the random joiners.

I crouched down to stow my guitar. This morning's performance had made me enough tips that I didn't need to ask for anything this time. I could leave now, avoid Melody, and make enough busking in Chicago and New York to pay the rest of the way to D.C.

But if I played another show here, I might have enough for the whole trip. And maybe, secretly, I wanted a chance to say goodbye to Melody.

Killian would've liked the stew served at faire. I could only finish half the bread bowl, while he would've eaten it easily, plus my leftovers. Nikolas and Troy, too. What would they think if they could see this modern, consumerist take on an old world? The children would have a ball.

Could I come here with my family? Take a vacation through time just for the fun of it?

I shook my head at my daydream and finished eating, hiding in a pub's dining area on the outskirts of the faire. After clearing the table, I claimed an unused bench and pushed it against a tree in the corner, deep in the shade. Hat low, feet propped up, I waited out the early afternoon.

My mind kept coming back to Loki. What had he done to be exiled, however temporary? Maybe my mother hadn't exiled me, but I'd grown up with a sense of abandonment. Knowing she loved me couldn't erase the trauma of the past.

I tucked one hand into my plaid pouch, and stroked the leather that covered Loki's blades. What would he do, if he were here? Would he watch? Would he take over? Would it turn into a massacre, or would it be the best day faire had ever seen?

Likely the latter, if his claim about running a night club was truthful.

A trio of loud men dressed in t-shirts and shorts interrupted my musings with a drunken rendition of one of my songs. It was hilarious, obnoxious, and a high compliment. I tipped my hat lower, pretending to sleep, while the brim hid my smile.

A while later, after the threesome of friends had drained their drinks and moved on, I emerged from my corner and set out in search of a stage that needed a performer, or a decent place to play roving minstrel.

I didn't get far before Miguel appeared, strolling beside me. "She wants to see you," he said in an undertone. Elbow out, he offered me his arm.

I almost refused, but this gave me a chance at closure where I never had it before. I'd delighted in Melody's power plays and many pleasures, in Miguel and Georgia. They'd been the highlight of this part of my life, so many years ago.

Ignoring the disorienting overlap of time, I took Miguel's arm. We walked down a lane lined with shops, turned left behind a tavern, and passed through a cast-only door. Out we went, into the staff campgrounds, where every sort of recreational vehicle and shelter made a village of their own.

Melody held court in a giant red-and-black tent outside her trailer, with all the doors pulled back. The airy, steel-and-canvas structure dwarfed her RV, providing shade for a host of people who looked hot, tired, and in need of a siesta. The Pirate Mistress sat on her throne; an antique sofa big enough for three if you got friendly about it. No one sat beside her, right now.

I let go of Miguel's arm and walked the rest of the way to face Melody. The stereo in the corner played tribal-sounding music with a backbeat, and incense wafted through the open space, covering for someone smoking a joint on a couch in the corner.

Melody leaned forward as I approached, her gaze dropping to my sword and dagger. She pointed with her chin, saying, "Your blades are magnificent."

My left hand went to my sword, my right to the weight of Loki's daggers in my pouch. "Thank you."

"Where did you get them?" She stood, coming closer in deliberate steps.

"That's a long story." My heart pounded with her so close. I didn't want her—not like I had before, but there was something potent here. An alliance.

Did a version of me in a parallel universe love Melody's soul? She had such fire.

With her face a foot from mine, making me look up to meet her gaze, she spoke quietly enough that no one else would hear. "What happened?" she asked. "You're different. The same woman, but more."

I smiled an apology. "I wish I could tell you."

Melody took my left hand and brought it between us. My ring shone. "You've never worn a ring before." Her mouth tightened as she touched the ring Killian had given me. "Now you have two."

I squeezed her palm before dropping my hands and slipping into lies and half-truths. "I found a patron. I actually wanted to talk to you." I tried to smile, but it must've come out wrong because she narrowed her eyes as

I went on. "I have to leave. Tonight. I've got a gig in Chicago and I just—wanted to say goodbye."

"That," she said, raising a finger, "was not what I expected."

"What did you expect?"

"That you ran away from a rich marriage and were finally showing your true colors." She frowned. There was no jest in her words, her gaze dead serious. "With the way you sang today, maybe you really are an enchantress."

I cocked my head. "Maybe I am." No sarcasm. It was the closest to the truth I could get. "My work here is nearly done."

"I'm not interested in letting you leave." She put her hands on her hips. "There may need to be spankings involved."

I grinned, shaking my head. "As much fun as that would be, I don't have time for such festivities."

"One more show?" she guessed.

I nodded. "One more show."

She stared at me for a long, drawn out moment. Finally, she spun to face the room, clapped her hands twice, and announced, "We have a mission. Our Siren is playing one last show. Let's make it the biggest this faire has ever seen."

And just like that, I had my own marketing team—one that would idly threaten as often as invite people to come watch my performance.

Melody sweet-talked a group of players into sitting out their time slot, securing a stage. As soon as they knew the location, our rogue friends went around hollering about my show. Georgia stood on stage, threw her arms into the air, and bellowed. "Beginning imminently, the Siren sings! Come one, come all, to the call of the Enchantress!"

As I sat to the side of the stage and tuned my guitar, Miguel watched me with sad eyes. "You're really leaving?"

"Yes." My smile wavered. I hated goodbyes, but this was better than what they'd gotten before, when I'd disappeared without a trace, leaving my van in the field.

"Then today is the best and worst day of faire." He took my hand and kissed it, rubbing his thumb over my fingers before letting go. "I got to be your champion for an afternoon, and listen to the most magical music in existence. And now, I have to say goodbye."

"I'm sorry." I swallowed. He really cared for me. I'd cared for him, too. The loss had hurt, and it gushed back as the memory emerged.

He handed me a business card. Miguel Xander, screenwriter and stuntman. It had a dragon logo, phone number, website, and email. On the back, he'd scrawled his home number and a note. *If you ever need a champion, call.*

With a bow, he left. Blinking back tears, I composed myself enough to sing.

A little over an hour later, I made it to my van. The rolling whine that came when I opened the side door deepened the sense of loneliness that crept over me. Miguel had offered to walk me out, but I'd told him no. It would be harder to avoid last kisses out here, things that were beyond me now.

I had a family. A beautiful family. I needed to get back to them.

Still, the sense of isolation grew. I was the only weaver, tasked with improving the fate of this complicated, multi-faceted world. I was sure I'd done some good here today, but would it last? Would people return home with a different perspective? Would they change things in their lives, or would the magic fade into a memory of a particularly bright day at faire?

I dumped my things on the bed, slid the door shut, and settled into the faint smell of wet dog, eying the explosion of belongings in the small space. Counting the money came first. My jaw dropped when I realized I'd made over a thousand dollars.

The most I'd made in a day before had been two hundred.

It's not like I'd asked for money—all my focus had been on increasing the awareness in each person of the importance of caring about others and living in harmony with nature. Yet people had thrown twenties in my guitar case. Someone had dropped a fifty. Love created generosity. Generosity gave rise to gratitude.

"May the cycle continue." I closed my eyes, took a breath of musty van air, and connected with the planet. With the sky. With the gods.

May the cycle continue. Love. Generosity. Gratitude.

The chant spun through my soul until I knew without a doubt that it was woven into the Tapestry. When I finally opened my eyes and looked at the clock, it was nearing the end of the day. Some people were entering the gates carrying djembes they'd retrieved from their vehicles for the massive drum circle at closing ceremony. Others were leaving, ready to head home with tired kids or drunken friends.

Wanting to get ahead of the traffic, I hastily stowed anything that might roll around, and hid my sword in my guitar case once again. I tossed my hat on the bed. Plaid purse with water, snacks, and Loki's blades went on the passenger seat.

Key in the ignition, I cranked the engine. The stereo came on, playing Tom Petty, and I laughed. I'd missed this. Thought it was gone forever.

Maybe the gods had given me a gift after all, asking me to come back.

CHAPTER 29
A LONG, STRANGE TRIP

THE GRATEFUL DEAD grooved through my speakers as I left farmland behind and entered the sprawling suburbia that surrounded Chicago. Troy would not like it here. Way too many people. And so many cops. I'd counted fifteen police cars on the way here, half of them on the side of the road with their lights on. The red-and-blue flashing triggered my anxiety even as I drove with cruise control on, two miles per hour under the speed limit. Now that I was in suburbia, there were even more cops. I picked out unmarked cars, always too clean, sporting an extra antenna or two.

My plan had been to head straight for the city, but I changed my mind. There was a place I used to park near one of the forest preserves that seemed like a good place to stay the night. Following old memories, I took an exit off the highway, and headed that way.

When I'd lived in a van, I never stayed anywhere too long, mostly because people complained and police started knocking on my window, telling me to move or making up excuses to search the vehicle. The spot I headed for now had once been a favorite, as had my adventures in the nearby forest to a place I'd dubbed "the faerie ring."

What would I find if I went there now? Were any elementals left? Could I coax nature spirits to occupy the forest again, to share it with humans?

Twenty minutes later, I pulled into a parking lot that bordered a complex of townhomes. Visitors could use the lot, and my soccer-mom-mobile fit right in. My ren faire costume did not fit in, however.

Once the blackout curtains were up and the windshield cover in place, the van became an island unto itself. I changed into leggings, and took some time to tidy up. Costumes hidden. Bed made.

It would be dark soon. I wanted to get into the forest before twilight fell. I could make my way back easy enough, but light would help my memory.

I refilled my water and supplies, slid Loki's knives beneath the sleeves of my long coat, and slung my plaid pouch over one shoulder, my guitar case over the other. Daggers in my boots, I slipped out of the van.

The forest I wanted to enter was to the south, but I headed away from it, into the rows of townhomes. Rule number one of sleeping in an apartment complex: look like you live there. A security car went through at a crawl, the guard behind the wheel eying me. I lifted my chin in a subtle hello, and he nodded back. Barely.

I kept on, the security car long out of sight by the time I reached the main road, where I waited to cross. Such a normal thing, standing at a stoplight. It sent my head spinning to be here. I'd changed so much, but time never stopped messing with me.

As the light turned red, a cop slowed to a stop along with a few other vehicles. The crosswalk turned, and I made my way across the road, walking right in front of the squad car.

I kept my eyes forward. Crossed with swift steps. And turned away from the forest again.

Technically, the forest preserves were closed at night. If the cop saw me going that way, he might follow me, and if he searched my guitar case, he'd find my sword, which was not something I wanted to explain. Nor did I want to have to call Eirian to bail me out. So, I walked away from the forest in a convoluted path, until I finally doubled back to an entrance on the other side of the preserve.

Cutting away from the road, I headed down a bike path, getting into the woods as fast as possible. Hopefully my green coat and brown guitar case blended into the trees. Even this path was too exposed. I needed a single-track trail.

A few minutes later, I found one, and followed it to the bottom of a gully. The path turned, and the wider one I'd been on was lost behind trees and bushes.

My detour had eaten up most of the daylight. Under the canopy of trees, shadows dimmed, hiding obstacles and berms made by mountain bikers. By the time night fell, I was still looking for the spot I remembered: a small circular clearing with a mound at the center where I'd gone before to sing and dream.

My toe caught on a root, and I stumbled forward. Would've been nice if I'd remembered to bring the flashlight from the glove box in the van. Probably better without, though. Cops would see a light moving around in the woods. So would anyone else who might be out here.

I crept along, enhancing my night vision by opening whatever receptors allowed me to see energy. As I fine-tuned the effect, I was able to see the forest in a subtle, bioluminescent-like glow. And as I studied the lines of light, I realized they all led where I was headed.

The faerie mound glimmered in my sight, and a thread of understanding told me it had once been an entrance to another world. That door had long been closed.

I listened for elementals , and for the song of the trees, but their voices were dim and few. Nothing like the symphony of awareness I would've heard if I was in this forest a few hundred years ago. There was sentience, to be sure, but it was guarded. Withdrawn.

What if I made a door?

A hasty plan formed. Inspired or reckless, I wasn't sure, but I was going for it. Opening my guitar case, I withdrew my sword. Dragon blade drawn, I strode to the top of the rise and held the weapon before my face.

Gentle. I mind-whispered instructions into the blade. *Gentle, now. Give me a little light. A little power.*

The sword lit along its edges with a golden radiance. I swung it around with a low note of song, then walked the circumference of the clearing, chanting quietly as I traced the edge of the circle. The third time I completed the loop, the light stayed, encompassing the mound in a soft yellow glow.

Back at the center, I held the sword, blade down, weaving my intention to align overlapping worlds. With another round of improvised incantation, I thrust the sword into the ground.

The night sounds went quiet. No insects. No cars or sirens in the distance. As I listened, the song of the trees crept in. Wind spirits. Forest dwellers. I could hear their music, but couldn't understand their words.

They didn't sound happy. I reached into my pouch and grabbed a square of chocolate I'd found in the van. "For you," I said, crumbling it up and tossing bits around the circle. I poured some water out of my canister in offering. Then I picked up my guitar.

Transparent forms shifted in the light. I was between where they were, and where I'd been a minute ago, sitting in the doorway I'd made. When I strummed the guitar, my back tingled with otherworldly attention.

As I sang, more translucent beings gathered in the space I'd created, my sword powering a sustained glow. After five songs, I stopped and bowed. "That music was an offering," I said. "And this door is an invitation. Some humans don't understand that we are all connected, but many people want to learn from nature. Should any of you wish to inhabit these woods, you may. It is your right. Your presence is needed here, on this beautiful planet."

I was acutely aware of the chance that this could go horribly wrong. I could be opening a portal to chaos. But I was a world-weaver, and it felt like the right thing to do.

"Peace be with you," I said, and wrapped both hands around the hilt of my sword. As I pulled it out of the ground, the golden glow faded to black. I blinked, heart pounding.

Insects sang. A siren sounded in the distance. No tree songs or wind spirits whispering in the branches, just a Saturday night in suburbia.

After cleaning off my sword, I sat down with my guitar again, and sang for a different audience. I hoped the nature spirits still listened, but the soft music I made was for the people who went about their lives, clueless that there was an armed dragon rider in the forest casting spells.

Awakening. Awareness. Love. Generosity. Gratitude.

Over and over, I poured the intention into the ground and sent it wide. They didn't need to hear the song for it to make a difference, did they? I could reach more people this way than if I had an audience.

When my inner sight showed the light of my work reaching into the city and shimmering on the lake, I stopped. And realized how tired I was.

As I stumbled through the darkness, back to my van, tired enough to take a nap beneath a tree, I wondered if all that magic had been worth it.

I only stayed in Chicago for a few hours the next day, singing one set in Lincoln Park and another near the art museum. I did my best to stay grounded, but the pressure of so many people in one place made me sick to my stomach.

Back on the road, I decided to skip Indianapolis altogether, and headed for New York. I spent the night north of Pittsburg, where I found a forest like the one outside Chicago. Repeating the ritual opened a new door. Another place where nature was invited to emerge, another spell to awaken those who lived nearby and far away.

By the time I rolled into the city the next evening, I was drained. Tired of singing, tired of casting magic. Tired of weaving worlds together. I just wanted to go home to my children and Nikolas.

I slept a wary night parked on a street near a subway entrance I'd busked at before, one ear open in case someone tried breaking into my van. The next morning, I took my guitar down the stairs and played while people waited for their trains. I'd made a false-bottom to my guitar case, hiding my sword beneath cardboard and thick cloth that cushioned the fall of coins people tossed my way.

Some commuters didn't hear me; the headphones they wore fed them their own music, creating their own little worlds. The magic in my songs reached them anyway, spells layered in soundwaves.

After an hour, I caught a train to Penn Station. I played a set there, then headed to Grand Central. I busked my way down to Prospect Park, and all the way back up to Central Park.

As I packed up, ready to catch a train back to my van, a young woman stopped before me. She twisted her hands around the handles of the duffle bag she carried, and said, "Your music is the best thing that happened to me today."

I smiled, trying to hide my fatigue. "That's kind of you to say. Thank you."

"I don't have any money to give you." She looked down, and I followed her gaze. Her shoes had holes in them, and her clothes had seen better days.

"Your words are gift enough." I fished into my pocket, where I'd deposited one stash of money, and brought out a handful of bills. "Here." I pressed it into her hand. "Take care of yourself."

"But this is yours—"

"Take it." I wrapped her fingers around the money. "I don't need it."

When the train pulled in, I left her there, tears pooling in her eyes. Finding a seat, I stood my guitar case up between my legs, and heaved a heavy sigh.

There were too many people like that woman. Too many in poverty. Would a song be enough to make people share what they could? Would anything I did ever be enough?

I rolled out before dawn the next day, stopping in Philadelphia for a morning set and some breakfast. I made Washington D.C. just before lunchtime, and parked in the first spot I could find. Not far down the street, trees grew in a small park, shading benches and a fountain. A good bit of foot traffic headed to the bustling restaurant across the way and the stores to either side. It was as good a spot as any to do my thing.

I placed my guitar case on the ground by the fountain, but my hand froze on the clasps as I noticed a group of suits walking past the park. Two had to be bodyguards; they were tall and fit, guns bulging under their jackets, earpieces showing, eyes darting everywhere. The man and woman they protected were politicians. I'd seen their faces too many times in the future to forget what they'd done. What they would do. These lawmakers and their cronies hoarded power and stole people's freedoms; their greed broke the economy while the ultra-rich took all.

Heartless humans. Did they deserve to live long enough to create their brutal legacy?

I sucked in a breath, shifting into reaper mode.

The woman with the long neck turned to the man with two chins, saying something with a smile so fake it was more of a grimace. The man looked across the street, where the sight of someone getting out of a limo made my blood run cold. His profile was unmistakable, his face a mask of con-artist innocence, a puppet ruler of the worst sort.

It wasn't quite a coup d'état, but it was damn close. These were exactly the kind of people I'd contemplated killing. I'd be doing the world a favor if I took them out.

I stood, one hand on my guitar case, and stared at the water in the fountain. I knew killing these people wouldn't get to the root of the problem—it wouldn't stem the greed for power and control that corrupted the government in this country and every other. Others would, no doubt, take their places. But I had a chance to remove key players from the gameboard.

There was no way this was a coincidence. This was fate offering me a chance to erase the horrors they'd do if I let them live. And I was going to take it.

Their lies and martial-law lockdowns would cause the deaths of many. Their wars would devastate the world. I had to stop them now.

Without drawing Loki's knives, I connected to their power. Their cutting accuracy. He'd hinted they could be used many ways, time to put that to the test. When I reached through my awareness, seeking the pulse of each target, I could hear their heartbeats as if the noise of the street didn't exist. All it would take was a little pinch. I could crush them from the inside with a thought by tapping into a power I'd never explored.

One Thor had never mentioned.

Loki's blades were teaching me, even now.

Fingers curling, I shot a decisive command to the man's body across the street. He convulsed, dropping to the ground, one guard rushing to catch him, another drawing his gun and swinging around in search of threats. I felt the bastard die. A silent vibration like harsh feedback from a mic made me shudder from my shoulders to my toes. His life force dissolved, his energy dispersed, and his body went still.

My stomach threatened to revolt, but I swallowed hard and turned my attention to the panicking politicians on this side of the road, whose hearts I held with a thread of thought. Their pulses raced. Bodyguards formed a wall around them, powerless to save them. With a twist of intent, I stopped their hearts and took them down.

Someone behind me screamed. Even though there'd been no shots, people started hitting the ground. I crouched down like I was as confused as everyone else. Like the reason I was shaking was fear for my own life, rather than the sickening gravity of what I'd done.

When the crowd started running from the scene, I went with them, leaving three bodies behind me. Murder in the name of the gods.

Was it any different than an off-books military operation? Didn't special ops go into other countries and take out violent drug lords and fascist dictators? Soldiers were assassins, and also heroes.

Does this make me a reaper, Loki?

He didn't answer. Not that I expected him to.

Ambulances raced past. I kept walking as sirens wailed and lights flashed, police cars pushing traffic aside to get to the scene. How would they explain what they found?

I walked far longer than I needed to, as if I could run from the doom I'd caused if I clocked enough miles. Around mid-afternoon, I stumbled up to a taco stand and ordered like I'd found an oasis in a desert. After my third taco, I looked around and realized where I was.

Pennsylvania Avenue. If I kept going, I'd be at the White House.

I finished my food, put a twenty in the tip jar, and headed down the road.

A while later, I came to an unoccupied bench and took a seat. Past trees and cars and fences, a white building sat like a castle. Was the President home today? If I played, would my music reach him? Would the magic penetrate past security checks and defenses, into the hearts of the people who worked in that house, and this city?

I pushed aside the guilt over what I'd done earlier, and got out my guitar. This would be my last set.

CHAPTER 30
NO REST FOR THE WEAVER

I SHOULD'VE CAUGHT a cab from the White House to my van, but my feet needed to move. Dead tired, and still running.

My mind replayed the same argument. I'd done the world a mercy, taking out those politicians this morning. I couldn't go around hunting them—wouldn't. There were too many governments, too many corrupt power players around the world. Even if I went full vigilante, I'd never get all of them.

But if they were right in front of me, I wasn't going to pass up the chance.

The gods wanted me to change the fate of the world. I'd done what I could do. Maybe I'd come back and do more, but not for a while. I needed to rest. Needed to be a mother.

I left my old belongings at a women's shelter, along with most of the money, signed transfer papers for the van, and my fake I.D., in case anyone else could use it. Then I took a bus out of town, and walked the rest of the way to an abandoned field near a state park.

The sun set through a haze of smog. Finally, when it was properly dark, I called Eirian.

He appeared beside me, his bulk blocking the distant noise of a highway. A buffer between me and the world.

How goes it, Weaver?

I groaned, and scrambled up his scaly hide. No saddle this time. *I'm ready to leave.*

He shifted beneath me. *Back to the village?*

Please.

In an instant, the field dissolved. My next breath tasted like salt water, the sea crashing below us. Eirian flew not far from the village of Thorson.

My ring hummed. Nikolas knew I was here.

We landed in the dark, to the sound of waves and crunching rocks. As soon as my feet hit ground, Eirian said goodbye and disappeared. No need for anyone to see him here. I huffed my way toward the warm glow of cottage windows, remembering the first time I'd approached this village. I was as tired now as I'd been then.

As I reached the house, Nikolas came down the steps, and took me in his arms.

"How long has it been?" I asked.

"Six days. How long were you gone?" He brushed hair away from my face.

"The same." I'd negotiated time on my terms. That was a victory, at least.

"Did you do what you needed to do?" Nikolas held my hands.

"I don't know." I couldn't keep the exhaustion from my voice. "I did what I could."

He put a hand at my back and walked up the stairs with me, opening the door.

It was all I could do to greet my children, change into clean clothes, and collapse in bed. The mattress shifted as Nikolas joined me, wrapping me in love, warmth, and the comfort of knowing he was by my side.

But that night, in the early hours of the morning, my dreams delved into prophecy.

Blue-coated troops invaded Nwetaka land, gunshots echoing off the mountains that sheltered their valley. The Nwetaka fought, outnumbered, against uniformed invaders who didn't discriminate. If they had a shot, they took it. Even if their target was unarmed.

In a flash of gold, Troy rode in on Sundance. The crack of his guns jolted through me, soldiers falling, bullets flying. Until an officer raised his rifle, and a blast shook the air.

My ring sent out a shriek that reached my soul, jerking me out of the nightmare, heart pounding, well on my way to a panic attack.

Nikolas woke beside me. "What is it?" He put his hand to his chest, exactly where Troy had been shot.

"I have to go." With a thought, I lit the lanterns. I only meant to light the ones in the bedroom, but I overshot and lit every wick in the house. Sounds of waking children filtered through the walls as I pulled on pants and tossed a shirt over my head.

"What happened, Shelta?" Nikolas followed me out of the room. "Why do I hurt?"

"Troy's been shot." My voice caught. "I have to go!"

Eirian, I need you now!

I couldn't explain things to Nikolas, too flustered to form words. I was reaching for my coat when he grabbed me, pulling me around to face him.

I sent him the scene, the story—all of it in a thought.

He staggered back. "I'm going with you."

I didn't argue. There wasn't time.

As I buckled on my sword, Ola burst through the door in her nightgown, Patrick behind her rubbing his eyes. "That was some waking." She scowled at Nikolas. "You pushed me right out of bed."

"Someone I love is dying." I stood before her, ready to go.

"I'll watch the children." She nodded; brow drawn. Did she see the scene that haunted me? Every second wasted was a second closer to Troy's death.

I didn't even kiss my babies goodbye. I raced outside, Nikolas beside me, his hammer hanging from his belt. Eirian landed on the beach past the village. Rúna swooped down with him, silvery-blue scales shining moonlight into Nikolas's upturned face.

I climbed onto Eirian's back, heart pounding, desperate to leave. Nikolas sat astride Rúna, who linked minds with Eirian, who tuned into my intent. Thus intertwined, we dropped through time and space.

With a blinding flash and sickening spin, we emerged above a scene so gruesome I almost heaved over Eirian's wings. Clamping my mouth shut, I searched for Troy in the carnage below.

It was exactly as I'd seen in my nightmare. Blue-coated soldiers surrounded the Nwetaka village, a massacre underway as both sides fired at will, some with focused precision, some with desperate abandon.

I found Troy crumpled on the ground, bleeding out while Diego stood over him, making good use of his rifle. With blood splattered over his golden coat, Sundance charged the nearest soldier, rearing up to bash the man's chest with a hoof. The Nwetaka fought valiantly, but the numbers were against them.

The cacophony got louder as we descended. Gunshots. Screams. The moans of wounded and dying. I searched the fray for Sarina and the two elders who had been at

Brendan's birth. I didn't see B'alam or Nemonte, but spotted Sarina bent over, tending to an injured warrior.

Eirian swooped low. I jumped with a battle cry and landed near Troy as my dragon turned, roaring at the mounted troops. Horses screamed, bucking their riders and trampling those who fell. Nikolas stood atop Rúna, surfing his dragon, who banked to cut off the army's retreat, her sharp-fanged snarl rumbling through the ground.

Nikolas jumped, landing with his hammer swinging. He hit one man, and five more fell, a thin flash of lightning blasting through them, from heart to heart. He would kill them all, my god-blooded Viking, to defend the Nwetaka and protect the dragons.

I dropped to my knees at Troy's side. He looked at me like I was a vision, the wound in his chest soaking him with blood. Tears streamed down my face as I drew healing energy from the earth and tried to force it through my hands, but panic impaired my efforts. This wasn't going to work if I couldn't calm myself, and I had very little time.

I slowed my breath and closed my eyes to the paleness of Troy's skin, calling on the Earth, on the elements. They responded, and my palms turned hot with energy, one over the other on Troy's chest. I sought the bullet with my awareness. It was wedged in deep.

I choked on my tears, using the magnetics of the earth to pull the lead out of his heart. When it hit my hand, I cast it aside like an evil thing.

Troy's breathing was becoming ragged. I had to mend him up or I'd lose him, and I had no confidence that the Tree would let me travel back in time to prevent this attack. I'd aimed for earlier today, but had been thrust here and now.

Thor's voice echoed in my mind: *The trick to healing is to make the necessary building blocks available, and let the body's intelligence direct the magic.*

I struggled, fear eating at me, desperately reaching for a sense of equilibrium. It was hard to ignore the gunfire, the screams, the stomp of horses and roar of dragons and thud of another body falling to the ground.

Inhale. *Cast a shield around my mind.*

Exhale. *Thicken it, shutting out all sound.*

Inhale. *Eternity exists in a second.*

Exhale. I reached energy into Troy's body, urging it to merge molecules into cells and cells into tissue, replenishing blood and bolstering his life-force.

I breathed, and he breathed.

And when I finally opened my eyes, he was awake, looking at me.

Troy put his hand to his chest and gasped. Skin covered the bullet hole that had been there a moment before. I let go of the magic and clutched him close, hands bloody, cheeks drenched.

"Shelta?" His voice was heavy with disbelief. "Am I dead?"

I shook my head. "I'm not about to let you die."

He held me with arms that contained surprising strength. Then he took my face and kissed me. When we leaned back, I looked up, and shivered.

The battle was over. Nikolas stood a few paces away, watching.

I couldn't read him. He'd blocked me from his emotions, and I saw fire in his eyes. Troy followed my gaze. This wasn't the time for introductions, though. There were others who needed healing.

I turned from them both and sought the wounded, who seemed to be everywhere. I had to call on Eirian for assistance after the fifth person.

As I moved to help another, I nearly tripped over Nikolas, who knelt beside a woman with a gunshot wound in her gut, holding her hand as she passed over. He bent his head, and I crouched next to him, whispering "I love you" in his ear before going to the next person who needed me.

Finally, I swayed on my feet. Nothing more to give. I stared at the rows of bodies that had been carried to a clearing nestled in a semi-circle of trees. Among them were B'alam and Nemonte. Someone had placed the elders' hands together, as if they walked hand-in-hand across the threshold to the next world. It sent fresh tracks of tears down my cheeks.

A touch at my back made me turn. Troy. Alive. We held each other for a long time, his hand on my head a miraculous thing. But when we stepped back, I looked for Nikolas. He stood on the outskirts of the village with the dragons.

Troy touched my ring, following my eyes. "Your husband?"

"Yes. That's Nikolas."

My insides turned as I watched them stare each other down. After a long minute, Troy walked over with me, and offered his hand to the Viking towering above us both.

Troy dipped his head as they shook. "Your actions saved many good people today."

Nikolas nodded, releasing the handshake and turning his gaze from Troy, to me, and back again. Not saying a word.

Troy opened his mouth, thought better of it, and walked over to the dragons. "You two are magnificent," he said, reaching his arms out.

Love surged through me. I leaned toward Nikolas, saying, "This is how deep our love runs. Through Troy. And Killian."

A muscle near his temple twitched. "I know it. But it's difficult, watching you with him, even if he has the same source within."

Troy turned back, looking from me to Nikolas. My men, sizing each other up.

"This is not an easy thing." Nikolas put a hand on the head of his hammer.

"No." Troy's hand went to his heart. His shirt was ripped, dark red with drying blood. His gaze settled on me. He'd nearly died.

Nikolas drew a breath that puffed out his chest, then let it go with a sigh. "I will stay a little longer, help you clean up this mess." He gestured at the uniformed bodies strewn across the clearing. "Then I'll take my leave."

"That's generous of you," said Troy.

Nikolas pinned him with his gaze. "You and I share a soul, and a wife. But we are different men. I think it's best we keep our distance."

I could've cut the tension between them with one of Loki's knives.

Troy nodded. "Agreed."

Nikolas held my eyes for a long moment, then strode off. He bent to grab a corpse by the leg, and dragged it away, adding to the pile the Nwetaka had begun downwind of the village. Rúna went to help, gathering bodies in her talons and using her wings to hop around, dropping them in a quickly-growing mountain of discarded flesh and bone.

CHAPTER 31
A SINGLE SURVIVOR

DIEGO AND SARINA came over, and bowed their heads to Eirian before turning to me and Troy.

"It's good to see you." Sarina's eyes held no hint of her usual mirth, and she had a smear of blood across her face. She'd lost her parents today.

"It's good to see *you*. I'm sorry I wasn't able to be here sooner." I looked down, holding onto Troy for balance, grief surging through deep fatigue.

Diego put his hand on my shoulder. "Our losses are not your burden, World Walker."

A whinny interrupted, and Sundance nosed in, wanting to be with Troy. The horse moved slow, ears back. Wary of the dragon.

When I turned away from Troy and his friends, I realized there were no more bodies to clear. Nikolas waited at the edge of the forest. I squeezed Troy's hand, nodded to Diego and Sarina, and slipped away.

The clack of an enemy's weapon being tossed in a pile near the mound of bodies made me jump. Heart sore, I walked over to Nikolas, avoiding the worst of the blood that stained the ground. When I reached him, I buried my face in his chest.

His fingers grazed my cheek, ever so slowly, making my skin tingle. His sigh held the heaviness of clouds burdened with rains that have yet to fall. "I cannot stay here," he said. "It's like having my soul stretched, to see you with him."

I blinked tears back. "I understand."

Nikolas pressed his mouth to mine. "You will return to me?" He kissed me again before letting me answer.

"Always." My voice rasped.

He lifted his gaze to the others, his eyes lingering on Troy. With one last caress, he strode to Rúna. Everyone's heads tilted up as the silver-blue dragon rose in the sky.

I shuddered as they disappeared. Nikolas had taken the life of every enemy soldier so they couldn't bring tales of dragons back to their superiors. He'd go home with that weight.

Perhaps not every soldier. Eirian used his most calming voice. *There is no threat, but there's a boy hiding behind a tree. He's wounded. I believe his life can be spared.*

With Eirian's direction, I walked to the edge of the trees, aiming to the left of where the young man was hiding. When I got close, I pivoted and fixed him with a hard gaze.

He couldn't have been more than sixteen. His uniform hung off his frame, and he leaned against a fallen tree with a bullet hole in his side. Brown eyes met mine, rimmed with red.

"I'm not going to hurt you." I frowned at his injury, wondering if I could conjure enough energy for one more. "Will you let me help you?"

He didn't say yes, but the sideways nod of his head was enough. I put a hand over the wound and tapped into a song of wholeness, asking his cells to restore themselves. By the time his skin closed, I was bent over on my knees.

"What's your name?" I asked between breaths.

"Samuel." He stared at his side. Touched his skin with a bloody hand.

"I'm Shelta. The Nwetaka are my friends. My family." I drew myself up and looked him in the eyes, a plan unfolding in my muddled mind. "Will you help me make sure this doesn't happen again?"

"How am I supposed to do that?" He glanced at his rifle, a few feet away.

I pushed to my feet, grabbed the gun, and rested it on my shoulder. "Get up."

He stood up, slow, holding onto a tree. Probably still in shock.

"Who ordered this attack?" I asked.

"General Rikes."

"Where's he based?"

Samuel swallowed, like he didn't want to rat out his superiors.

I caught sight of Troy, who stood a few paces off, gun drawn. Watching my back.

"Listen, Samuel," I said. "You have a choice. You can help me, and swear on your life to keep quiet about the dragons, and I'll let you live. I'll even give you a bit of gold so you can leave the army behind. Or, you can be difficult, and end up as a snack for my dragon."

Far too little meat on that one. Eirian's teasing tone made it hard to keep a straight face.

"H—help," Samuel stuttered. "I'll help you."

"Good choice." I nodded. "I'll need the general's location."

He blew out a breath. "There's a camp a few days' ride from here. They're running land acquisition campaigns in every direction."

"Not anymore, they're not." I started walking, and Samuel was smart enough to keep up.

CHAPTER 32
A THREAD OF CHANGE

TROY STRODE BESIDE me toward Eirian, frowning. "Where are you going?"

"To put a stop to this." My gaze dropped to the hole in his blood-soaked shirt.

Samuel lagged behind, and I tossed a glance over my shoulder. He held his side, where he'd been wounded. Maybe I hadn't healed him as much as he needed, but I'd done what I could. More than I should've. No energy left to tend myself.

My feet dragged; eyelids heavy.

"I'll come with you." Troy put his hand on my arm.

"Best if you didn't." He didn't need more people hunting him.

He pitched his voice low. "You can barely stand."

My eyes closed of their own volition, and I rocked on my feet. "Get me to my dragon."

Black sucked at me, the world a swaying blur. Then, stillness.

Warmth.

Breath.

A deep, steady heartbeat.

I opened my eyes to a rose-tinted sky, laying against Eirian's belly, his wing spread above me like a stained-glass dome. Troy stood a pace away, bathed in red light, arms crossed. He looked terrible.

I shut my eyes again, resting in Eirian's energy. He fed me in slow waves like a tide, restoring the reserves I'd overspent. I thanked him with complete surrender. Trust. Gratitude.

Finally, I stretched, and sat up, blinking.

Troy nodded, worry narrowing his eyes. "Better?"

"Much, yes." I scratched my head, something nagging at me. The kid! I got to my feet. "Where's Samuel?"

Eirian lifted his wing, folding it against his back. *I kept an eye on him.*

Samuel got to his feet and cleared his throat. "Your dragon told me to wait here."

"Right. Good." I looked down, grimacing at my blood-soaked clothes. My stomach grumbled, empty and angry. "Maybe we should get a meal and a bath before we go."

"Sure." He nodded, eyes wide. "Yes, Ma'am."

The sun dropped low as I returned to my dragon alone, clean, and wearing a borrowed dress that didn't fit me or the mission I was off to accomplish tonight. Eirian had gone hunting, had a bath of his own in a nearby lake, and returned bearing gifts. He hummed as I opened the saddlebag he'd conjured through time.

What made you so happy? I asked, my hand brushing over soft leather I didn't expect.

A gift. From your patron. Eirian was positively elated. He stretched his claws out, curling them into the ground like a cat, leaving great scratches of freshly-exposed soil.

My patron? I pulled out the leather ensemble: a pair of tailored pants, a long, graceful tunic, and a sleek coat. Black leather dominated the pieces, but the coat and tunic had accents of red. To match my dragon.

The Keeper. Eirian confirmed my guess.

You popped back to Asgard, then? I giggled, giddy with Loki's gift.

Eirian didn't respond with words, just a wash of joy laced with mischief. A dragon, keeping his secrets.

I changed beneath his wing. The pants and tunic fit perfectly, the long coat falling to my ankles. I narrowed my thought to a tunnel of focus, and sent a whisper to a single god.

Thank you.

For a moment, I heard music. Laughter. Then, it was gone.

The clothes made me feel invincible. I returned the dress Sarina had loaned me, kissed Troy, and left him with her and Diego. Twilight fell as I led Samuel back to Eirian. He wore a clean shirt under his tattered army uniform, and looked a great deal better than he had before, though his eyes were no less haunted.

As we flew in the direction he gave me, Samuel's terrified mutterings became whispered words of awe.

"Gives you a different perspective, doesn't it?" I looked over my shoulder at him.

"Yes, Ma'am, it does." He nodded, taking in the canopy of trees, shadowy mountains, and deep blue sky, the first stars of night twinkling.

We landed half a mile from a makeshift base. Before we left Eirian, I fished in my saddlebag and pulled out a purse I'd been given in the Realm of the Gods, retrieving three gold coins. They clinked against each other in my palm as I closed my fingers around them.

Eirian disappeared, fading through the Tree so he didn't draw attention. I stood before Samuel, whose mouth hung open. Taking his hand, I gave him the gold.

He stared at the coins with bloodshot eyes.

"Do you want to continue to serve in the army?" I asked, hoping he'd want to leave on his own account.

He shook his head. "I didn't want to be a soldier to begin with, but my father said it was the best way to make me a man."

I cocked my head. "Well, now you have money to start your own life. You can decide what kind of man you want to be. Hopefully not one who kills people to steal their land."

With a shaky breath, Samuel said, "Never. Never again."

I swallowed. "Good. Let's go find General Rikes."

The night deepened as Samuel and I strode into the army camp. Canvas tents dotted a field where men huddled around fires. I held my head high, heart cold. That these men were here was wrong in so many ways. Most of them were probably decent people trying to survive the struggle of life, but following orders didn't excuse the crimes they committed.

Samuel led me to a tent at the center of the encampment. When two soldiers stopped our march and asked who I was, Samuel said I'd helped him return from the battle— that he was the only survivor. That news alone seemed to dumbfound our challengers. I'd left my sword with Eirian, trusting Loki's knives and my ability to kill with a thought, and since I appeared to be an unarmed woman, they didn't think I was a threat. The fools.

A guard cleared our admittance with his commander, and Samuel and I stepped past the canvas door into the lantern lit interior of the general's quarters. Once we were in, I put up a barrier so no one outside could hear our conversation. The grey-haired, mustached man eyed me with curiosity.

"General," said Samuel, "this woman has a message for you." We'd agreed not to use my name, and I was glad the boy remembered.

"Where is your commanding officer?" asked the general, ignoring me. Like I was of no consequence.

Underestimate me at your peril, Sir. I knew he couldn't hear my thoughts, but perhaps he sensed the intent, his eyes flickering my way.

Samuel cleared his throat. "Dead, Sir."

The general made a low sound of discontent, his mouth drawing tight. "How many others have returned? I didn't expect you back until tomorrow at the earliest."

"None, Sir." Samuel's voice was heavy with remorse. "I was the only survivor."

The general's eyes narrowed as he fixed me with his gaze. "What's your message, Ma'am."

"I'm here to tell you to pack up and leave. And to give a message to whoever has been ordering these 'land acquisitions,' as you call them. No more. You take no more land. If people want to settle out here, they may do so in a respectful manner, but this is not your territory to take." I anchored into the ground beneath me, seeking a root of the Tree, weaving my words into the Tapestry like a decree.

"Is that so?" He crossed his arms, a sick sort of smile playing across his face. "And why would I listen to you, pray tell?"

"Because I killed the men you sent. If you send more, their deaths are on you, as is your own suffering."

He barked a harsh laugh, indignant, shaking his head at Samuel. "Where did you find this wench?"

"Sir, you'll want to take her seriously." Samuel's eyes widened with warning.

The general's eyebrows rose, but he obviously thought the boy was making things up.

Time to convince him.

I sent my awareness into the earth beneath the general's feet, and he promptly sank up to his waist in mud. He struggled, but couldn't get free. With a slight movement of my hand, I tipped his lantern over and set his desk on fire. He yelled, but I'd encased the tent in a shield. No sound escaped, nor the flicker of flame. No one came to his aid.

After a minute of him screaming at me, I extinguished the fire, leaving him stuck in the mud. "Are you ready to listen, General?"

He glared at me. "What are you, some sort of witch?"

"Oh, I'm far more than a witch." I took a step toward him. "I'm the daughter of a goddess, and I don't give a damn what you think about me. What I do care about is that you leave the Nwetaka alone. Leave all the Indigenous people alone. They are protected. Any man you send into their territory will be killed. The trees will hang your soldiers in their branches and bury them beneath their roots. The earth herself will open up and swallow them whole."

To be certain he understood, I buried him up to his neck with a sucking slurp of liquid earth. His eyes bulged, properly terrified, sweat trickling down his temples.

"On your life," I said each word carefully, binding them with magic, "do you swear to leave this area and abandon your mission of displacing the Nwetaka and any other Natives that live on this great, wide land?"

"Yes," he croaked.

"Will you release this young man from duty?" I gestured to Samuel.

"Yes," he said. "Immediately, if that's what he wants."

"Good." I returned the general to his feet, on solid ground.

He touched the soil that clung to his clothes, gaped at his charred desk, and looked at me with a great deal more respect than before. It was based in fear, but that was fine. I needed him to be afraid of me.

I turned to the boy beside me, and said, "Goodbye, Samuel."

"Safe travels, ma'am," he replied.

Without another word, I dropped the sound barrier and erected a shield of invisibility around myself, effectively disappearing before their eyes. I moved toward the door, waiting. I wanted to see how this played out.

Looking years older than he had when we'd entered, the general fixed his eyes on the young man before him. "Samuel, is it true that there were no other survivors? Did you see the battle?"

"I saw it all," confirmed Samuel, his voice breaking on the last word. "No one survived, Sir."

The general gave a shaky nod. "Then here's the story we're going with: your regiment was ambushed, and the land there was worthless anyway, so it was all a waste. We'll pack up tomorrow and get the hell home. As soon as we get back to civilization, you're free to go your way."

"Thank you, Sir."

"There'll be no mention of that witch, or what she did to me, is that clear?"

"Yes, Sir."

"Dismissed," said the general.

When Samuel exited the tent, I went with him, dropping the invisibility so the guards saw me leave. "Keep walking," I whispered to Samuel, who had the sense not to act surprised to see me.

As he escorted me to the edge of camp, the general called everyone in to notify them of their new orders, so the boy and I had no eavesdroppers as we said goodbye.

"Are you really the daughter of a goddess?" he asked.

"I am."

"I believe you." He swallowed. "You've given me a lot to think about."

"Good." I shook his hand, and walked away. Maybe what I did here would turn the tide on this timeline. Maybe the troops would stay away. Maybe Samuel seeing things differently could start a chain reaction. Whatever the case, I'd done all I could that night.

I rendezvoused with Eirian, and took to the skies.

The darkness helped me hide when we returned to the Nwetaka village. I snuck back to Sarina's dwelling, wishing I had more time. Diego promised to send Sundance home at first light.

Troy climbed up behind me on Eirian, and held me as we flew the distance home. Soon, we slept by the fire, with furs and sheepskins cushioning our bodies. Our safe place.

But when morning came, achingly soon, I readied myself to go. I'd left our children behind, after all. There was no breaking it to him gently, I just out and told him as he stoked the fire.

"Troy, I have to go."

His gaze masked sorrow with affection. "I know, Shelta. It's alright."

I tilted my head. "You're amazingly gracious, you know that?"

"I love you. How can I be anything but kind?" He smiled and leaned close, his kiss ripping another scar in the tapestry of my heart.

PART III

~

CHAPTER 33
STRETCHING TIME

OVER THE NEXT FEW days, I spent nearly every waking moment with my children. Then, Ola took them for an afternoon, giving Nikolas and me time to ourselves. He sat on one side of the smooth wooden table, me on the other, sipping tea.

I'd told him everything that happened as soon as I got back, but he hadn't said much about the whole ordeal. I hadn't pushed, giving him space. Now, it seemed, he was ready to talk.

Nikolas cocked his head to one side. "Seeing you with Troy was difficult, but it gave me a chance to consider how hard it must be for you, to be torn between three men."

"It is, indeed." I drew a slow breath.

He pushed a strand of hair away from my face, calloused fingers brushing my cheek. One side of his mouth lifted. "There was something beautiful about seeing you with him, Shelta—as much as I resisted it—because I know your love for Troy, and Killian, is the same love you have for me. I don't want to share you, even with myself, but I realize it's difficult for you, as well."

I crawled into his lap, whispering sweet words between even sweeter kisses. He understood me like no other.

Time passed in that easy, comforting way that happens when all is well. Winter was long and cold, but the magic of the Northern Lights filled our nights with wonder, and there was warmth inside, with the company of family and friends.

I snuck a visit to Killian at Yule, promising to come back for a longer stay in the spring, and spent two weeks with Troy to ring in the New Year.

Being a mother kept me busy, but Nikolas, Ola, and the older children were always there to help, as was the community as a whole. What a vast difference between that coastal village in medieval Norway and the world where I'd grown up. The village was isolated, but everyone who lived here belonged. It made modern civilization seem lonely and detached.

As the weeks went by, a nagging pressure built in my head. Finally, I went into the forest alone, and reached for the goddess.

Brighid? I traced patterns on the bark of a tree. *Mother?*

Daughter. Her presence rustled branches and filled the wood with potency.

I sense impatience. Urgency. I didn't want to name the thing I was avoiding.

You sense correctly. There is much to address in the world you left behind.

I knew it wasn't just her, that she was only passing on the council's collective will, but rebellion flared inside my chest. *I wish to live my life without being responsible for an entire world's fate.*

Your choices are your own. But you're a Weaver, as are your children, and the Tree will call you if you do not seek it out. A chill breeze gusted, then vanished, along with the goddess's attention.

My breath misted the air, the quiet leaving me strangely lonely. I hadn't meant to get angry at my mother.

At least I had my answer. My choices were my own.

I'd return to the Tree when I was ready. And I wasn't. So, I put the task off.

But the longer I did, the more I got the feeling that I was running out of time.

CHAPTER 34
BELTANE

WINTER TURNED INTO spring, and Beltane approached. The village prepared for weeks, gathering a massive pile of driftwood on the beach for a bonfire.

Beltane morning, I stirred together ground oats, eggs, honey, milk, and the last of the dried berries from the summer before, wishing for ingredients I'd always taken for granted. The children played in the backyard while I cooked. Julia's voice mingled with Brendan's, singing a song that they'd made up. My daughter was a year old—I'd given her Beltane as a ceremonial birthday, since she was born out of time—and my heart surged with gratitude for her light.

They were my joy, my children. I'd promised myself I wouldn't have them, and it would've been easier by far if I hadn't, but I had. And I was glad.

Nikolas had been hinting, lately. A few days ago, I'd stopped taking the herb that kept me from getting pregnant, having thoughts of the child the gods foretold, finally feeling ready. One child from each father lent a sense of balance to my existence, woven as it was through time and space.

The front door burst open, disrupting my train of thought with a swirl of wind that made its rounds through the house even after the door was shut. Nikolas strode over, moved my hair to one side, and kissed the base of my neck. Running his hands down my sides, his thumbs brushed my breasts, and I wondered if he planned to take me to bed then and there.

"Hello to you, too." I bumped him with my hip.

Nikolas took a folded cloth from his pocket, and held it out to me. "This tea is from Ola," he said. "For tonight."

Herbs from Ola weren't a surprise, but I always got them from her myself. Nikolas had never presented me with his sister's medicine, and I couldn't read the look on his face. "Why for tonight?"

"It's Beltane." There was so much mischief in his grin he reminded me more of Loki than Thor. "If a child wills itself this night, the blessings of nature will be that much more potent. This tea will help."

My tongue traced the edges of my teeth. "When should I drink it?"

"Take half now." His eyes shone like deep ocean lit by sunlight. "The rest before dinner."

I put a pot of water over the fire, and Nikolas pulled me close for more kisses.

A while later, the children returned, and I sipped my tea, more focused on my family than the herbal concoction. Julia was enchanting with her blonde curls and sparkling green eyes. She had no trouble keeping up with Brendan, careening about with surprising grace for a one-year-old, and her vocabulary blew me away.

Brendan spoke with clarity and ease. He made a mess as well as any child, but he also helped Dagný collect the plates when the honeyed bread disappeared. At the bowl that served as our sink, Brendan climbed up his "helper's ladder" to assist Dagný with the dishes, handing them to Leifr, who set them out to dry.

Together, we paraded outside into a bright, mild day. The children bounced with excitement that was shared by everyone around.

Most of the action happened at the ancient ash tree at the center of the village, around which children played and people danced. I sensed the joy of the tree to be circled in such delight, adorned with spring-green leaves and colorful ribbons. The afternoon rang with music, and I added my own, bringing out my guitar and singing until the sun began to set.

After dinner, I had my second dose of tea, which left me buzzing. Ola stayed with the children while Nikolas and I went out into the night. A bonfire blazed on the beach, circled with drummers pounding large instruments that set a deep, driving rhythm. The ocean crashed loud, the stars shining nearly as brilliantly as they had at the circle of stones.

Whoops and trills accompanied the drumming. Dancers ringed the flames, throwing shadows on the ground. Nikolas and I entered the fray, and I let the nectar of the night strip my inhibitions away.

The waves grew higher, the earth more alert. The sky shone with a gibbous moon. The day's celebrations had been about abundance and community, while tonight was about fertility. Sensuality. Couples kept disappearing into the darkness.

Hot from the dance, the fire, and my husband's wandering hands, I drew him toward the shadows. Our feet fell quick over pebbles and sand on our way to a sheltered cove in the cliffs. We passed other couples, pressed into alcoves or behind large rocks, and I couldn't help but glimpse them tangled together, tasting salty moans in my throat. The tide was coming in, but it didn't matter. Not to two demigods on a night of passion.

When we reached the cove, Nikolas lifted me, hands under my skirts. I wrapped my legs around him and returned urgent kisses. He was like his own bonfire. Hot. All consuming.

He growled, put me down, and we flung our clothes up to a dry ledge. The wind blew, but elemental magic cocooned us, keeping the cold at bay. The saltwater that surged at my feet was warm instead of icy. Rather than knocking me off balance, it held me steady. His doing, of course. My husband.

We pressed together, legs tangled. When I reached down and wrapped my hand around him, Nikolas moaned into my mouth. He tasted of honeyed mead and magic. He lifted me up, and a wave splashed us as I lowered onto him, my songlike sigh lost in the rush of the ocean.

The drums echoed off the rocks. Nikolas held me from beneath, from behind, and I wrapped around him, as if we could turn into one being. Every sensation was heightened by magic. Nikolas inside me, surrounding me. The ocean spanking me as the waves grew higher. Cries of ecstasy coming from lovers along the beach.

We came together in an explosion of love and lust and fulfilment. The tide had claimed our hideout, but we didn't part. We shook and melted and panted in our ocean hot spring, whispering each other's names between breaths.

Finally, we climbed up the rocks and stood naked in the wind atop the cliffs, watching the massive fire from afar as it blazed against the dark of night.

When we were dry, Nikolas wrapped us both in his fur-lined coat, and held me from behind, gazing out over the endless expanse of ocean. I closed my eyes to the surge within me, surrendering to the man who held me.

Even with my eyes closed, I could sense the brilliance of the stars, nature's song swirling around us. It climbed up through the soles of my feet, tingled as it danced across my fingers and palms, played in my bloodstream and kept time with my heart.

What I heard was far more than music. It was nature's response to the intentions woven into every festival in every community that celebrated that night. It was the Tapestry at work, the sentience of the World Tree at play.

Opening my eyes, I saw a flash of light as a star streaked across the night. My breath moved deep, and my mind struggled to comprehend the entirety of the universe. Merlin would've told me to relax into it, but I couldn't, because as the falling star glittered out of sight, there was a tug of awareness in my womb. A spark of life made itself known as it traveled to where it would grow within me. Behind me, Nikolas's breath caught, and he moved his hands to my lower abdomen. Clearly, he felt it as well.

I welcomed the little sprite, a mother's smile on my lips. Honoring the most potent magic of all: the ability to make life.

CHAPTER 35
AN UNWELCOME CALL

A month later, in the quiet of an afternoon when Brendan and Julia were sleeping, I'd stretched out on a fur near the hearth for a nap. Nikolas and the older children were away doing various tasks and giving me quiet, knowing I was tired from the early stages of pregnancy.

A knock came at the front door, which Ola opened, letting herself in. I sat up, and she came over to kneel beside me, her lips turning down, a crease between her brows.

"There is something you must do before this child can come," she said. "You've given the gods your word on something, yes?" Ola's eyes were sharp, like she didn't like the message she'd received any more than I would.

"Yes," I conceded. "I was hoping to wait a while longer."

She shook her head. "You must go. Get this thing done or the child cannot come."

The seer had spoken.

Familiar fear swept through me, and I shut my eyes tight, reaching out to my mother. I spoke with as much patience as I could—which was admittedly not a whole lot. *Brighid, must I do this now? I already did some world-weaving. Let me have this child before I do more.*

She spoke clear in my mind. Like she'd been waiting. *You are needed, Shelta. What you've done so far is good, but it's only the beginning.*

I'm pregnant. I wanted to stomp my foot like a child. *I'm happy here. I'm needed here.*

You are needed there as well. Her voice carried starlight, reminding me she spoke for a collection of stellar beings, not only herself. *Billions of people are desperate for change. They pray to the gods for intervention, yet we can do little to help. You can do more.*

I don't want to leave Julia and Brendan, I protested.

Take them with you. They've chosen this path. They are weavers, too.

I opened my eyes and stared into the fire, liking her idea less than leaving them behind where they'd be safe. *When must I go?*

There is no time to waste.

As Brighid withdrew, so did the sense that I was watched by the stars, and I breathed a little easier. A very little. I turned my gaze back to Ola with a forced smile.

"It is not easy to be chosen," said Ola, who'd saved her own mother as she came out of the womb, stepping into her role as healer before she'd taken her first breath.

I wasn't the only one living a complicated life, touched by the gods. "I need to find Nikolas," I whispered.

"He's on his ship. I will stay with the babies." She watched me as I got up and had a sip of water. But as I slipped my arms into my coat, Ola gave me a warning. "Shelta, you need to be careful with the one who grows inside you."

"Of course." My voice caught in my throat. What had she seen?

Walking to the docks, I reached out to Eirian. *I've been called.* Images and emotions tumbled from my mind to his.

The dragon's response came with eagerness. Like he was looking forward to this. *When would you like to leave?*

Tomorrow.

I'll be ready.

The dock's wooden planks creaked beneath my feet. I found Nikolas inspecting the rigging of his ship. "Are you planning a voyage?" I asked.

"Yes." He placed a coil of rope on the deck. "I hope you will go with me."

I shook my head. "I'll be going on my own adventure."

The smile on his face faded as he realized what I meant. He held out a hand to help me board, and I promptly sat on one of the ship's benches.

"This is interesting timing," said Nikolas.

"I don't like it either. Ola came with a message from the gods. No putting it off any longer." I didn't tell him what his sister had said about the child. Didn't want to make him worry.

"This is what you agreed to in Asgard." His voice was gentle, even if disappointment weighed it down.

Breath whistled through my nose. Closing my eyes, I recalled countless times when I'd wanted the world to be a better place. I remembered telling Killian when I met him that I would change things if I had the power to do so. Now, I not only had the power to make big changes, but the gods had explicitly asked me to.

Time to face the music.

CHAPTER 36
FOR THE LOVE OF TREES

EARLY IN THE morning, Brendan and Julia held my hands as we walked to the dock. I gave Nikolas, Frøya, Leifr, and Dagný each a hug and kiss, and saw them safely aboard the *LófiDanu*. We waved as they glided through the fog into the open water.

Then, I towed my children back through the village to Ola's house. She met me outside, handed me my guitar, and slung a bundle over her back. We walked together in silence, and I appreciated her company as we entered the forest.

While I'd helped prepare food for my family to take on their voyage, Ola had made provisions for me. Already queasy from growing a baby, the added nervousness made me wonder if my first act in my original world would be to revisit my breakfast.

Five weeks pregnant. Not the best time to go travelling. Still, if I absolutely had to answer the call before this child could be born, better to get it done and over with.

Ola and I made our way to a clearing, where Eirian waited, resplendent as ever. He wore his saddle, and I wondered if he'd magicked it on himself, or had help from someone in Asgard.

You are magnificent, Eirian, I told him. Ola stroked his forearm. His pleasure came through our bond like a mighty purr, his enthusiasm helping to ease my reluctance. The dragon was excited to go. I might as well try to enjoy the journey.

Ola helped me tuck Julia and Brendan into their soft, warm nests, and I secured the food, water, and whatever other goodies she'd packed in my magic saddlebags.

She squeezed me in a hug, gave me her blessing, then stepped back to the edge of the trees. Eirian spread his golden-red wings, and propelled us above the fog, into the cloudy sky.

Are you ready, Weaver? He asked before making the transition between worlds.

I took a deep breath. The answer was no, but I said, *Ready as I'll ever be.*

Where would you like to begin?

Same year as before. 2010. Different location. Hopefully, I could make enough change in a small slice of time to leave the world alone after that. Shouldn't people be able to work out peaceful ways to coexist on a planet together?

Shaking my head, I cleared my mind. Going down that rabbit hole of thought wouldn't help me now. With a deep breath, I honed my focus and sent Eirian an image, affixing the spot in my mind.

Let's go.

A moment later, the brilliance of the sun blinded me, a green jungle spread out beneath us. We descended into a steamy day, and I stowed my coat away.

"The Amazon Rainforest," I told my children. Brendan and Julia squinted in the brightness. "This is the world where I was born, though it was far from here."

"Far," said Brendan.

I smiled. "Very far."

Julia giggled.

When I looked around, I realized we shared the sky with an airplane. Culture shock made me shiver. It was a commuter, far enough away that I was pretty sure they couldn't see us, but it sharpened my awareness. I created an optical shield around Eirian, making us invisible to anyone who might look our way.

The next task was to figure out where to begin. We were high enough that I could see much of the rainforest as it stretched over the land. In many places, the thick, green cover was broken by wide tracks of clear-cut.

There. I pointed with my mind so Eirian knew where to go. He dropped his left wingtip, banked around, and glided over the spot.

A crop of soybeans had been planted where trees and medicinal plants once grew. A few workers farmed the huge field, which was otherwise empty.

Shaking my head, I took a deep breath and reached for the source of power I was going to wield, but when I called to the elementals, I received no answer.

They'd hidden. Withdrawn.

Growing trees relied on the willingness of the nature spirits, and if the ones who existed here couldn't hear me, or didn't trust humans enough to help, none of my half-baked plans would work.

I need you to drop me off, I told Eirian, searching for a spot at the edge of the clear cut, where the jungle looked thickest. *There. Just get me close enough to jump.*

I grabbed my bag, freed my legs from their straps, and waved to my children. They waved back. Eirian dipped, I dropped, and my boots hit the ground with a thud. I rolled, holding the hilt of my sword so it didn't jab me in the gut.

My invisible dragon wheeled back into the sky, and I sprinted into the foliage.

The forest watched me. Suspicious.

Slowing, I reached into my pouch and brought out some of Ola's herbs. "Elementals," I cooed, holding the leaves and flowers in the palm of my hand, "I'm here to make peace. Here to help."

A breeze picked up out of nowhere and took the treasure, petals dancing on air, guiding me deeper into the forest. I followed bits of dried leaves and faded flowers, climbing over roots and vines, coming to a clearing not unlike the fairy mound in the forest preserve. This one was bigger, and infinitely wilder. Plants and trees ringed the space, the hill at the center covered in growth. Pink flowers, purple leaves, green of every conceivable color. A bright yellow snake watched from a tree branch, a lizard rustling leaves below.

A narrow path led in a circle around the rise, and I walked it once around. Listening.

The nature spirits who lived here had invited me to their sacred space. I brought out more herbs, and sprinkled them around. "I'm here to open a door," I told them. "I will help you regrow the forest. Will you help me?"

Yes. Whispers of agreement came at me from all around, below and above.

I set to work, placing crystals at the four compass points. Then I drew my sword, called its gentlest light, and walked around the circular path three times. Stopping at the labradorite stone Nikolas had given me at the standing stones, I drove the blade into the ground. Then I stood, went to the next crystal, and plunged one of Loki's knives into the earth. My dirk went in at the south, the second of Loki's blades in the west.

Emerald light melded with the golden glow from my sword, and I felt Loki's presence in the charge that pulsed through the space. With a slow breath, I braced myself, and set my intention clear. Then I knelt, palms on the earth, and let loose bright beams of light.

Blue-green rays of energy spread out from my hands. In my mind's eye, I watched the light expand, covering the miles-long area of clear-cut. The crop of soy disintegrated, becoming compost for the forest. I sensed the alarm of the humans in the area, and asked the nature spirits to keep them safe as we worked.

With the energy I fed the elementals, the rainforest replenished itself. I drew nutrients from deep in the earth, growing saplings into mature trees. I didn't stop until there was no noticeable difference between that which had been cleared and the surrounding jungle.

How the people would find new work, I didn't know. Hopefully their next job wouldn't be cutting down the trees I'd just grown.

Thanking the forest, I collected my blades and stones, and climbed a tree so Eirian could pick me up. Nature spirits rushed in, crossing from where they'd retreated, coming out of hiding. I'd opened another door. Another portal. And this one was far larger than the ones I'd created with just my sword.

I repeated this ritual of regrowth a dozen more times before Eirian flew over an area where trees were actively being cut. My gut cramped as the pain from the trees hit me with violent force. I knew anger didn't help, but it flared up anyway.

To motivate the humans in and around the machines, I sent down a bolt of lightning. They took the hint, clearing the area with haste.

The elementals had retreated from the pain of the forest being razed, agony I couldn't block out, though the people below surely had. My breath shook.

One by one, I made the abandoned machines disappear, relocating the logging equipment a hundred feet underground, distributing the molecules to their original states. In essence, I composted the cutters. Next, I called on the elementals I'd awoken in other areas to help the ones here, and together we regrew the forest. As green took over, I let go of the spell. Nature would do the rest.

Let's take a break, I told Eirian.

Fatigue pulled me down. My shield kept the sun from burning us and allowed me to work unseen, but I'd moved a lot of energy, and a lot of machinery.

What the hell am I doing here in my first trimester? I didn't direct my thought to Eirian, but he hummed a soothing vibration in answer.

We turned away from the jungle, swooping down to a wide, deserted beach. The ocean sparkled blue, seagulls wheeling away as Eirian landed. After a meal, Brendan and Julia played under the dragon's watchful eye. I had a swim in the ocean, then a nap with my babies.

I need a way to do this faster, I said to Eirian when I awoke.

We could fly higher. He sent me a zoomed-out aerial image of the entire continent.

I grinned at him. *Brilliant.*

All aboard the dragon again, Eirian gained altitude. I contacted any jungle elementals that wanted to participate, which was a great many at this point. I'd opened a lot of portals, and they were being well used. Some nature sprits were leaders, architects of the grand design. These stayed connected to me even as the distance between us increased.

Eirian rose higher than I'd ever flown with him before. Already, we'd healed many scars on the land, but it was shocking how much of the forest had been demolished. I reached out to those areas, especially the forest that surrounded them, and initiated regrowth en-masse. If there were settlements with farms that fed the locals, or pastures for animals, I left the area alone, otherwise, I encouraged the jungle to grow wherever it wished.

This time, I sourced from the stars as well as the earth. As I was finishing, Eirian broke into my thoughts with a warning.

It seems we've been detected, Weaver.

I let go, and the magic I'd been working fell like glitter to the ground, fear spreading through me like frost. Fighter jets approached, four of them streaking toward us with alarming speed, close enough that I could see their missiles.

Let's relocate, shall we? I said to my dragon friend. Eirian and I linked intentions, and a moment later, we soared effortlessly over the Pacific Ocean.

No land in sight, blue water as far as I could see. I dropped the shield and tried to regroup; my focus shaken by the dread that spiked from seeing bombers flying toward my children.

"We help the ocean now?" asked Brendan.

"Yes, baby," I said. "Good idea."

"Go swim?" asked Julia.

"Not right now, sweetheart."

"Swim?" She tried again.

"Later, my love," I said softly.

The children sat up in their nests and looked out, secured by leather straps. Julia giggled and Brendan squealed in delight as he pointed at dolphins doing playful acrobatics, as if they were saying hello.

Though I enjoyed the solitude of flying over the ocean, it was only a few minutes before I saw the reason I'd sent us to this particular spot, and the promise of peace receded before it had settled in my heart, replaced by seasickness that had nothing to do with the waves below.

An island of trash floated in the water. The dolphins stayed well clear of it, at least. I'd read about mass amounts of plastic and other garbage that collected in patches, brought together by ocean currents. It disturbed me to see how much there was, even more so when I closed my eyes to assess the true extent of it. There was far more beneath the surface.

My approach for this dilemma would be similar to the way I'd disposed of the machines in the jungle. *Let's go higher, please, Eirian.*

Strong wings took us up, and I reformed the shield around us. With help from the stars and water elementals, I sent the garbage deep beneath the ocean floor, back to its original, natural state.

When I'd finished that bit of weaving, exhaustion slammed into me.

Enough for now.

"Do you still want to go swimming?" I asked Julia. She gave an enthusiastic reply, and I asked Eirian to find us an uninhabited island.

We spent the rest of the day basking on white shores, playing in turquoise waves, and eating the food Ola had packed us. Evening brought a beautiful sunset, and the babies, who hadn't slept all day, passed out in their nests well before dark. Unable to sleep, I laid on a blanket atop the sand, and let my mind wander.

It had been a successful first day, all things considered. But tomorrow's project was far more of a gamble.

Improving the state of the environment was important, for sure. I could regrow trees, but they'd probably be cut down again. Humans would continue to wage wars, with too many struggling through poverty while others were consumed with greed.

So many people craved change, yet most felt helpless to create it. I knew the feeling well; I'd felt the same way often enough. It would take a collective shift in the hearts of the human race to make the world a better place, and I didn't know if that was possible.

Running my fingers through the sand, I closed my eyes and felt the life that grew within me. Each baby came into the world so perfect and innocent, yet so many grew into bitter adults, defeated by the toils of life. I wanted to invoke the pure spark within each being in such a way that their inner light shone more powerful than the illusions of separation and despair.

Tomorrow, I would sing their hearts awake.

I managed to sleep for a handful of hours before Julia woke at dawn. After she settled, bird song and waves lulled me into a receptive state, and I listened to the planet.

So much beauty. So much life. A many-layered song revealed itself, with the voices of growing trees, playful dolphins, peaceful whales, tiny tree frogs, grape vines, fields of corn, caves of crystal, glaciers, and mountains. Yet discord reverberated through the notes, distortion coming from the myriad ways humankind brought pain to each other and the planet.

Elementals noticed me listening, and started approaching me with petitions to help their causes. Rivers and lakes desired protection and cleaning, salmon and cod needed time to bring their numbers back to plentitude. Tribes of animals were being hunted to extinction, while mining destabilized the land. On and on it went.

Overwhelm struck me full-force, and I curled up on the sand, my body racked with sobs. How could I help them all?

Eirian arched his wing over me, and the voices stopped. Waves and bird song were the only sounds. The sun's first rays shone through the dragon's skin, bathing me in ruby light.

Brendan woke to find me wiping my eyes.

"Why you crying, Mama?" he asked, crawling out of his bed.

"Oh, baby," was all I could say.

I rocked him, though I was the one who needed consoling. His small arms wrapped around me, and he nuzzled close.

I didn't rush our departure. Instead, I allowed myself to enjoy it as much as I could. Brendan and Julia played in the sand and waves. Eirian went for a swim in the ocean and came back with a belly full of fish.

I ate one of Ola's sweetbreads, then turned my mind to the task before me. I was going to sing a song to wake the world. If each person could find their own passion for life, for living in harmony with one another and the world around them, then my world-weaving services would no longer be needed.

But when I tried to conjure the song where I was, the island's isolation made it elusive. It would be easier to accomplish in a place where there were more people, and where music already had a strong hold. New Orleans would be perfect.

I'd send my magic up through the waters of the Mississippi River, down through the Gulf of Mexico, and out through North America. We'd cover Central and South America today, then continue once Eirian rested. Africa, Europe, Asia, Australia... I'd do a round trip tour of the planet, singing all the while.

And then, I'd take my children home, and leave this world to figure itself out.

"Okay, my dears. Let's go for a ride." I packed up, strapped Brendan and Julia into their nests, and settled into the saddle. *To New Orleans.* I showed Eirian an approach over the Gulf of Mexico.

He linked with my intent, and we dropped through space and time in a blink, coming out over grey-blue water and a bright orange flame that stole my breath.

A drilling rig blazed like a torch, surrounded by water. Oil spewed from a hole beneath, suffocating everything it touched. Every creature caught in it, every lingering elemental, every drop of water cried out in an overwhelming chorus of pain.

Anger. Hurt. Betrayal. Death.

I doubled over, aching like I'd been punched in the gut.

Eirian's dismay washed through our connection, as did his concern for me. Low in my belly, a throbbing discomfort demanded attention. Everything was wrong at once.

Grinding my teeth, I made a sharp movement with my hand, plugging up the hole in the bottom of the Gulf. I filled it in so that no more oil could leak out, then sent the newly risen oil back where it belonged, freeing the animals that had been coated in sludge. I lost track of time, working until people stood on the decks of ships and looked at the water in confusion.

And then the telltale roar of fighter jets made me look up. Shaking from exertion, I clutched the saddle to steady myself.

What next, Weaver? Eirian asked.

Did they see us on their radar? I thought of all the ways I could take those fighters out of the sky, trying to retain compassion for the people who flew them. But as I wrestled my thoughts, pain stabbed through my abdomen. *Get us out of here,* I told Eirian.

With a roll, he dove for the water. I held my breath when it looked like we were going to hit the surface at speed, but instead of crashing, we blinked out of the world.

CHAPTER 37
DYING AND HEALING

EIRIAN LANDED IN the dragon field outside Asgard. I clutched my belly, flooding my womb with healing energy, but the spark that had been there was gone.

Pain seared through me as blood begin to flow. Gasping for breath, I prayed.

Brighid, I need you.

She appeared in an instant. Thor was there, too, taking me down gently. I curled up next to Eirian, the agony increasing.

"My children." I gasped.

"They will be cared for," answered the goddess.

"My baby." Through the blur of tears, I looked to my mother.

Her eyes were green fields of sorrow. *You must let it go, Shelta. It's not yet time for this one.*

It took a moment for her words to sink in. I thought for sure she would do something, that she'd make it right. Rage swelled through me. How dare the gods not fix this? I'd been on an assignment they'd demanded of me.

Thor put his hand on my shoulder, but I pushed him away and glared at them both. "This wouldn't have happened if you'd just let me be."

"Shelta," my mother began.

I cut her off with a howl of pain, thick with anger. This was their fault, these gods who refused to save my child's life.

Brighid frowned at Thor, who reached toward me again. He didn't touch me, but his palm glowed, fingers unfurling. A current of calm claimed me like a river of ice, and swallowed me whole.

When I woke sometime later, alone in a familiar bedroom, I could only blame myself. I'd lost our child. Nikolas would be devastated when he found out.

I drifted in and out of consciousness, feeling like I'd been run over, until the door opened.

Nikolas came in, grave concern lining his face.

"Nikolas," I whispered. "I'm so sorry." I couldn't look him in the eyes.

"Shelta," he murmured. Such a sad sound. "You are not at fault."

Oh, but I am, my love, I spoke to his mind, not wanting to frighten the children. *If I'd been able to shield myself, to cut myself off from the suffering I'm supposed to be fixing, this wouldn't have happened.*

You don't know that. The child will return when it is time. Nikolas sat on the bed and brought me into his arms, eyes shining with grief.

"What about your voyage?" I asked.

"I sailed home as soon as I felt your need." He stroked my hand. "The ring called me. Ola is with the children."

I nodded, numb.

Nikolas held me as dawn stole the darkness. His quiet strength helped, but I was fragile. My body and heart hurt like hell.

In the morning, Brighid returned, and Nikolas gave us the room, walking off with Airmid and my children. My mother's emerald eyes caught my own.

"Shelta." She sat next to me and took my hand, her touch like a cool, fresh spring. "You left here before you had time to master your training, and I'd barely begun with Brendan and Julia. Now we have an opportunity to work together again. But first, you need to rest."

I knew the miscarriage wasn't her fault, not really, but it was still hard not to hold it against her.

After five days of resting, taking healing baths, and reading books that Merlin sent along with my meal trays, I couldn't handle it any longer. My body was wrecked. Weak. That needed to change. As if it was part of my training, neither my mother nor Thor had offered me a quick-fix healing. It was up to me to deal with my own mess.

The children were with my mother and Airmid; Nikolas was off somewhere with Thor. I knew I had to reclaim my power, and that I'd have to let go of my anger in order to access it.

Not an easy task, but I had a dragon to help. *Eirian? Weaver?* Companionship filtered through our bond.

I need you.

How can I be of service?

Well, for starters, I need enough strength to get to an exit. Think you could help me with that? The dragon field seemed impossibly far when a mere trip to the bathroom took effort.

Dragon laughter filtered through me, like purring thunder. *Happily.*

I crept out the door with a soft dress flowing around my legs, escaping from the confines of my room. Eirian bolstered my reserves with his own, preventing the lingering fatigue from slowing me down. When I reached the dragon field, he was there, shining crimson and gold in the sunlight. Waiting for me.

He sheltered me with his wings as soon as I reached him, granting me the privacy I wanted without being asked. When he lowered his head, I rubbed my hand over the smooth scales of his face. Leaning against his foreleg, I wrapped my arms around as much of him as I could, and breathed deeply.

"Are there any wild places in this perfectly manicured world?" I asked.

There's a secluded lake ringed by an ancient forest that I quite enjoy. Would you like me to take you there?

Please.

I scrambled into his saddle and strapped myself in. When he spread his wings, the thrill of flying briefly eclipsed my melancholy.

We flew over the sprawling, glittering palace, and passed Merlin's tree at the end of the gardens. Beyond, mountains sprouted from the earth and the ground rose higher and higher. As we cleared a ridge, the sparkling expanse of an ocean came into view. My breath caught in my throat, and I forgot, momentarily, the weight I'd been carrying, giving over to awe.

We didn't go to the sea, but to a lake nestled in a valley not far from the coast. Enormous trees grew all around, reminiscent of the redwood forests on the coast of California. The thought brought regret rushing back. I'd wanted to regrow those forests, as well.

We can return. Eirian spiraled down to a clearing by the lake.

I didn't answer. I wasn't sure I could face that world again.

You will grow stronger, Weaver. When you're ready, we will return.

I couldn't see it, but I knew I needed to try. I *did* want to return. As scared as I was at messing up again, I wanted to make things right.

Except I'd lost the child. That could not be undone.

I slid down the dragon's side and let my bare feet touch the ground. I stood there for long minutes, one hand on Eirian's hard scales, two feet in the cool, soft moss that grew near the lake.

When I reached out to the nature spirits, I found them vividly present. Clearer than ever. They were well aware of my dragon and me, watching, waiting to see what we would do.

Faeries. Sprites. Spirits. I could see them all. There were stout gnomes, tall dryads, and transparent water nymphs. As I looked around, I found so many varied beings that the place didn't seem secluded anymore, and yet their existence took nothing away from the peaceful atmosphere.

When I told them why I'd come, to heal from a deep hurt, they drew back, giving me privacy.

Leaving my dress on the mossy ground, I walked naked to the edge of the water where an outcropping jutted over the lake. Sunlight shone down, showing dark green. "I forgive myself," I said out loud.

I didn't believe it. Not even a little.

So, I repeated the words like a mantra, again and again, chanting them until I could change my own story.

I accept myself completely. I love myself. I forgive myself. I claim my power.

When actualization began to seep in, my strength returning, I opened my arms wide. The sun warmed my back and cast my shadow on the clear lake before me.

With a deep breath, I dove in.

The water made me gasp. It was cleansing I sought, and cleansing I received; the cold lake freed me from the muck I'd been carrying around. My moan of release echoed across the surface, as did my cries of grief.

After a long swim, I emerged and laid on the mossy ground until the sun warmed me all the way through. With each breath, each thought, I wove wholeness into my reality.

I love myself completely. I accept myself completely. I trust myself completely.

By the time the sun lowered behind the towering trees, I'd found the conviction that had been lost to me. I dressed, left some herbs for the elementals, and faced my dragon.

It is good to see you well, Weaver, said Eirian with a heart-smile. *Are you ready to go back?*

Almost. Hang on a minute. I vaulted onto his back and reached into the saddlebags, seeking my pouch of crystals. When I found it, I pulled out a polished piece of rose quartz from my original world, and blew a breath of gratitude into the crystal. The stone sparkled as I stood in the saddle, and tossed it into the center of the lake. For the child I'd lost. For the elementals who'd given me space to heal.

The rock fell with a clear, bell-like note that pulsed from the lake and all through the forest. Nature spirits danced as Eirian launched himself into the air.

Flying over the Realm of the Gods, I wondered if I was weaving even now. I'd dropped a crystal from one world into a lake in another. Did that ripple through the Tapestry?

Could elementals from this place find their way through the doors I'd created?

Feeling strong for the first time since I'd arrived, my mind started scheming. To move forward, I needed to fulfil my obligation to the gods and have done with it.

CHAPTER 38
NEVER UNDERESTIMATE A WIZARD

UP UNTIL NOW, I'd eaten in my room. In hiding. Healing and grieving, yes, but wallowing a bit, too. Holding a grudge against the gods.

Tonight, I dined in the main hall with Nikolas. My blue dress with golden embroidery matched the gilt and glitter of the hall, but I still felt out of place.

We sat at the same table as last time, with Brighid and Airmid next to Brendan and Julia in their high chairs. Thor sat next to Lancelot, Guinevere, and Arthur, leaning toward me with quiet mention of how rare it was to see the three legendary lovers out together. Even Merlin emerged from his tree, sitting on my right while Nikolas sat to my left.

"Exquisite mead, this." Merlin smiled as he held up his glass. The crystal made the honey-colored liquid dance with light. "Have you been enjoying my books?"

"Yes." I couldn't be mad at my eccentric tutor. "Especially the one that describes the World Tree in the context of music."

"Ah, yes." Merlin smiled. "*Conducting the Symphony of the Universe*, by Glorielle Raccá. The author was quite the weaver herself. Too bad she was lost. She would've taken a liking to you."

My smile faltered. There'd been so many weavers lost. Was I doomed to their fate?

Merlin patted my hand and topped up my goblet. "Have some more mead, dear. It helps to keep your head straight."

Which pretty much set the tone for the evening. The food was divine, the company jovial. But what intrigued me the most was the family-like dynamic of the legendary trinity: Arthur, Guinevere, and Lancelot. After dinner, Guinevere switched seats with Merlin, and leaned toward me like we were long lost friends.

"You wonder how this came to pass, Weaver?" Her gaze darted to her lover, then her husband, her raven-black hair shining in the gold-tinted light of the hall.

"Yes." My voice caught, and I whispered the rest. "My heart belongs to three men who share the same soul."

"We are capable of loving more than one person," she said, her voice slipping beneath the conversations around us. "It's a lot simpler to love just one, but it doesn't always work out that way. Eventually, Arthur accepted that I loved them both. I couldn't help but love them. It nearly destroyed us, but in the end, we prevailed."

I scooted closer to her on my overlarge chair. "What happened?"

She tipped her head toward me with a barely-there smile, trusting me with the truth of a legend that had roots wrapped deep in the World Tree. "Arthur knew I could not choose, and if Lancelot was cast out, it would break all of our hearts. They used to take it in turns, to quest or stay with me, giving each other space... Sadly, our comrades could not reconcile the breach of tradition. Our love came at the cost of Camelot. Try as we might, we were unable to stop its demise. It's a burden we carry, especially Arthur. My heaviest burden is my inability to bear a child. But we have each other, and we have this place. In the end, Frigga offered us solace."

My gaze moved to the goddess queen who sat at the raised table with King Odin. As I sought her, Frigga looked to me. I bowed my head, and she inclined hers ever so slightly in response. Guinevere loved more than one man, like I did. And they were able to get along.

"It's almost like Camelot here." I wanted to hug her, but refrained. "Thank you for trusting me with your story."

She took my hands and gave them a squeeze. "We're grateful to have you and your children here." Her gaze moved to Brendan and Julia.

Seeing how she looked at the children, I brought Brendan over and introduced them. A minute later, he was sitting on her lap, and Guinevere's smile made her face light up. I studied the silver streaks in Arthur's hair, the lines on his face, and the affection in his eyes as he looked at his queen. Everything about him was regal. An immortal king in a hall full of gods.

Arthur met my gaze, and his voice slid into my mind. *I know you're due to quest again, Weaver. Would you like to speak before your journey? Perhaps I can help.*

My eyebrows rose toward the gilded ceiling. *That's very kind of you.*

He tipped his head. *I'll find you before you go.*

As I reeled from the honor, Thor leaned toward me with a half-grin, and said, "Odin would like you to sing."

I looked to the dais and met Odin's gaze, feeling his call without the slightest move on his part. I squeezed Nikolas's hand, left the children under the watchful gaze of my mother, and headed to the stage beside the high table of

Asgard, where an immortal minstrel sat in an armless chair and tuned my guitar.

"Do play a lively number for us, won't you, Weaver?" called Merlin, glass held high. "I feel like dancing!"

I climbed two oversized steps and went to receive the guitar Killian had given me. I wished he could see me here, that my Maclean family could see me here. Troy wouldn't like the crowd, but Killian would love it. He'd beam with pride, like Nikolas did.

I curtseyed to Odin and Frigga, then settled into my seat and got things started with a feisty tune that roused the dancers in the room. Merlin twirled in the aisle near our table, taking Guinevere's hand before either of her lovers. The old man moved with a bounce I didn't expect, spinning the black-haired queen. My mother danced with Brendan, while Airmid swayed with Julia. Nikolas stomped his feet and clapped his hands in time with the music, and he wasn't the only one adding rhythm. A minstrel joined in with a set of hand drums, and when I nodded my encouragement, more players emerged with their instruments. The hall resounded with music.

With a tip of my head and slight variation in the tune, I signaled the end of the song, and when the refrain wrapped up, every musician finished together. I cheered with the crowd, then launched into something new, conjuring lyrics inspired by the wizard's display of youthful vigor. The other minstrels listened, then, one by one, added to the song.

Never underestimate a wizard,
For he'll spin you 'round with ease.
You may think him weak or old,

In truth he's spry as a breeze.

No, never underestimate a wizard,
Or believe you know his mind,
Quick as a bolt of lightning,
He'll change, and then you'll find,

There's no end to his ability
To amaze, surprise, astound.
Never underestimate a wizard,
Or he'll spin you right around.

Each musician made up a verse, and then members of the audience started making up more, the collective merry-making getting increasingly louder. Merlin punctuated the music with small fireworks and timely shouts of "Hey!" and "Ho!"

It was one of the most festive, enjoyable evenings I'd had the pleasure of living.

I woke the next morning hungover from mead, dancing, and making love until dawn. I'd only been awake for five minutes when Nikolas told me he needed to leave. I blinked, understanding, and hating it anyway. His children needed him. The village needed him. Yet I never knew when I'd see him next, or what would happen before I did.

Out on the dragon field, I drank in every detail of him. Eyes the color of a bluebird sky, hair glinting gold in the sun. He kissed me thoroughly, then strode into the center of the field and lifted his hammer to the sky. In one powerful stroke, he brought it to the ground, and with a clap of thunder and flash of lightning, he was gone.

Julia and Brendan, who were climbing on Eirian's paws, startled at the sound. Julia yowled, giving me no time to dwell on my own thoughts. I scooped her up and tried soothing her, but it didn't work. Brendan joined in, bursting into tears. Tempted to join them, I sat on the ground, with both children on my lap, and swayed.

Eirian hummed softly behind me, which helped, but there was still a void left empty. Three men held my heart, and they were all so far away.

CHAPTER 39
DIG DEEPER

I SPENT THE DAY with my children, distracting myself from the emptiness of Nikolas's absence. We explored a mammoth library, with every book imaginable organized by worlds, and a courtyard that housed a menagerie of birds, tended by a feathered goddess.

By the evening, my head pounded. The calm I'd found by the lake had vanished. Healing myself only worked for a fraction of an hour before the throbbing returned, and I entered the dining hall with my brain feeling like it was trying to escape my skull.

My mother took pity on me. "Drink this," she said.

The goddess situated Brendan and Julia in padded chairs as I sipped a greenish infusion of herbs and honey. Halfway through the glass, my head cleared.

Guinevere sat to my right tonight, with Arthur next to her. Lancelot was elsewhere, giving the queen and king time together. After dinner, Arthur challenged Thor to a blind taste test of the selection of wines and spirits. Thor pushed his chalice toward Arthur, closed his eyes, and said, "Begin."

Arthur poured clear, honey-colored liquid, the corner of his mouth twitching toward a smile.

Thor brought the glass to his nose, then to his lips for a taste. "Glastonbury mead."

"Right you are," said Arthur. He followed that up with three white wines, one from Atlantis, one from Lemuria, and one from northern Austria. There was a Pinot Noir from Bordeaux, a Syrah from New Zealand, and a blend of grapes from Mount Olympus.

On it went. By the time Thor swirled his second brandy around, he was leaning back in his chair, eyes still closed, telling stories.

The next day, mastery school was back in session. Brighid showed up altogether too early in the morning, asking, "Are you ready?"

"Sure." Bring it on. Anything to procrastinate another shot at the weaving I'd failed twice. Would once more be enough? Would anything I did ever be enough?

Brendan and Julia were unusually fussy, clinging to me with half-hearted noises of protest. My mother, in her infinite wisdom, had brought food for us all, including a cup of coffee, which brightened my mood considerably.

"What do I need this morning?" I stood before my wardrobe, which was magically stocked with all my belongings. Glory to the gods.

"You will want your sword," she answered, intent on keeping Julia from hitting her brother with the breakfast cutlery.

"Thor, then," I murmured, wondering if gods got hangovers.

Reaching past my dresses, I brought out the rider's uniform Loki had given me, black leather with dark red flares. Did my mother know where I'd gotten this outfit? I loaded up with daggers, knives, and sword, and braided my hair. On the way out the door, I asked, "What will Brendan and Julia do while I'm in lessons?"

"They have their own lessons."

My stomach churned, unsettled on too many counts. "What kind of lessons?"

"Similar to yours, adapted for younglings. They are weavers, Shelta. It will be to their benefit, and yours, for these children to explore the powers they possess here, where we can guide them."

It made sense, but it also sounded a lot like stealing their childhood. They ought to be playing with sticks and rocks and discovering the world like normal children.

I carried Brendan, while Julia rode in her grandmother's arms. Brighid led the way to a room full of instruments that looked like toys, most of which glowed with light. Airmid came forward with a sphere hovering above her hand, and the children were immediately enthralled. I left them there, and stepped back into the corridor.

Alone again. Still out of control of my life.

Perhaps control was an impossible illusion. Even the gods seemed unable to avoid catastrophic mistakes and things turning out very differently than intended.

Thor met me in the courtyard, the hammer at his side super-sized. I eyed it warily as I approached, and said, "Good morning. How are you feeling after last night's festivities?"

"Perfectly fine." He grinned at me, and drew his hammer. "Good morning to you."

I pulled my sword, then retrieved my dirk when I saw Thor draw his sword as well.

A weapon in each hand, we circled each other. I placed my feet carefully, noticing every detail, from the soft fold of grass beneath my boots to the gurgle of the fountain at the side of the lawn.

"You seem to need practice doing battle without getting tangled in the snares of anger," Thor said lightly, as if he were commenting on the overcast sky. "I would like to help."

"Fabulous." He'd singled out my biggest weakness. I was in for a fun morning, then.

Thor laughed his easy laugh, then lunged in left-handed with his sword, and so began an indeterminable hour designed to knock me off balance at every opportunity. What made it bizarre was the contradictory way he radiated love, but did everything possible to make me angry.

As he swiped at me with his hammer, Thor said, "You know, your world has a long way to go before its people can be free from the slavery and oppression of your leaders."

I spun to avoid getting clobbered. "Not my world. And, yes." I swung my sword, grunting. "I know."

"What are you going to do about it?" He wasn't even breathing hard.

"Whatever I can." Sweat dripped down my forehead.

A graceful step, a charming smile, and a small bolt of lightning rattled my shield. "You could just remove the oppressors," he said, baiting me. "It would be the easiest solution."

I arced a blast of electricity his way. "I dabbled in that, but it doesn't stop similar people from taking their place."

Thor jumped straight into the air, summersaulted over me, and made a smashing effort with his hammer on the way down. I dove out of the way, then rolled to my feet.

He stopped abruptly, standing at ease. I panted, bracing for his next move.

"You could gather them up in one place and talk with them," he said brightly.

I laughed. "Talk sense into the human race as a whole? Good luck."

Thor sheathed his weapons. Without warning, he lunged forward and pushed out with his hands, blasting me off my feet. I crashed against the brick wall of the courtyard, fifty feet away from where I'd been standing. On impact, my dirk and sword flew from my hands.

With a thought, the hilts of Loki's knives dropped into my palms, vibrating with power. "What the fuck was that?" I gasped, sore, shaken, and pissed off.

"A trick of the wind." Thor raised an eyebrow at my daggers. The blades shone slivery-green. "I was wondering if you'd bring those out."

"What of it?" I challenged him. My shoulder throbbed from where I'd collided with the wall.

"Come on, then." He spread his arms out.

I ran at him, then slid to a stop, and let one of Loki's blades fly with the cutting intention of piercing through Thor's shields and doing actual damage to the god. He could heal himself with a thought, and deserved a bit of what he was dealing out.

The knife sliced through the air faster than Thor could get his hammer up to block, and sunk into the god's shoulder. "Ha!" I let out a triumphant yell, then opened my hand and *called the blade back*. With a thought, it returned to me.

Thor looked at the blood dripping down his arm, then at me, eyebrows furrowed, mouth halfway between a scowl and a smile, like he wasn't sure whether to be impressed or annoyed. "Loki's been teaching you."

I crouched down to wipe my blade on the grass, and proceeded to ignore his comment. "You want me to heal that for you?"

He scoffed, and I took another look at his shoulder. The skin had already closed, the wound gone. "Let's have a chat, shall we?" Thor went to the fountain, took a pitcher of water out, and rinsed the blood off his arm over the nearby shrubbery.

I tucked my knives away, gathered my sword and dirk, and joined him on the bench, a knot forming in my stomach. "Sure. Talk."

He smiled. "You don't need to be defensive. I don't care if you've trained with Loki. He can be quite an effective teacher, at times."

"I haven't been training with him." I touched my forearm, a knife beneath the leather Loki had given me. My patron. The Keeper of Lost Souls and Stories.

"You've been *entraining* with him, then." Thor nodded, looking me over, decked out in his brother's handiwork. "He's taken a liking to you, but you're just his type. He adores artists, survivors, rebels. And, of course, there's your dragon."

I said nothing, waiting for Thor to give me a lecture like my mother, or at least a warning.

But he didn't. All he said was, "Loki has his heart in the right place. Whatever he's been in the past, he's something entirely different now. His influence looks good on you."

"Thanks, I think." I let my guard down, and reached for a glass of water from the fountain. It was cold and clean, and helped wash away the shock of being thrown against a wall. "I'd say I was sorry for stabbing you, but that's the first point I've gotten in the history of you beating me while sparring, so, sorry, not sorry."

Thor laughed. "It was well done."

"Do you talk to your brother much?" I asked.

"On occasion. In fact, the last time we spoke, he mentioned you."

I swallowed, imagining Eirian flying in a distant sky to keep from turning my thoughts to the memory of the black cave where I'd summoned Loki. "What did he say?"

Thor tipped his head, eyes narrowing. "He shared his opinion that the council is out of line, pushing you into weaving when your children are only babies; that the worlds have been amiss for so long, letting it go another few years wouldn't matter. He's protective of you, his Song Weaver." He shook his head, adding, "He has a point."

My jaw dropped. "Of course, he does. If I'd been left alone to have my child, I wouldn't have lost it." Finally, I had a chance to voice the accusation I'd been fighting since it had happened.

He nodded, solemn. "The majority of the council felt that the urgency of balancing the World Tree meant a weaver was needed immediately, and you're the first person in ages capable of doing what needs done."

"Why didn't you heal me when I arrived?" My voice cracked.

He dropped his gaze. "The spark was already lost," he said. After a moment, he looked into my eyes. "That same spark will return to you."

I pressed my lips together, holding back the anger that wanted to rise. "I know you think I'm the weaver destined to change the fate of the worlds, but I'm only one person. The task is too great."

Thor put his hand on my shoulder. "Do what you can. In the not-so-distant future, you will have more help."

"What does that mean," I asked.

"I cannot say." He laced his fingers together. "I'm not sure how that part of the Tapestry will unfold."

I brought my fingers to trace the dragon at my neck, afraid to find out why the creases in Thor's forehead deepened as he looked away from me.

I ate an early lunch in my room, head spinning with the events of the morning. When I finished, my children piled through the door full of excitement, telling me everything at once.

"Mama, we played apesifters!" Julia exclaimed.

"Shapeshifters," Brendan corrected. "Red and blue and…"

"Purple n green an rainbow." Julia twirled around.

Brendan bounced on his toes, making shapes with his fingers. "We made tringles and spears and they floated!"

"You made triangles, spheres, and a variety of other shapes and colors, yes." Brighid translated their enthusiasm. "And you made them float around the room with your mind, didn't you?"

"Yes." Julia sang a little song, racing around with her arms out. "Zoom!"

"Yes, sometimes they zoomed." Brighid grinned.

I received a mental image of glowing objects travelling through the air, changing shape and color, spinning and bouncing. I saw Julia standing with her hands outstretched as if she conducted an orchestra. I felt Brendan's excitement to be doing something so engaging, feeling so powerful.

And then it hit me that the one transmitting this image wasn't Brighid. It was my son.

"Do you see, Mama? Do you see it?" Brendan asked as I turned wide eyes to him.

"Yes," I said, blocking him from my conflicted thoughts on this development.

As impressed as I was with his newfound ability to project his thoughts, I didn't want my children to be able to see into my mind, or bombard me with their feelings. The volume they were capable of when upset was quite enough as it was.

I looked to Brighid, and spoke through a telepathic channel intended only for her. *Aren't they a bit young to mindspeak? Shouldn't they learn something of self-control first?*

They are learning, Weaver, extremely quickly.

Perhaps too quickly.

That afternoon, I knocked on Merlin's tree-house door, ready for a relaxing few hours of books and snacks. But Merlin had other plans. He strode out with his tall, gnarled staff in one hand, a leather satchel slung across his chest. "Adventuring we go, Shelta!" He waved for me to follow, and kept on walking, brown robes billowing behind him.

I stayed where I was. "Uh, Merlin? I was hoping for tea and scones and a quiet afternoon discussing your current favorite flavor of jam."

"My dear Weaver." Merlin stopped abruptly. "Where's the fun in that?" He frowned at me in a wizardly way, then set off at a brisk pace.

I hustled after him along a path behind his tree, into a forest I was sure hadn't been there a moment before. Ferns grew as tall as the wizard, huge trees vaulting into the sky. When a bird the size of a dragon flew overhead, I was intimidated enough to speak up.

"Merlin?"

"Don't worry, my dear," he said merrily. "He's looking for larger prey than you or I."

"Did you shrink us?" I asked. The scale of things was seriously out of proportion.

"Not at all. Isn't it marvelous?"

"Impressive." I tuned my senses to our surroundings, half-expecting something to jump out at us from behind a car-sized leaf. Insects and birds sang multi-layered songs that made them sound like they were far larger than they had any business being.

After a while, Merlin slowed his pace and motioned for me to stay silent. We rounded another colossal tree root, then he stopped, and beckoned me to stand next to him.

"This is what I wanted to show you," he said, his voice barely a whisper.

It was a pond, or really, by the scale of things, a puddle. And in that puddle, the most beautiful flowers bloomed. They were like lotus flowers, so small they would fit in the palm of my hand. Some were orange and pink, some yellow with orange, giving off a soft glow. They floated among flat, blue-green leaves, growing far beneath the towering canopy, where the sun couldn't reach.

Confusion overwhelmed me on many counts. What were these delicate flowers doing in this over-sized world? For what purpose had Merlin brought me to see them? And why were we creeping up on them without making a sound? Surely the flowers didn't care if we talked.

I raised my eyebrows and looked at the wizard as if to say, "What's the point of all this, man?"

"The Lumen Flower," Merlin murmured. "This is the only place in all the worlds where it grows." He looked away from the flowers and turned his sharp grey eyes on mine. "Can you guess why I've brought you here, Shelta?"

I thought about it for a moment before saying, "To show me something that defies the world around it?"

"Exactly!" He nodded. "And at the same time, no."

I waited, hoping he would make some sense of it all.

"It does defy its surroundings," he agreed. "It grows where there is no sun, tiny in a land of large, where it could be crushed by the feet of nearly any creature native to this world. And yet, it's perfect as it is. It needs the exact conditions of shelter these trees provide, never buffeted by wind or flooded by rain."

Fascinating as that was, I still didn't understand why we were there.

"They have one mechanism that allows them to survive in the event of a threat," he said. Then he walked forward, flapped his arms, swung his staff, and yelled, "Hullo there!" marching right into the water with a fierce look on his face.

The flowers vanished instantly. Or so I thought.

I noticed a reflection in the water, and looked up. There, about fifty feet in the air, the whole colony of Lumen Flowers hovered, roots and all.

The wizard, now standing knee-deep in the puddle, looked up and smiled. He seemed tickled by the way the flowers teleported themselves to a safe place, waiting for the threat to leave so they could settle back into their home.

A minute went by, then he looked at me and asked, "Are you coming, Weaver?"

To which I answered, "Where?"

"To tea, of course." He held out his hand, waiting for me to join him in the pond.

Bewildered, I walked into the water, and took his hand.

A blink of time later, we stood next to Merlin's house. Sloshing in my boots, I followed him to a stone table and pair of comfortable chairs set out beside the back entrance to his tree. From his leather satchel, Merlin pulled a selection of scones and jam, with plates, cups and saucers, and a piping hot pot of tea. I concluded the bag had been empty the whole time, and he simply conjured the items at will.

Lastly, he pulled from the satchel a pair of Lumen Flowers sealed in a glass-like shield. He held them reverently in his hand: blue-green leaves, dark-brown roots, tiny pink-and-yellow petals shielded from the sun by the shade of his tree.

"I thought I'd try to grow them here," he said, and waved his hand toward a bare patch of ground that promptly turned into a muddy puddle. He carefully lowered the captured plants into the water, then grew the shield to keep the wind out.

I sat in the chair, watching Merlin pour tea, wincing as my mind protested the increasingly bizarre events of the day.

"You will find," the wizard said as he offered me a scone, "that the more you embrace what you don't understand with the openness of wonder, the less you resist. And the less you resist, Weaver, the easier things will be for you."

Riddle received, I took a sip of tea, willing my mind not to implode.

The next morning, Thor switched tactics. Instead of practicing combat and trying to rile me up, we did yoga and meditated. It was a welcome change, but he was far more serious than he'd been before, which told me our time was coming to a close. Soon, I'd need to go finish what I started.

"The trick," Thor said in a trance-like voice as we transitioned out of meditation, "is to find this sublime centeredness in the heat of battle."

A trick indeed. I couldn't imagine maintaining a sense of contentment when faced with a fight to survive. "How am I supposed to find peace when it goes against the instincts of fight or flight?"

"Do a handstand," he instructed.

It took me a second to realize he meant do a handstand, right now. I got up, settled my hands in the grass, and kicked up in the center of the lawn. While I was upside down, Thor upped the ante.

"Lift one arm," he said, as if he'd asked me to wiggle my toes.

Straddling my legs for balance, I shifted my weight and carefully brought my right arm to the side.

"What are your children's names?" he asked.

"Brendan, Julia, Frøya, Leifr, and Dagný," I said, beginning to sweat. "And Charlie."

"What things did you love from your original world?"

"Coffee. Music. Chocolate."

"What was the most frustrating thing about your original world?" Thor asked, adding, "Switch arms, Shelta."

I switched arms. The move made me wobble. Thinking was not helping my balance, and he'd given me quite a thing to think about.

"I'm not sure." My words came out choppy.

"What's the first thing that comes to mind?"

"Money. Inequality. Poverty. Greed. Waste. War. Oppression." I was on a roll. "The way humans thought they were more important than the rest of nature and plundered it in the name of profits. The way the powerful exploited the weak."

My tirade made me lose balance, and I fell over, letting the momentum take me to the ground. Sprawled on the grass, I looked at the god who towered over me.

"See?" I flopped my hands out. "I was fine until you asked me to think of unpleasant subjects."

He nodded, unperturbed, then sat on the grass so I didn't have to look so far up to see him. "You would be fine if you could master your emotions."

"I'm human. Emotions come with the territory. It's part of my charm." I smiled a big, toothy grin, mocking myself.

He shook his head once. "You can master your emotions, Weaver, but it may take a dire situation for you to learn to do so."

"I don't like the sound of that." I sat up.

He shrugged. "It's the truth, even if it's not agreeable. Every weaver faces a time where the only way to get what you want is to master self-control. The power you wield is severely limited when anger and fear blur your focus."

I frowned at him.

"If your children were in danger, how would you feel?" Thor leaned back on his hands.

I was ready to fight at the mere suggestion. "I would do whatever it took to protect them."

"What if the only way you could protect them was to remain calm?"

My heart beat faster at the thought, jaw tensed, ready to run. He wanted me to contradict instinct.

"Dig deeper, Shelta," Thor said. "I would not ask this of you if you weren't capable. It would serve you well to practice now, here, while you're safe."

His words stayed with me as I walked back to my room.

Dig deeper, Shelta.

He'd given me quite the motivation to do so.

The next day, when I knocked at Merlin's door, King Arthur answered it. I took a step back, and dropped into a curtsy. Somehow, he intimidated me a good deal more than Thor or the wizard.

"Good afternoon, Shelta." Arthur bowed, his movements graceful while mine felt awkward. His silver-streaked hair shone in the sun filtering through the canopy of Merlin's tree. "Would you care to accompany me for a walk?" he asked. "Merlin has given me the time he would otherwise have with you today."

"That would be lovely." I stepped into stride with him, and we made our way along the path that meandered the lush grounds.

"I care a great deal about the world from which we both originate," he began. "I've traveled there on occasion, throughout the ages, to do what I could to assist."

"What was it like for you when you went back?"

"Frustrating, mostly," he said with a subdued smile. "Wonderful and sad."

"Were you a world-weaver?" I asked. How many had retired? How many were left?

"Not like you're thinking, assisting the entirety of the World Tree. No, I had great hopes for my contribution to that specific world. Camelot was to be a mecca of cooperation, arts, philosophy, and growth." Memories thickened his voice. "It began that way. And then judgement and hatred tore it apart. It's sad to have so great a dream, only to watch it collapse. To be forced to let it go."

"I can imagine." The disappointment of my latest weaving pulled at my heart.

"Our dreams are not so different." Arthur glanced at me. "They both require people to respect each other and live in ways that allow for the prosperity of all."

"It seems like a lot to ask from the human race." It was nice to have someone who understood my struggle. I'd found a comrade in a legendary king.

"Would you care to share your ideas with me?" He turned a hand up, revealing a scar that ran across the outside of his palm. "Perhaps I can offer suggestions to enhance your strategies."

"That would be welcome. The best idea I've come up with is to compose a song and broadcast it across the world, invoking each person's sense of compassion and desire for freedom. I'm hoping people naturally rise up and make a better world for themselves. I mean, I can't be expected to do it for them. I'll help by encouraging elementals to return, and restoring nature, but I want them to do the rest."

"Perfect. You are the Song Weaver, after all." He stopped beside a fountain, water burbling over a statue of a mermaid. "It seems to me, that if you include your freshly-awakened populace in the work that needs to be done for the planet as a whole, they would feel more involved. People like to be able to take action, to have a sense of accomplishment."

"I hadn't thought of that." The breeze blew my hair, and I tucked a stray strand behind one ear. "How do you suppose I do that while riding a dragon and trying to evade military strikes?"

Arthur stroked his beard. "It was the same for me when Camelot lost its way. Too many battles on too many fronts, and not enough consensus in the ranks. Perhaps you can seek leaders who already devote themselves to the tasks you envision, and position them to instruct those who wish to join their cause."

"You're a genius." My mind started spinning with names of people to recruit. But first, I wanted to talk with another strategist.

One I'd last spoken to in a dark cave.

CHAPTER 40
IMMORTAL PERSPECTIVE

INSTEAD OF GOING inside to find Brighid and the kids, I circled around, following pathways lined with benches, sculptures, and sometimes faerie lights. The grounds became wilder as I headed away from the manicured promenade, into a shadowy stretch of woods.

When I found a narrow path snaking away from the palace, I took it, stopping in a secluded clearing a few minutes later. The trees created a quiet, private refuge. Using the razor focus of Loki's knives, I erected a shield of secrecy like the one Eirian and I had created back in the cave, and sent a call to a single god.

Loki. Would you care to join me?

Song Weaver. His words came through with a rush of emotion. *A moment, if you will.*

Of course. As soon as I sent the thought, I realized the energy that had been tangled in his transmission. Seduction. Lust. I hurried to give him an out. *Later's good, too. Didn't mean to catch you at a bad time.*

Laughter came out of the woods. Loki emerged with his jacket rumpled, shirt unbuttoned. "You didn't catch me at a bad time. It was rather good, actually."

I cleared my throat. "You didn't have to come."

"Oh, that would've happened either way." He flashed a toothy grin.

Blushing, I struggled to remember what I wanted to talk to him about. His open shirt was a distraction, showing the scar that ran diagonally across his chest. Over his heart.

"You must have so many stories," I murmured.

He looked down, and buttoned up his shirt. When he lifted his gaze, the play had gone out of his eyes. "Indeed. But you didn't bring me here for stories, did you?"

"Not really." Although I'd gladly listen if he was willing to share. "I was hoping you'd be able to help me. I want to visit specific people in my original world without actually being there."

"And you've come to me for this because?"

"That's what you did in the cave, wasn't it?" I asked.

"Astute. I projected myself into your sanctuary of darkness."

"How do I do that?"

He stalked closer, hands smoothing his black jacket with purple undertones. When he stopped an arm's length away, his voice dipped lower. "The same way you opened dimensional portals last time you were weaving."

"With the blades you gave me?"

Silver sparks shot through his eyes. "You open a doorway to the correct place and time, then you can sit inside it and send an image of yourself wherever you want to go."

"Right." Easy. No problem. "Do you have any helpful tips?"

"Well, you might set parameters as to who and what can come through. If you're projecting, you want a one-way portal. If you're bridging worlds, consider what else might lie on the other side before leaving the gate open."

I took a step back, fear dropping through me. What had I done? "Should I close the ones I made?"

His eyebrows rose in mild interest. Like it didn't really matter. "It's not necessary. I think giving easier access to elementals is a good thing. It should be entertaining to see what comes through."

"Entertaining?" I frowned. Was this a game to him?

"Intriguing, might be a better word." He lifted his hands. "Shelta, nothing you do will be without consequence. None of us know what will happen until the weaving is in motion."

"You sit here and watch it all happen, immune to the fallout."

"Immortal, yes." He brought his hands together in front of his chest. "But not immune."

I looked down, remembering that he'd been exiled, and stared at his thick-soled boots. Black, with distressed gold accents, they looked ready for dystopian warfare.

"It does give a different perspective," said Loki, "watching generations of mortals pass like the tides. So many lives. So many deaths. After a while, you become detached."

"But you got attached, didn't you? To Eirian's last rider."

Closing his eyes, Loki said the name like soft, mournful music. "Roáve." When his gaze met mine, his eyes were dark as the forest around us. All the silver gone. "Some attachments are hard to avoid. There's a fine line between being detached and uncaring. Better to take a turn with passion every so often than to become numb to the passage of time." He straightened, lifting his chin. "Better to risk failure than become insignificant."

His last words made the corners of my mouth twitch up. "You could never be insignificant, Loki." I stroked the knives at my wrists.

"Some would prefer it if I were. But that is not my fate. Nor yours." He slipped a hand into his pocket, then extended it toward me, his oversized fist concealing a bundle.

I turned my palms up, and he handed me a trio of narrow items as long as my hands from fingertips to wrist. Sheathes of dark leather protected wands of crystal. When I slid one out, it shone blue with a faint silver glow. Its current made my fingertips spark.

"One for you, and one for each of your children." Loki stepped back.

"What are they for?" I tucked the crystal back into its pouch, buzzing with energy.

"Power. They are energy reserves and conduits of magic."

I swallowed, afraid to ask but needing to know. "What's the cost of using them?"

"The risk is always the same: the bigger the weaving, the more likely you are to have threads go astray. These can amplify the outcome, good and bad."

I eyed him. "What's your motive?"

He lifted an eyebrow.

"I appreciate the gifts." I rubbed my thumb over the leather that protected one of the crystals. "I just wonder why you're helping. If there's something you're hoping to get out of it."

A slow smile crept across his face. "I consider myself your patron, Song Weaver." He paced to the left, walking around me in a lazy circle. "Please take these as tokens of appreciation for your music. Nothing more." He stopped before me again, his gaze as sharp as the knives resting along my forearms. "Is that an arrangement you can accept?"

I slipped the crystals into my pouch, then held my hand out to him. "Gladly."

Loki's hand dwarfed mine as we shook. "Excellent. Well, if that's all, I have a previous engagement to attend to."

I laughed, and waved him off. He disappeared, leaving me alone in the woods.

I pondered his words as I retraced my steps on the winding path. It seemed the crystals he'd given me were like the ones in the belt Nikolas wore. Raw energy, but with Loki's silver magic woven through. More power. More responsibility.

I wasn't about to give them to my kids.

As I neared the dragon field, Eirian swooped down with two other dragons. Confused, I opened my mind to his. *Hi! I didn't realize we were meeting now.*

We weren't, but come. Your children have called their dragons.

They've what? I started jogging, clutching my bag so the crystals wouldn't bang around. *Do you know the dragons they called?*

Eirian's laughter rippled through me. *I know them well. They are my offspring.*

Oh! I'd never even thought to ask if Eirian was a father.

Fear not. Pride and amusement washed through our connection. *Duer and Niya will take excellent care of Brendan and Julia.*

When I made it to the field, there my mother, standing well back from my tiny children who were face to face with enormous dragons. Airmid watched from a few steps away, smiling like all was well in the world.

I strode over to Brighid, took a breath in a failing attempt to calm myself, and said, "Don't you think you could've consulted with me before doing this?"

"Doing what?" she asked, like giving toddlers their own dragons was a perfectly normal thing to do.

"This," I whispered aggressively, gesturing toward my kids. "They're too little."

"They are young, but they'll benefit significantly by having their dragons. And they're the ones who asked. Brendan said, 'When do we get our dragons?' and I told him, 'Whenever you're ready,' and they both agreed they were ready now."

I gaped at her. "And you thought that was a good idea?"

She looked pointedly past me. "Yes."

The instinct to protect my children grappled with the beauty of their dragons. Niya crouched before Julia, turquoise scales and wings gleaming in the sun. Brendan had his hand on the nose of a pearl-white dragon whose face was shaped so similarly to Eirian's, I had no trouble believing Duer was his son.

When Julia noticed me standing there, she said, "Mama! Come see!"

I reached a hand out, and Niya touched her snout to me, her voice sonorous in my mind. *I am Niya. It is good to meet you, Song Weaver.*

And you. I struggled to keep my frustration hidden. This was happening whether I liked it or not. *Hello, Duer.* I walked toward the white dragon.

Well met, Mother of Brendan and Julia. He turned golden eyes my way. *I feel your hesitation. I promise we will protect your children with our lives.*

Biting my lip, I nodded in acknowledgement. *Thank you for watching over them.*

Brendan tackled my leg, and Julia tugged on my hand, both overflowing with things they wanted to tell me. The subject turned quickly to flight.

"Will you lift me up?" asked Julia.

At first, I thought she meant in my arms, but she was clearly pointing at the saddle Niya wore—with a miniature seat. Duer had a similar one, and Brendan bounced around, saying, "Let's go flying!"

I shook my head, but my quiet "no" was lost in the enthusiasm. As my mother went to Brendan, I struggled to discern if I was being overprotective or if I was the only reasonable person on this field. Before I could come to a conclusion, my mother and Airmid had marched up to the dragons, offering to help my children up. My babies.

"Wait just a minute!" I shouted.

The field went quiet, and everyone looked at me. Two goddesses, two toddlers, three dragons, and a handful of immortal spectators.

"Where are you going to fly to?" The words caught in my throat. I didn't want to let them go, and I didn't want to be the one who held them back, either.

"Just above the field," Brighid answered.

I wasn't really asking her.

Niya answered in my mind. *We will only take them in this sky, above you. They're too young to world-jump on their own.*

Yes, Duer agreed. *We defer to you until they are grown. We will keep them safe.*

"Let me help you up then." I jerked my head to tell my mother and Airmid to back off. If my children were going to fly away from me, I was going to be the one to strap them in and see them off.

The saddles had restraints for their legs and torsos, and I triple-checked each harness before climbing down. Then I stood back, conjured my warmest grin, and waved.

"Have fun!" I called. "Come back soon!"

Julia and Brendan waved. "I love you," said Brendan, with Julia as his echo.

Their dragons launched into the sky. Eirian followed, adding his wingbeats to the gust that buffeted me. I watched for several minutes on the edge of panic, but my children stayed in their saddles, their dragons doing lazy circles above the field.

I spun toward my mother, prepared to give her a piece of my mind, but she spoke first.

"The council has suggested that you travel through the Heart of the World Tree."

That threw me. "The what?"

"The Heart of the World Tree," she repeated. "It's a vortex of power that will enhance your abilities."

I had a pouch full of crystals so powerful the thought of them made me tingle. "Nah, I think I'm good."

She frowned. "This is your greatest chance for success."

My gaze darted to Airmid, who nodded, adding, "Whatever transformation the Heart provides, it will be exactly what you need to realize your purpose."

"Transformation?" I didn't like the sound of that.

"Think on it, Shelta," said my mother. "I know this all seems like a lot for you," she lifted her gaze to the dragons in the sky, "but we are doing everything we can to help you and your children. The council foresees great things from them."

"Is that so?" I fought to keep the anger from my voice, sugarcoating my next words with a smile that didn't reach my eyes. "Well, I'll ask you and the council to kindly keep my children out of your prophecies."

Her lips went flat, and I looked away. Above me, sunshine flashed on crimson, pearl, and turquoise scales, and as beautiful as it was, the sight gave me an ominous chill.

CHAPTER 41
PLANS AND PORTALS

THAT AFTERNOON, as my children slept off the aftermath of their exhilarating ride, I went back into the forest where I'd met with Loki. Instead of summoning the god, I called Eirian.

His bulk barely fit in the clearing, but he managed. I wanted him with me for what I was going to do. Eirian craned his head around to look at me, smelling of ocean and brimstone.

I put a hand out to stroke his neck, and asked, *Have you ever been through the Heart of the World Tree?*

He went still at the mention. *Yes.*

I stepped back to see him better. *The council has suggested it. What's it like?*

It is different each time. His claws dug into the mossy ground, turning up rich, brown soil. The earthy scent infused Eirian's words with a sense of gravity. *The first time, I was young. Going through the Tree's Heart made my body larger and stronger. My scales and wings changed from amber to crimson, and my abilities advanced considerably. Other times, the vortex has given me insight into the Matrix of Knowing, and guided me to precisely the place and time best for my journey.*

That doesn't sound so bad. Why did the thought put me on edge, then?

No, it's not bad, but it is intense. And one never knows what will happen inside.

Uncertainty. My nemesis. *Well, before we get to that, I need to gather a team of people on the ground and see if I can get some help to carry out my plan.*

I am here to assist. He settled in, lying like a giant cat in the clearing.

I sat with Eirian at my back and took out Loki's knives, driving them into the ground on either side. A hum surrounded me. I set my intention, creating a one-way portal to my original world, a few days after I'd last been there.

Sitting in a sphere of energy beneath my dragon's wing, I set out to visit the people I'd put on my mental list. Community organizers. Environmental champions. Scientists. Journalists. Inventors. Activists. Actors. Musicians. Even a few politicians I thought might not be completely corrupt. I'd chosen people with influence, people who'd shown a passion for helping others.

Of course, I'd never met any of them, so, much of my mission would be getting them to trust me. My first stop was to visit a woman named Jo who'd spearheaded hugely-successful grassroots campaigns to eradicate poverty through community programs. I found her sitting at her computer, and projected myself into the chair opposite her.

"Hi," I said with an awkward smile. "I apologize for showing up like this but—"

She jumped to her feet, picking up a coffee mug and making like she was going to throw it at me. "The hell you doin' in my house?"

"I'm here to help." I kept my hands where she could see them. "And I'm not really here, anyway. If you throw that mug, it'll just go through me."

Jo threw the mug. It passed right through my image, dropping onto the chair.

I stood up. "Have you heard about the forests regrowing?"

Incredulous, she looked at her computer, then back at me. "I was just reading about it."

"That was me." I conjured a ball of light in one of my palms to help her believe. "I'm coming back to do more. I thought you and I could help each other."

Coming out from behind her desk, Jo put a hand on her ample hip. "You think I'm gonna make a deal with a ghost?"

"I'm not a ghost," I protested.

"What are you, then?"

"I'm a—demigoddess." I put my hands out. "They call me a world-weaver. I'm not sure how to define myself, honestly. I'm someone with power to make important changes, but I can't do it alone."

Jo crossed her arms, wrinkles lining her dark face. "What kind of changes do you want to make?"

I clasped my hands, seeking calm from the dragon supporting my body's weight, warmth and steadiness that was with me, even if my mind was far away. "I want to help bring freedom to all. To bring balance. I want you and those you work with, those you help, to have far more support than you have now. I want the kind of programs you've spearheaded here to be replicated all over the globe. Resources for families, for single parents, for elders, for veterans, for those struggling with addiction or any kind of health issues. Accessible programs to benefit mental health.

Community gardens, local food, local forests for everyone to enjoy and respect."

She put her hands out, stopping me. "I see you've put some thought into this."

"You have no idea." I laughed, shaking my head. "I'm going to sing as many people awake as I can, so they make choices that align with the goodness in their souls. I'll put out the call, but it will be up to each person to decide what they want to do next. People will need leaders like you."

She pressed her lips together. "What do you want me to do?"

"Be ready." That was it, really. "Plan for a flood of volunteers and funding, so you can put people to work. Be ready to take action on a massive scale, if my plan works anything like I'm hoping it will."

"You're a demigoddess?" She narrowed her eyes. "Not an angel?"

"Not an angel." I shook my head. "Nothing like that. I'm the child of a mortal and an immortal, but I don't claim divine parentage."

"You're not a prophet?" She eyed her bookshelf, where a copy of the Bible sat, surrounded by a number of esoteric titles.

"Not that either," I conceded. "I have no idea how this will play out, but I'm taking one more shot at helping this world shift practices of oppression and destruction."

"One shot?" Jo tapped her fingers on her arm, her perfectly-sculpted nails painted a sparkling midnight blue.

I hadn't meant to tell her that. "One more, yes. I don't want to be a savior." I wanted to be a mother, to be with my family, to turn my back on the strife of billions. Was their suffering my responsibility? Could anyone bear that burden? "This world needs to save itself. I know people are capable, they just have to wake up and create new systems that work in the interest of the collective, rather than the few."

She studied me for a while. Her scrutiny made me sweat, though my projection stayed cool and calm.

"When are you putting out this call?"

"Two weeks from now." That was my plan, anyway, if I could jump to a specific date.

Jo nodded her head. She went straight to her desk and started writing notes in a flurry of production. I returned to Eirian, my projection vanishing, leaving her chair empty but for the thrown mug.

I repeated this process countless times. Each person I approached went through a range of reactions: surprise, distrust, amazement, curiosity.

Each time, I did what I had to so they'd believe. With some, I could simply put on a show. I had more than one cross thrusted at me as if it would banish my projection. I tried to stay compassionate and have a sense of humor, but it was hard not to get frustrated when people shouted at me, calling me the devil. One man started going on about women and original sin, and I got so fed up I flipped him the bird and disappeared.

Almost as bad were the people who thought I was a sign from God. One woman wouldn't stop chanting, repeating a mantra silently while I tried to reason with her. In the end, she promised to help, but didn't accept my claim that I was neither angel nor demon.

Most people were simply skeptical, like Jo. Once they'd accepted that I wasn't a hoax, I asked if they would help focus the changes I hoped to spark with my song. And other than a few who wouldn't accept any of my arguments, almost everyone I contacted said yes.

Weighed down by fatigue, I took a break.

We could continue tomorrow, offered Eirian.

With a groan, I got up to stretch. *I'd rather do it all in one go. I want to get this done, rest for a day, then finish the weaving and get the gods off my back.*

When you're ready, then. The dragon shifted, adjusting himself.

After a few minutes, I sat down and retrieved one of the crystals Loki had given me. It slipped easily out of its soft leather sheath with a jolt of energy. "Yeah!" I grinned at Eirian. "Now that's what I'm talking about. Let's do this."

Three hours later, the crystal was still buzzing. I, however, was slipping down Eirian's arm, ready to sleep in the clearing. Swaying, I wrapped the crystal, returned it to my plaid pouch, and stood up to leave, or tried to. My knees buckled, and I crumpled into my dragon's side.

Eirian? What happened?

He peered at me from above. *You used the crystal to fuel your work. Did you also draw from it to replenish yourself?*

I whimpered. Always a learning curve with these things.

Even with the crystal's rejuvenation, walking back to the palace took an unreasonable amount of effort. It was all I could do to eat, put the children to sleep, and fall into bed. When I woke the next morning, I had an energy hangover that rivaled the worst ones I'd ever had from partying.

When Brighid and Airmid came to gather the children for lessons, I informed them that it would be our last day. Their faces fell, but they smiled at Julia and Brendan, taking them by the hands and leading them off for whatever adventures they had planned.

I was due to face off with Thor, but I could barely stagger to the courtyard. He stood in the center of the lawn, arms crossed, observing as I went straight to the bench by the fountain.

"No sparring today," I said by way of greeting.

He came over to sit by me. "You've been using Loki's gifts."

I narrowed my eyes. "How do you know?"

"We spoke last night." Thor conjured a mug of water from the fountain and handed it to me. "His creations always have a shadow side, but then, most things do. It brings balance."

"Sleep brings balance." I chugged some water, put the mug down, and collapsed spread-eagle on the grass. "Is it possible to use the crystal he gave me without feeling like death afterwards?"

"Yes." Thor leaned forward on the bench, elbows on his knees. "If you use it for shorter periods of time, you'll be fine. And you will build up a tolerance."

"Is there anything else that would provide the same kind of benefits without draining me like this?" My bones ached.

"There are other tools, but they all take some getting used to."

I sat up, retrieving the crystal I'd claimed as mine. The other two were back in my room, packed with the children's things. I slid the crystal out, laid it on the ground, and poured fountain water over it. Like I could cleanse it. "Why didn't my mother give me something like this? I've spent more time with you than I have her."

Thor frowned. "Your mother, in her wisdom, has given you as much space as she can. It's easier for you, and easier for her."

"Because I'm mortal and I'm going to die anyway?" I leaned back on my hands, too tired to care how my mother felt about me.

"You're not quite mortal, Shelta, nor is the rest of your family. You have a high-concentration of star blood. Your lovers are my descendants, and your children are god-blooded."

As I stared at him, I saw Nikolas in his eyes, heard Troy in the quiet of his voice. The cut of his jaw was the same as Killian's.

"You're the matriarch of the next wave of world-weavers," said Thor. "Your mother distances herself so the council cannot accuse her of overstretching her influence."

"And you? Are you part of the council's meddling?"

He answered my prickly words with an easy smile. "The council nominated me to train you, and Merlin."

I fell to my back on the grass again. "Any chance you want to magic me into recovery? I may have done too much yesterday, and I'm hoping to leave tomorrow."

"How many people did you contact?"

I sighed. Just thinking about it hurt. "Ninety-three."

Thor lowered down to his knees beside me. "That's—a lot of projecting, Shelta. Even with the crystal providing extra power, that's an impressive weaving." He put his hand on my shoulder. "And since you asked, yes. Of course. I'd be happy to help."

Energy flowed into me. Warm. Tingling. Healing. I closed my eyes as Thor washed away the fatigue, replenishing my life force in a way I couldn't manage on my own. Every breath became a miracle of light. Time dissolved. Boundaries blurred. The planet beneath and the sky above melded into one. When the magic receded and Thor took his hand away, I blinked my eyes open.

"Thank you." I pushed myself up. "Does it drain you to heal me?"

He sat back on his heels, hands on his thighs. "Not really. If I had to heal a thousand people in a day, that would be a challenge, but one is nothing."

"A thousand!" I thought of the healing I'd managed after the battles I'd fought.

"When you're ages old, Shelta, you learn a trick or two."

"Right." I got to my feet, mindful of my limits.

I needed more power. More endurance. If going through the Heart of the World Tree would give me an advantage, I'd take it.

The god stood up, and nodded to me. "You're ready, Weaver."

I made a sound that wasn't quite a laugh. "As ready as I'll ever be."

Thor's eyes shone with something like sorrow. "I will miss our morning engagements, but you will do well."

"I hope it's enough." I bent down and scooped up the crystal, sliding it into my pocket. "I don't want to go back to my original world for a long time after this." I pinned him with my gaze. "And I won't let the council force me into it again."

"Understood." He tipped his head in acknowledgement. "It is not up to you to put everything right, only to turn the tide."

"Do you believe I can?" I needed to hear it.

"You know I do."

CHAPTER 42
THROUGH THE HEART OF THE WORLD TREE

THE NEXT MORNING, I stood on the field with my children, our dragons, and a small gathering of legends. Thor and Merlin. Arthur, Guinevere, and Lancelot. A scattering of immortals who'd come to see us off. My mother and Airmid were with Brendan and Julia, saying goodbye. I shook my head at the scene. I'd adjusted to the idea that my kids would be safer on their own dragons, but I couldn't digest how young they were.

"They're just babies," I said to Thor.

"They are far more than that, Shelta," he replied.

He was right. They were extremely advanced little people, trained by goddesses.

"They're happy," said Merlin, grinning at my children, who were clearly enamored with their dragons.

We all watched Brendan climb up Duer's tail, staggering across his gleaming white back before sliding into the high-backed seat of his saddle. Brighid moved to buckle him in.

"A dragon rider if I've ever seen one." Lancelot beamed at my son.

"They're awfully young to be riding." Guinevere's voice held the same misgivings as mine. At least someone didn't think I was being overprotective.

"The greatest gift we can give those we love is our trust," said Arthur.

And the freedom to spread their wings, Eirian added.

"It is not always an easy gift." Arthur's gaze shifted to Guinevere and Lancelot.

"No, it's not." I hugged Thor, and Merlin, and Guinevere, shaking Arthur and Lancelot's hands last. The goodbye held a degree of finality.

I didn't plan to return to Asgard anytime soon.

My mother and Airmid had secured my children in their saddles, but I jumped up to Duer's shoulders to check Brendan's straps anyway. After assuring myself he was as safe as he could be, I wrapped my arms around him, kissed his forehead and both cheeks, and sighed when he hugged me back with all his strength.

"I'll be okay, Mama," he said.

"I know you will, baby. I just love you so much."

"I love you, too."

I squeezed his hand, then slid down, and repeated the process with Julia. She was so little in my arms, such innocence in her voice as she said, "Love you, Mama."

Back on the ground, I thanked Airmid for all her help, then faced my mother. "I guess I'll see you when I see you."

"Blessings on your journey, my daughter." Brighid put her arms around me, and I hugged her tentatively. She was still a mystery, but I was glad to know her.

Not long ago, I'd been an orphan helplessly tossed through time. Now... Whatever else I'd become, I was no longer helpless.

Eirian shone crimson and gold as I climbed up and strapped in. Loki's crystal rested in its pouch on my weapons belt, and I had my sword and dagger at the ready.

Knives up my sleeves, I tipped my head to my friends on the ground, then gave the command to fly.

Up we rose, three dragons and weavers in an early morning sky.

So, how do we get to the Heart of the World Tree? I asked Eirian.

The nearest access point is the Forest of Ancients, he answered, flying west. Niya and Duer banked with us, and we headed toward a dark stretch of land in the distance.

The forest was aptly named, with massive trees that we flew over on our way to a glow in the distance. The pull of magic grew stronger the nearer we got to the World Tree, which towered over the others. Its branches twisted, adorned with multicolored leaves that sparkled in the sun.

Eirian aimed for the column of light above the Tree. *Are you ready, Weaver?*

My heart raced. *Yes. Let's go.*

The dragons dove, nose down, into a blinding rainbow of light. Pressure squeezed through me, blasting my mind open. I could sense Brendan and Julia on their dragons, but I couldn't see them through the shifting of time and space.

And then, in a rush, the pressure evaporated into an otherworldly calm that held me in the palm of eternity. We'd reached the Heart. The eye of the vortex.

With an expanded perspective that tasted like omniscience, I saw order hidden beneath the chaos of existence. I *understood,* as if the workings of the cosmos unfolded in one moment, simple and complex, all the mysteries of life revealing themselves at once.

Too soon, we entered a whirlwind of light, and the understanding faded, along with the uncanny sense of calm. Music surrounded me, streaming through me, a melody planting itself in my brain. The song I'd been seeking.

Finally, we broke through, into the atmosphere above the Atlantic Ocean, with a brilliant-blue sky and a floor of clouds below. As I looked from my dragon to my children, the consequences of our journey knocked the wind out of me.

The Heart had changed us all.

My babies were gone. Grown. Two children stared at me from their saddles. They were mine, no question, but Julia and Brendan looked like they were now seven or eight years old.

The World Tree had stolen part of their childhood.

I choked, struggling to breathe as I turned my head from Brendan to Julia and back again. The dragons had changed, too. Eirian glimmered gold, barely any red left on his scales and wings. Niya had darkened to a deeper blue-green, and Duer had lost the shimmering pearl he'd had before, his white scales taking on a shade of grey that would blend well with storm clouds.

But I didn't care about the dragons, or whatever melody I might've gotten out of the Heart of the World Tree. My babies' youth had been stolen. I shouldn't have taken us through.

So many moments we'd never get to share... Tears streaked across my cheeks.

"It's okay, Mama!" Julia's voice came clear over the wind.

"This was our choice," Brendan said. "Please don't cry."

It took everything in me not to start sobbing. Shredded.

Oh, my sweet, beautiful babies.

My dragon heard, his presence strong and silent within.

Was this the moment Thor had warned of? He'd said I'd be faced with a time when the only way to protect my children was to remain calm. Right now, I needed to find a sense of peace not only to protect my children, but the entire planet. I was here to weave harmony, not this mess of betrayal, sorrow, and anger sloshing around inside me.

Eirian, shield us, I pleaded. *Shield this world from my grief. This is not how I wanted to begin.*

It is done, Weaver, came his gentle response. *Take your time.*

"Mama." Julia again. Her voice was so different. "It's okay, really. Now we can help you."

I could see her more clearly than I should've been able to with that much space between us and tears in my eyes—as if my vision had been enhanced by our journey. Julia's long, brown hair blew in the breeze her dragon's shield allowed through.

"We wanted this, Mama," Brendan said, his black hair nearly as long as his sister's. "This is the way it had to happen. Please try to understand."

Oh, I understood. Didn't mean I had to like it. But even if I wanted to rage at the gods for meddling, fighting wouldn't do any good. Nothing would fix this.

With concentrated effort, I slowed my choppy breath.

"Are you mad, Mama?" Brendan asked.

"No, my love. I'm not angry with you."

"I'm sorry we made you sad." Julia rode her dragon like she'd been born to it.

"It's okay, sweetheart." I tried a smile.

"Are you going to be okay?" she asked.

"Yes, baby." I wiped my cheeks. "I might keep calling you 'baby,' even though you're not babies anymore. Is that okay?"

"Yes, Mama." They said in unison.

"Can we help you now?" Brendan asked. "We really want to help. Duer does, too."

"And Niya. We didn't want you to feel alone anymore."

How many times can a heart break? As young as they were, they'd realized how overwhelmed I'd been, how much pressure the gods had put on me.

I made my voice as clear as I could. "Yes, you can help. The plan is to bring harmony to the planet, and the people. Freedom. Peace. Empowerment. Love. Can you help me sing the song? Did you hear it, at the end of the portal?"

"Yes, Mama." Their voices sounded on either side of me. My children. World-weavers.

Ready, Eirian? I asked. My chest was tight and a knot hardened in my belly, but I ignored it and pretended I had everything under control.

I am ready, Weaver.

Down we went, through the clouds, soaring above the wide blue ocean below. We started at the southern tip of South America. I planned to work our way north, then spiral around to cover the whole planet, using small jumps sparingly and flying faster than any plane could, shielded by the dragons. The horizon loomed as we sped toward it.

I closed my eyes, opened my mouth, and let the music come.

A wordless song swept across the sky with an echo of the music I'd heard in the Heart of the World Tree. Julia and Brendan joined in, harnessing the power of their dragons and the intention that linked us all.

Our job was to wake people up, to bring consciousness to the masses. After that, it was up to the ninety-three people

I'd contacted, and anyone else who wanted to make change, to take that energy and keep it going.

The clear, innocent voices of my children blended with mine in perfect pitch, sometimes singing in harmony, sometimes matching my melody. Instinctively pulling out the crystal Loki gave me, I sent the song into crystals all over the planet, deep beneath the earth and close to the surface, arteries of minerals that conducted the energy of the earth and amplified the music.

We flew high and fast, covering ground quickly. Below, South America spread out, from sea to sea, mountains running like a spine through it all. Central America snaked through wide swaths of ocean, then Mexico, and the vast expanse of North America.

We called the entire planet to return to its thriving, vibrant truth. The longer we sang, the more I could feel waves of response. People were joining in the song.

Some resisted. Some refused to heed the call, or blocked out the melody entirely. Freedom for all threatened the lies some had dedicated their lives to, and they were unwilling to let them go.

We were over Asia when the first fighter jets entered my awareness, and I stopped our song. Brendan and Julia went quiet, as well, looking toward the planes.

We're going to move now, I told them through our heart-mind link. *Eirian, let's go.*

New Zealand, next, then Australia. We sang for the oceans, for the islands, for all of Asia as we took another approach from the east. When we passed over the Himalayas, the song was amplified so powerfully I stopped to catch my breath, basking in the beauty of a composition that had taken on a life of its own.

We'd nearly completed our circuit when a pair of jets caught up with us over the North Sea. Our shields made us invisible to others, but clearly didn't fool radar or whatever other instruments the fighters employed.

I sent Eirian our next location, and we jumped.

Seconds later, we soared over coastal California. Brendan and Julia commented on the coast's rugged beauty as we headed to an area where one of the activists I'd contacted had gathered a group of people. I'd promised regrowth of the giant redwoods, and I was here to deliver.

Hope warmed me as I called to the trees, which sprouted up to tower over houses, obliterating clear cuts and lining the highways.

You are a part of this. I sent the thought to the people on the ground. *Be the stewards of these trees. Help them grow.*

No sooner had I finished my motivational speech, than fighter jets came screaming in. More of them this time. It seemed every military on the planet had heard about the strange phenomenon in the sky, and they all wanted to catch us.

We ran. But dragons can only time-jump so many times.

We went to three more points. Each time we worked with people on the ground, each time leaving as aircraft threatened our airspace. I was reaching my limit, relying on the crystal more than I wanted to.

Body heavy, discouragement closed in like a shroud. Would any of this be enough?

Finally, way out in the Caribbean, I stared down the U.S. Air Force, tired of running away. Maybe their intentions were peaceful, but if they engaged me, I'd turn from a bringer of goodness to a force of destruction. I didn't want to do that. Better to slip by as an unidentified flying object and never be found.

Pointing my blue crystal like a wand, I sent a last blast of light into the earth. As it spread throughout the planet, all the doors I'd opened glowed in my inner sight. Nature spirits flocked to the bridges I'd made, and the forests around them thrived. I saw worlds layered on top of each other, symbiotic. They vibrated with the energy of the weaving.

It's up to you now, I told the ones who cared, the ones who listened and hoped and dreamed. Those who had heard the song. *Blessed be.*

The gods couldn't expect more of me than this. And if they did, that was too bad.

"Let's go home," I said to my children and our dragons. "The people of this planet can make their own changes from here on out."

CHAPTER 43
HOME AT LAST

AS SOON AS I caught sight of Thorson village and its sheltered bay, the shock I'd pushed aside hit me full force. My children had lost years of their childhood to the Heart of the World Tree, and I wasn't sure if I'd ever forgive the gods.

Niya and Duer landed next to Eirian on the beach, unafraid of being seen. Nikolas and his children ran out to meet us, with Ola and Patrick following, along with most of the villagers, who marveled at the dragons.

Mouth open in dismay, Nikolas stopped in his tracks in the rocky sand, and watched Julia and Brendan unstrap themselves from their own dragons. Our children. Grown.

I slid out of my saddle, hitting the ground hard. Grief and defiance shook fists in my chest. The council of gods had suggested the Heart of the World Tree, and I'd sacrificed more than I was willing. From now on, if I made a weaving, it would be on my terms.

My choice.

I fell to my knees to hug Brendan and Julia, tears making salty tracks down my cheeks. When I finally let them go, Nikolas offered me his hand, pulling me to my feet and into his arms.

"Are you hurt?" he asked, his mouth near my ear.

I held him, trembling from wielding energy and the onslaught of emotions. "Hurt, yes. Injured, no."

He all but held me up, one arm around my back as Leifr, Dagný, and Frøya came over, Ola and Patrick behind them.

Nikolas's sister eyed Julia and Brendan with a furrowed brow. "My, how you've grown," she said. Julia's smile faltered, and Ola put her hand on her shoulder. "Come to tea and tell me all about it."

Nikolas held my hand as we trailed them back to the village, my oversized saddlebags carried by Leifr and Patrick. Dagný held hands with Julia and Brendan, who were now the perfect age to be her playmates.

Behind us, the dragons took flight, drawing an awed murmur from those who watched.

Until next time, Weaver. Eirian's voice was an embrace all its own.

Until next time, my friend. I sent a blast of love, my heart to his.

The dragons soared toward the clouds, Duer blending in beautifully, Niya a teal streak of speed, Eirian glimmering gold. Then they blinked out of sight.

Three nights later, I walked alone beneath the full moon, breathing salty mist from the waves, witnessing the ocean's song. Out of necessity, I'd adjusted somewhat to the transformation of my children, but it was a line that should not have been crossed.

I would never be at the beck and call of the gods again. I didn't need to shout it out or visit Asgard to tell them. They knew.

I wanted to hate them, but I couldn't quite. I had to believe they were doing their best to help, even when it sparked disaster, which was the reason the gods weren't supposed to intervene in the first place. Every action spawned unforeseen consequences.

My children might be weavers, but I would shelter them from that responsibility for as long as I could. Part of protecting them was turning my back on the world I'd agreed to save, my promise to the gods fulfilled to the extent I was willing to do so. Walking away from that obligation meant not visiting that world again. I'd never know what came of my intervention. I didn't even want to know.

The best I could do was hope humanity made good decisions and that I hadn't screwed anything up too badly. How had the old weavers managed?

A ghostly scent of berry scones clashed oddly with the sea, and Merlin's words echoed in my mind. *You will find that the more you embrace what you don't understand with the openness of wonder, the less you resist. And the less you resist, Weaver, the easier things will be.*

Sometimes resistance was called for, but I couldn't change what I'd become, or the things that had happened to my family. All I could do was move forward. And in order to live the life I wanted, I had to leave my original timeline behind.

There were only three worlds I wanted to weave. Killian, Troy, and Nikolas were my anchors. I would do what good I could in the places where my family dwelled. Surely that trinity would assist the rest of the Tapestry, rippling out, as everything I did was destined to do. I couldn't escape my responsibility, but if I lived on my own terms, I didn't need to resist it.

I'd gone from a woman lost, to a weaver who'd found her home.

Above me, the stars shone. Behind me, the village slept, as did my family. And before me, the ocean was both the dancer and the music, breathing against the shore.

THANK YOU FOR READING!

If you enjoyed this book, please leave a review!

Reviews can be posted wherever you purchased this book, at Goodreads, Amazon, and Bookbub, or shared on social media if you have friends who might enjoy the read. Even a short review is helpful, and very much appreciated.

If you love this story, or any other book you read, please tell people about it. There's no higher compliment for an author than having their book personally recommended by readers.

AUTHOR'S NOTE

In the process of creating a fantasy where alternate histories and parallel worlds exist, I've taken many liberties. For instance, my portrayal of Duart Castle and the lore of Clan Maclean are mostly the conjurings of my imagination. I've reinvented myths and legends. The Nwetaka tribe is also a fabrication, as the Shoshone would've been the Native residents of that area of Wyoming had this tale taken place in our actual history. Even so, I've tried to represent each human and historical element of this story with respect. It is my intention as an author to explore imagined possibilities in ways that inspire hope and an awareness that we are all connected: people, nature, and the cosmos.

ACKNOWLEDGEMENTS

Writing is a solitary endeavor, but it takes a community for a book to become something extraordinary. To everyone who has encouraged and supported me on this journey, thank you!

Special thanks to authors Elysia Lumen Strife, Nina Castle, and Jenna McKinley. Your insight made this story what it is today. To Sir Lachlan Maclean and Alison Canham from Duart Castle, thank you for your blessings on these books.

Lastly, I want to extend my gratitude to *you*, the reader. Without you, this story would be nothing but lonely words on paper. I hope you enjoyed Shelta's adventure, and that it came to life in your imagination.

About the Author

Leia Talon writes fantasy and speculative fiction with romantic elements. Her lyrical approach is influenced by a lifetime of turning emotions into poetry and songs. She lives with her family in the mountains of British Columbia, where nature sparks her imagination to run wild.

The overarching universe of *The World Tree Chronicles* opens with *Shelta's Songbook*, a standalone collection of Shelta's poetry and short stories, complete with love letters from an immortal. To be notified about new books, sign up for Leia's newsletter at www.LeiaTalon.com.

Connect online:

www.LeiaTalon.com
Twitter.com / LeiaTalon
Facebook.com / LeiaTalon
Instagram.com / LeiaTalon

The World Tree Chronicles